P9-DWE-994

PRAISE FOR

The Roughest Draft

"Real, raw, and heartfelt."   —*USA Today*

"*The Roughest Draft* is a book about books, and a breathtaking meditation on the ways in which fiction can be a space to expose and write large our most vulnerable truths. . . . Complex and achingly romantic, *The Roughest Draft* feels as if it's a palimpsest for Wibberley's and Siegemund-Broka's most deeply held beliefs about writing and each other—a profound collective story inked out for all of us to find ourselves on its pages."   —*Entertainment Weekly*

"*The Roughest Draft* has it all: romance, rumor, and intrigue, and you won't want to put it down."   —Shondaland

"Wibberley and Siegemund-Broka deliver on what they've always done best: imperfect characters who you want to follow all the way to the end. There's fire-hot tension and yearning and resentfulness and fights and steamy romance, but there's also beauty in the way the story depicts the uncertainty of creative careers, working as a team, and individual growth. If you have a case of winter blues, this is the novel to pick up."   —BuzzFeed

"Emily Wibberley and Austin Siegemund-Broka are the dream team from heaven. Starting as YA authors and shifting their power-house kingdom into adult, *The Roughest Draft* absolutely gives me *The Hating Game* vibes for a new generation, but sweeter. And maybe steamier?"   —Oprah Daily

"This novel is that rare piece of writing that needs no editing, haunts your sleep, and leaves you wishing it was longer when you turn the last page."

—Jodi Picoult, #1 *New York Times* bestselling author of *Wish You Were Here*

"I love, love, *loved* this book. It sucks you into a slow, sexy burn from page one and keeps you hooked with its layered, heart-wrenching honesty. This is contemporary romance at its best!"

—Lyssa Kay Adams, author of *A Very Merry Bromance*

"Together, Emily Wibberley and Austin Siegemund-Broka produce a seamless voice that is compulsively readable. Their characters spark to life immediately on the page and are so real and relatable that I'm still thinking about them days later."

—Jen DeLuca, *USA Today* bestselling author of *Well Traveled*

"There isn't a single page of *The Roughest Draft*, not one, that doesn't contain a sentence I had to reread twice just to savor. I'm going to be thinking about this heartbreakingly lovely, vividly emotional book for a long time. These authors are masters of their craft and their writing is such a treat to read."

—Sarah Hogle, author of *Twice Shy*

"Searingly insightful and achingly romantic, *The Roughest Draft* is a sweep-you-off-your-feet celebration of love and creativity in all its mess. Emily Wibberley and Austin Siegemund-Broka plunge readers into the world of co-writing with a depth and vulnerability that is sure to delight and fascinate."

—Sarah Grunder Ruiz, author of *Luck and Last Resorts*

"*The Roughest Draft* offers the most tantalizing romantic tension with a giant helping of swoon."
—Trish Doller, author of *The Suite Spot*

"*The Roughest Draft* turns the act of co-writing a novel into one of the most soulful expressions of love I've ever read. Smart, tender, and deeply romantic, this book is an unforgettable, page-turning knockout." —Bridget Morrissey, author of *A Thousand Miles*

"Utterly engrossing and beautifully wrought, *The Roughest Draft* is an intimate and authentic portrayal of human connection and the creative process. An exquisite love story that will leave you spellbound and longing for more."
—Libby Hubscher, author of *If You Ask Me*

"A deeply emotional meditation on the psychological perils of success within a passionate romance." —*Booklist* (starred review)

"This will-they-or-won't-they romance is perfect for readers who enjoy friends-to-lovers, or anyone pursuing a passion project professionally. For fans of Emily Henry's *Beach Read*, Minnie Darke's *Star-Crossed*, and Christina Lauren's *Twice in a Blue Moon*."
—*Library Journal*

Titles by Emily Wibberley & Austin Siegemund-Broka

The Roughest Draft
Do I Know You?

Wibberley, Emily, author.
Do I know you?

2023
33305254130465
ca   01/25/23

Do I Know You?

EMILY WIBBERLEY & AUSTIN SIEGEMUND-BROKA

Berkley Romance
New York

Berkley Romance
Published by Berkley
An imprint of Penguin Random House LLC
penguinrandomhouse.com

Copyright © 2023 by Emily Wibberley and Austin Siegemund-Broka
Readers Guide copyright © 2023 by Emily Wibberley and Austin Siegemund-Broka
Excerpt from *The Roughest Draft* copyright © 2022 by Emily Wibberley and
Austin Siegemund-Broka
Penguin Random House supports copyright. Copyright fuels creativity,
encourages diverse voices, promotes free speech, and creates a vibrant culture.
Thank you for buying an authorized edition of this book and for complying with
copyright laws by not reproducing, scanning, or distributing any part of it in any
form without permission. You are supporting writers and allowing Penguin
Random House to continue to publish books for every reader.

BERKLEY is a registered trademark and Berkley Romance with B colophon is
a trademark of Penguin Random House LLC.

Library of Congress Cataloging-in-Publication Data

Names: Wibberley, Emily, author. | Siegemund-Broka, Austin, author.
Title: Do I know you? / Emily Wibberley & Austin Siegemund-Broka.
Description: First edition. | New York: Berkley Romance, 2023.
Identifiers: LCCN 2022021597 (print) | LCCN 2022021598 (ebook) |
ISBN 9780593201954 (trade paperback) | ISBN 9780593201961 (ebook)
Subjects: LCGFT: Romance fiction. | Novels.
Classification: LCC PS3623.I24 D6 2023 (print) | LCC PS3623.I24 (ebook) |
DDC 813/.6—dc23/eng/20220523
LC record available at https://lccn.loc.gov/2022021597
LC ebook record available at https://lccn.loc.gov/2022021598

First Edition: January 2023

Printed in the United States of America
1st Printing

Book design by Alison Cnockaert

This is a work of fiction. Names, characters, places, and incidents either are the product
of the author's imagination or are used fictitiously, and any resemblance to actual persons,
living or dead, business establishments, events, or locales is entirely coincidental.

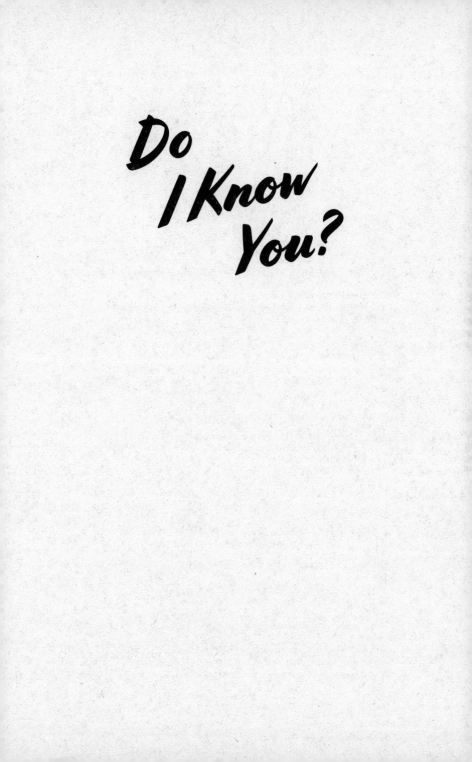

Do I Know You?

1

Eliza

SAY SOMETHING.

I watch my husband out of the corner of my eye, imploring, wishing he would end the silence filling our car. In the window past him, the ocean glitters, unchanging. The California coastline should inspire wonder, with its rippling cliffs and its crystalline expanse, even when you've spent hours watching the water through the windshield. Instead, the thing I notice most is how it just keeps going.

Say something.

Graham doesn't. He drives, his long fingers clamped on the pebbled leather of the steering wheel, his posture stiff. The quiet, interrupted only by the occasional *whoosh* of cars passing us, prickles over me like the start of a sunburn.

Is this how this week will be?

I told myself it wouldn't. I've told myself that pretty much every day since Graham's parents handed us an envelope over dinner containing a weeklong, all-expenses-paid romantic getaway at the Treeline Resort to celebrate our fifth wedding anniversary. I convinced myself the week would be wonderful instead of awkward or claustrophobic. What couple wouldn't want to celebrate five years of marriage at a five-star hotel famous for its romantic ambience?

The quiet filling our car says it knows. Determined, I fight off my discouragement. I wish Graham would speak up, would offer something up into the silence—even comment on the weather—but he doesn't.

It's not only him not speaking, I remind myself. Screw sitting here waiting. Maybe I need to be less narrator, more main character.

I clear my throat. "We're doing good on—"

"Just three hours to go—" Graham quickly cuts in.

"Time," I finish, then wince, hearing the unintentional overlap of our voices. It's less like cutely finishing each other's sentences, more like two supermarket shoppers coincidentally reaching for the same shelf. Less unison, more collision.

I don't blame him for cutting in, for intuiting exactly what I was going to say. Every exchange my husband and I have managed in the past twenty-four hours has consisted of nothing except this one meaningless subject. When we should leave, how long the drive is, whether we should take the 1 or the 5 freeway. Unable to help myself, I glance over, wondering whether Graham shares my desperation to change our conversational flat tire.

He does. He shifts in his seat like someone's stowed rocks in the soft leather cushion under him.

I remember the way I described Graham Cutler to my friends and my parents fresh off our first dates. *He's tall,* I'd said. *He's got blond hair, a cleft chin, intelligence in his eyes. The kind he could use to eviscerate rhetorical weaknesses, but he doesn't, not with me.* We'd met and chatted with each other on a dating app, and when we got together in person, these observations were the first I connected to the personality I'd gotten to know on my phone.

The problem is, they're what I hear now. Observations. I've been married to Graham for five years, and when I look over from the passenger seat, my mind does nothing except reproduce the list of identifying marks I jotted down in my head when me met. *He's tall. He has blond hair.*

It hasn't been this way forever—in our newlywed years, Graham turned, the way spouses should, into swirling slideshows of happy memories, never-ending excitement to catch up over dinner or share something funny one of us found online.

Gradually, though, it's gotten harder to feel like I *know* the man seated next to me, despite knowing I love him. It happened not through fights or rifts, but through late work nights, quick conversations instead of real ones. Our starkly different careers don't help—the high-profile San Diego law firm where Graham is planning to make partner, the many audiobooks and voice-acting jobs I've recorded in the past five years. Complacency converted into unspoken questions and discussions never had. Five years into our marriage, I'm left with only my catalog, once eager, now rote. Learned. Repeated.

He's tall. He has blond hair. He is my husband.

Part of me wonders whether Graham's mother gave us this gift knowing we're having difficulty finding the spark. Helen has never been a particularly generous gift-giver despite being a member of a Marina del Rey yacht club. When I got home and googled the hotel, seeing the price per night confirmed her meddlesome motives.

Of course, Helen's response would be to force us into this situation, which is frustrating in principle no matter how much I might be looking forward to cucumber water in the lobby. The Cutler family way is to walk through fire, while mine is to walk in the other direction. It's why I haven't spoken to my sister in months. I don't *enjoy* retreating—I've just concluded it's the safest thing for me. For everyone.

No, I chasten myself. *Eliza, you will enjoy yourself, damnit. You will not surrender to three more hours of traffic-related small talk.*

My internal pep talk surges confidence into me, like I felt when I spontaneously shoved my new lingerie into my suitcase under my running shoes and my e-reader. It's red, lacy, and designed for exactly one purpose, which is *not* day-to-day functionality. My best friend, Nikki, gave it to me to celebrate this anniversary. While packing this morning in the bedroom of the house we rent in San Diego's summer cottage neighborhood of La Jolla, I chose to ignore how out of place the lingerie was in the present context of Graham's and my marriage, how far we've started to feel from spontaneity or surprise. *I'm going for it,* I decided, stashing the collection of lace and straps in my suitcase.

"Hey," I say, latching on to a conversational handhold. "I wonder if this hotel has milkshakes."

Every sliver of my focus is on Graham's reaction to this subject change. When he smiles, despite the sun shining through the windows since we left our hometown's morning fog behind, I feel warmth for the first time in the hours we've been on the road.

Until he replies. "Milkshakes?" he repeats, cool confusion in his voice. "Why would we want milkshakes?"

My heart plunges. Right off the cliff outside. Right into the endless ocean. I wonder if Graham knows what he's done. His straightforward stare says nothing of my dashed hopes.

"I don't want milkshakes," Graham goes on. "I want *banana* milkshakes."

I hear myself laugh. The sound is quick, echoing joyously in our car. Now Graham grins fully, half Cheshire cat, half high school boy pleased to have earned his crush's laughter. *I'm the crush,* I remember delightedly. I'm not just the person he goes to bed with—I'm the person he still plays games with.

On the first night of our honeymoon, we lost track of time exploring the streets of Santorini, returning to our hotel famished with only five minutes until room service ended. The understandably perturbed kitchen staff explained they'd cleaned up for the night except for the ice cream supplies, and the other guests had polished off everything but, inexplicably, the banana ice cream. If we wanted, they offered, they could make us banana milkshakes.

We did. We spent the first night of our honeymoon watching midnight descend over the water, drinking banana milkshakes.

"What will we do if they don't have them?" I reply, pitching my voice breathily, putting on the register I used for the wonderful new historical romance novel I'd just finished recording. Today, I'm a damsel in milkshakeless distress.

When Graham replies, I recognize the gravitas of his client-phone-call voice. "I think we have clear claims for tortious vacation interference or negligence of frozen treats," he informs me. "Wrongful death if my wife perishes from banana milkshake deprivation is harder, but there's precedent. Depends on the inclinations of judges in this circuit."

"Better hit the books then, Mr. Cutler."

"Will do, Mrs. Cutler."

"Is this pro bono work?"

"Out of the goodness of my heart, Mrs. Cutler," he promises.

I smile, relaxing into the passenger seat, the stress releasing from my shoulders. I shouldn't feel so relieved. It's just—so many of my conversations with Graham lately, while pleasant, have felt insubstantial. Missing something. Like the filler dialogue I sometimes record for video game parts instead of the main story. Banana-milkshake banter felt real. It felt like *us*.

Emboldened, I pivot in my seat, crossing one white sneaker under me. The canopy of trees unexpectedly soaring over this stretch of road filters the sunlight in patterns while we drive, speckling the dashboard in ever-changing leopard spots. "For real," I prompt my husband. "What do you want to do when we get there?"

I watch the moment it happens. Graham's expression doesn't change—the relaxed hint of his smile, the fixture of his eyes on the road—except, something *does* change. Some secret spark shuts off in him. Photographs of sunlight look like day, but they offer no warmth. Nothing grows in the sort of false light now glinting in Graham's eyes.

"I don't know," he replies with forced casualness. His hesitancy is its own flashback, reminding me of his studious reserve when we first met, when courtroom experience hadn't yet put confidence into him.

I press on, patiently struggling. *We were just having fun, weren't we?* "Well, *I'm* just looking forward to having the gorgeous room to ourselves. The ocean view, the trees, the hot tub . . ."

Graham just nods.

"This is going to be good for us," I say, then immediately regret my choice of words. I can't ignore the implication in them. Saying this trip will be *good* for us is prescriptive. It's vitamins served on a silver platter. I sound desperate, chasing the nameless shadows creeping into the corners of our marriage lately.

"It will," Graham says. It's the end of the conversation.

When the road swerves, my thoughts do the same. I retreat into sudden insecurity, ignoring the spectacular path our car is now winding into the sagebrush mountains. Are our memories the only things we have left? If so, why even go on this trip? Why drive these six hours into the green hills of Northern California if we're only going to cloak ourselves in reminiscence when we get there?

No. I refuse to give up. We haven't even gotten to the hotel. I know retreating would be easier, occupying myself with the sample I need to record—

Right then, I get the perfect idea.

The sample my producer sent me is not video-game dialogue. It's not nonfiction essays. It's not commercial voiceover. It's . . . sexy. Very sexy.

Maybe it could reset the tone for this trip. Loosen Graham up. It could be, dare I say, fun.

Glancing up, I find my husband still focused on the road. "Hey," I say innocently. "Would you mind if I record something?"

2

Graham

"WOULD YOU MIND if I record something?"

I'm embarrassed by how quickly the rush of relief comes over me. It's just—the out Eliza's given me is preferable to the grating howl of the question never far from my thoughts when I'm with her. *What do I say? How do I be interesting enough, funny enough, fun enough for* her?

I don't remember how I ever pulled it off, how I charmed Eliza Cutler, née Kelly, into marrying me. I sometimes feel like a fraud, some con man who managed to scam her into thinking I was worthy of her. Every day, every hour, every conversation, I come closer to her realizing I'm so much less interesting than the man she thought she married. The less I say, the more time I have before she sees through me, and I'm holding on to every precious second I have left.

Even under normal circumstances, it's difficult these days to conjure up conversation interesting enough. It's insurmountable now, when I'm preoccupied with how this very same worry will taunt me for one whole week of hikes, hot tubs, and hotel champagne with Eliza, uninterrupted.

The ocean outside my window was supposed to relax me. I picked PCH—the Pacific Coast Highway—for the sweeping scenery, the glittering sea right past the cliffs on which we're driving. I'd hoped it would remind me of the picturesque surroundings I'm heading toward. Instead, it's only made me more uneasy. It's one thing to feel our distance in the stiflingly familiar house neither of us has had time to clean in months. It's something else entirely to feel it on vacation, nestled in the stunning forested hills of Northern California.

"Of course not," I say. "The road noise won't get in the way?"

She unlocks her iPhone. "It's just a sample for my producer to give me feedback," she says.

Eliza is a voice actor, primarily for audiobooks and video games. When we met, she was voicing the villain for an indie computer game, copies of which I purchased proudly. It stings to remember helping her rehearse, reading opposite her for long nights on her old green couch. She played a powerful sorceress, and I found myself enchanted by other kinds of magic watching her talent come to life.

She shifts in her seat, unfolding her foot out from under her. I know her long legs get stiff on lengthy drives. *She's gorgeous,* the voice in my head says. No matter what, it's the first thing I think whenever my eyes find her. She's the most gorgeous woman I've ever met. Shoulder-length hair, once chestnut, now streaked with gold courtesy of the San Diego sun. Wide, intense eyes the color of the mist La Jolla is wrapped in every morning. Small, serious mouth. Utterly gorgeous.

Just . . . a gorgeous person who I happen to live with.

It's the second thing I think whenever I see my wife. The dif-

ficulty we've had connecting recently. I remember when her dancing eyes, her smile, were invitations into shared laughter and easy
conversation.

Now they're like the elegant details of the paintings I studied in
the art history class I took in undergrad. It was the only B that I got
in college.

I wish I could make casual conversation with her, the way I
would with a stranger or acquaintance. In those cases, I could ask
about their homes, their jobs, their childhoods. I've been com-
mended on my small talk, in fact. The managing partner at my
firm says I make clients comfortable, like they're old friends.

With Eliza, I've already asked those questions. I asked them
over dinners and coffees when we started dating in LA. When I still
couldn't figure out why the confident, funny woman sitting across
from me in the hipster café on La Cienega or in the incredible Thai
place on Sunset had swiped right on me, one UCLA law student out
of thousands of young professionals in the city. Even now, her responses from back then have the luster of young love when I remember them. *Grew up in Evanston. University of Chicago for college.
One sister, older. Moved to LA for acting.*

Yet, lately, I've started to feel like what I know is the biography
of Eliza Cutler, not Eliza herself. I knew the whole Eliza once, the
quirks, the impulses, the passions, the idiosyncrasies. Now, I can
sense new gaps in our knowledge of each other, ones I don't know
how to fill, not when I'm worried every inquiry will draw her closer
to uncovering the inadequacy in me—or when I feel like even having these questions is some incriminating sign. How do I *get to
know* the person I'm spending the rest of my life with?

Shouldn't I know her already?

I deeply wish I did. My devotion to Eliza, to our marriage, to our *relationship*, to the extent it's something different from our marriage—which it is, intimate instead of institutional—is unwavering.

It's something I don't know if my friends or even my parents really understand, even now. In litigation, half of the fight is just confronting the supposition of guilt, the presumption of where the problem lies. If I dared explain these issues, I know how everyone else would rule on our marriage, because I've heard their doubts before. I remember the unconvinced nods when I mentioned I'd met Eliza online. I remember the order of our friends' reactions when we told them we'd gotten engaged—first shock, *then* joy. I remember my mom's probing, insistent questions put to her twenty-three-year-old son, judgments in the form of delicate queries.

None of those doubts ever mattered to me. None of them matter now. Even when I don't know whether I deserve her, I know I want to spend the rest of my life with Eliza Cutler, née Kelly.

I just don't know *her*.

Eliza opens her recording app and hits record. I try not to move or make unnecessary noise while she starts into her selected excerpt. Her voice changes pitch just slightly, her diction shifting, her delivery coming more firmly. I recognize one of the many voices she has in her repertoire. It's always a little uncanny to hear. Not because it's vastly different from her normal voice—Eliza wouldn't force her vocal cords into unnatural shapes for so long it would risk destroying them. No, it's precisely the similarity I find unsettling. It's her, yet subtly transformed. Like there's this other person hiding within my wife.

While she reads, I let my mind return to my own work. I have one of the most important cases of my career waiting for me when we return home. I've spent the past five months doing depositions and marshaling other discovery to consolidate our position. What's left is prep for several of our key witnesses, the tech executives we're defending from claims they violated the terms of the sale that would save their company from bankruptcy. I'm on the trial counsel team, which means it's on me to craft the information we have into the story they can tell on the stand.

In truth, I'm sort of screwed. Getting everything in order will require some very, very long nights when we get back. But I refused to be the husband who couldn't take a one-week vacation to celebrate his fifth anniversary.

I'm running through the terms of the purchase documents in my head, feeling reassured by my recall of each warranty and covenant, when I catch what exactly Eliza's reading.

"I undressed my husband deliberately, the patience its own pleasure," Eliza says in focused, eloquent syllables. "I never needed to wait with him. Which made me want to, until I could no longer."

I blush.

Eliza continues on crisply. "We were together now, not ourselves except who we were with each other. I was no longer the vacation planner from Ontario, he no longer the consultant from Connecticut. We were bodies in motion."

It is now nearly impossible not to shift in my seat. Even the dappled ocean out my window starts to seem more insistent than iridescent, the reflected sun like a splinter in one side of my vision. *Possibly the scene will end here,* I tell myself. *Leaving the rest to the imagination, with literary finesse.*

It does not. "I felt myself grow wet with expectation," Eliza pronounces.

I have to clench my jaw while my wife's voice goes breathy, describing the character's mounting pleasure while her own chest heaves with—with echoes of sounds I haven't heard in I don't want to think about how long. Out of the corner of my eye, I notice the glance she shoots me. *She wants something,* I realize. I just don't know what.

Or maybe I do, and I just don't know how to give it.

"Fingers under his waistband, I took his firm cock in my hand," Eliza practically whimpers.

Suddenly, in my head I hear one thought like a twig snapping in a silent forest. If she were to narrate our real-life sex scenes, her description would sound nothing like this.

"Could you not?" I cut in, hearing something stung in my voice, then I control my tone. "I mean, could that wait?"

Eliza stops sharp and faces me. "You ruined my take." There's no frustration in her simple sentence—only other things I don't want to dwell on, like betrayal. She's not wrong to recognize how far my comment was from long nights on her green couch.

"Sorry," I say honestly. "But maybe you could do that . . . literally any other time? We agreed—no work on this trip."

"We haven't reached the hotel yet," she points out.

I never knew the sun could feel so cold, so unlike light. When we curve from the mountains onto the next flat stretch of seaside highway, it's like the heat is drained from the car. Because now, from its submergence in Eliza's statement of fact, I hear exactly what I expected. Disappointment.

Of course she's disappointed, hisses the insistent voice in my head. I'm disappointed in myself, too. I wish I could be the type of guy to pull this car over to the side of the empty chaparral road, who could inscribe Eliza's exhaled words onto her stunning body. I don't know where or how I've misplaced the part of myself that once would have. I don't know if it's work burnout or existential pressure or what. I just know Eliza wants it back.

God, so do I.

"Graham . . ." Eliza begins, her voice heavy.

I can't. I can't hear this right now. I want to pretend for just a little longer that I'm not sinking into a hole I can never climb out of. "Remember our first vacation?" I venture with desperation I know I'm not hiding. "In Ojai? With the horses?"

"Of course I do," Eliza says, then goes quiet.

I stare straight forward, focusing on the seemingly endless stretch of flat highway in front of me. It's clear what she's not saying. She's not content just to dwell on what was. If I glanced over, I'm certain I couldn't stand the sight of my shortfall on her perfect face.

When she speaks next, there's no misreading her resignation. "I do need to send out this sample tonight. Do you really mind?"

I know I can't say no, not when I've just flung what she was *really* hoping for off the perilous cliffs outside. I palm the steering wheel, my mind reaching for some sort of compromise. "Could you maybe not read . . . *that* scene?"

"What's wrong with *that* scene?" Crossing her legs, Eliza studies me.

I resist the urge to look at her, keeping my eyes on the road. "Come on, Eliza. You know what's wrong with it." I feel myself frown. I've had easier settlement negotiations with plaintiffs over millions of dollars.

Eliza is silent for a moment. When she replies, there's hurt in her voice I didn't intend to cause. "Yeah," she says, "I guess I do."

I wish I knew what to say. I push to wake up the parts of my brain experienced in this, in finding the perfect resolution of rejoinder. The way forward. I want to explain—I *need* to explain how I'm not rejecting *her*. I'm rejecting . . . myself, sort of. If I can just explain, she won't be thrilled, but she'll understand.

When the first words I want to say find their way to the tip of my tongue, though, Eliza's phone vibrates.

She looks down to read her screen, her brow furrowing. When she gives the shortest laugh under her breath, then sets off typing with white-nailed fingers flying over the keyboard, I know what she's doing is nothing career oriented. She's replying to Nikki, with whom her texting conversation never ends, it only pauses for several-hour stretches.

Out of the corner of my eye, I notice pink painting the base of Eliza's neck. I know Nicole Edleson well enough to guess she's asked something invasive about Eliza's and my sex life. In fact, I've known Nikki longer than I've known Eliza. She was my friend first. One of my freshman-year hallmates in college, Nikki was there for coffee runs while I was studying for the LSAT, and I was there for moral support while she was interviewing for engineering jobs.

Even so, when I introduced her to Eliza, Nikki didn't need long to pick her new favorite. It was not me. I couldn't even blame her— I, too, was smitten with the girl I'd been chatting with online for weeks.

One day, Eliza herself will go the way of Nikki. She'll realize there's someone better out there. She'll leave me behind.

While Eliza texts, I feel discomfort constricting my chest. I don't know how to fix this. Not just this conversation—*this*. This quiet expanse we're wading through, together but separate.

I don't break the silence. Instead, I let the sparkling ocean mock me the rest of the drive.

3

Eliza

WHEN I STEP out of the car, I can finally breathe—though this place is breathtaking. We're on a cliffside with forest surrounding the inn, dark green trees soaring high into the sky. The scent on the wind is the resinous sweetness of wood meeting with the bitter salt of seawater.

It's *nearly* enough to lift my spirits. But not quite. If the drive up was any indication of how this anniversary getaway will go, I'm not heartened. Graham knows I'm trying. Trying to be fun, trying to be flirty, trying to find the spark. I don't understand why he won't let the light in. Why he's suddenly so self-conscious.

He walks stiffly ahead of me, his frame one of sharp corners like he's made of matchsticks, though these never catch fire. He's heading for the wooden doors of the hotel's understated, geometric entrance.

I can hear the ocean past the inn. I suspect the water would be visible over the edge of the cliff, but in the nighttime, everything is black. I know the hotel boasts gorgeous sightseeing trails—I couldn't help clicking through every photo on the website. In a hopeful flicker, I imagine going on an early morning walk with Graham.

Then the memory of the smothering quiet in the car descends over me. On instinct, I start strategizing how I'll find my way down to the picturesque pathways on my own. Maybe I could schedule a morning massage, then take my time returning to the room.

Immediately, I feel guilty. I shouldn't be fantasizing about spending time away from my husband, especially not on the very first day of our anniversary retreat.

Once more, I breathe in the night breeze. Fortified, I follow Graham inside.

The Treeline Resort, our home for the next week, is maddeningly perfect, like enjoyment of its every lovely detail waits just out of my reach. It's modern in an earthy way, sculpted with wood and stone in uneven lines meant to evoke nature. I walk into the large lobby, unable to help drinking in the pristine design and inviting low light. Behind the reception desk, a waterfall bubbles quietly.

"Checking in?"

The hostess smiles welcomingly from the desk. Her name is Rosie, I read on her name tag. She fits here, her sleek black hair and impeccable slate-gray dress matching the cool, clean simplicity of the place.

"Cutler," Graham replies gruffly.

I frown. Unless he's in court, Graham doesn't have an edge to him. He's not one of those guys. The Graham I know is congenial, even boyishly charming. I've been to his firm's parties with him. I know his colleagues like him for this—for how when he's not shredding the plaintiff's case, he's ready with a genuine smile, a firm handshake, and a clever compliment.

I'm a little surprised to see his sharpness come out now. I embarrassed him in the car, I realize, which he's metabolized into frustration via the commonest of male equations. I didn't mean to. I was trying to have fun. Now I don't know how to fix it. I *do* know he'll be irritated when we get to our room and I tell him I still have to finish recording my sample. Grimly, I play the conversation out in my head. *No. I said I'd send it in tonight. Probably thirty more minutes? Yes, Graham, it includes the words "heaving breasts."*

The hostess—Rosie—doesn't seem to notice Graham's tone. With unchanged cheer, she types our name into the computer. "Will you be celebrating anything during your stay?" she asks.

Graham darts me a glance.

I feel my eyebrows flit up. Close to confrontational.

"Our five-year wedding anniversary," my husband grinds out.

Now Rosie's expression changes. Hearts practically pop into her eyes. Her pleasant smile melts into one reserved for the mushiest of romance. In fact, for someone who probably encounters plenty of celebrating couples in her line of work, her enthusiasm seems remarkably genuine.

"We have a number of experiences programmed this week," she says excitedly, simultaneously tapping keystrokes into the computer. The printer next to her whirs, producing a new sheet of crisp white paper. "Some are mixers designed for those here for our dating workshop," she continues, "while others are more intimate and designed for couples. I recommend those. You're too late for dinner, but our bar will be serving food for the next two hours."

I take the paper, trying to look grateful. Glancing down, I catch sight of *cliffside picnic, stargazing, basking pools, yoga.* I read it as *strained silence during cliffside picnic, strained silence during stargazing, strained silence in the basking pools, strained silence during yoga.* Rosie beams while I fold the list, which I shove into my bag.

She returns to her hidden screen. "I have you all set for—" Confusion swipes the smile from her face.

My heart lifts. *Did Helen mess up the reservation? Or was there a computer error, leaving us roomless with no other rooms available in the hotel? Will we just* have *to drive back home tonight?*

"—two rooms," Rosie finishes.

I look to Graham. He shifts next to me, leaning forward like he wants to see for himself. "That can't be right," he says.

Rosie keeps clicking, eyebrows furrowed, until understanding flits into her expression. "This was our mistake. When your reservation was made online originally, it was for one of our standard mountain-view rooms. But then a Mrs. Helen Cutler called to reserve the honeymoon cliff suite instead. Looks like the computer made a new reservation rather than an upgrade." Evidently relieved to have uncovered the problem, Rosie smiles with renewed warmth. "It's no problem. We won't charge you for the duplicate booking, of course. I imagine you'd prefer the honeymoon suite?"

Graham nods like someone's offered him the choice between hearing bad news or bad news. "Yeah, we'll—"

"Hold on."

The words leap out of my mouth.

Four confused eyes find me. I don't blame them. I'm not sure what I'm going to say next either, but the start of some vague idea is catching in me. Graham's features show plain weariness, and when he speaks, his voice holds unhidden exasperation. "Eliza, we should take the suite."

"Of course," I say. "But—"

What's made me hesitate is the vision forming in my head of what this *vacation* will really look like. If we check into this honeymoon suite together, it's going to be the car ride, but worse. The images of the rooms I saw online carousel through my head— soaking tubs big enough for two, California king–sized beds covered in rose petals, champagne in sweating buckets. Graham and me being hit over the head with romance won't suddenly rekindle our spark. It'll feel like pressure.

Maybe—maybe what we need is space.

"Let's keep both rooms," I say.

The next seconds fill with charged silence, empty except for the consistent warbling of the waterfall.

Graham gives Rosie a rigid smile. "Could we have a minute?" he asks Rosie. The gruffness is gone. I've honestly never seen him so effortfully *polite*, not even when we tiptoe past every conversation we're not having in the confines of our house. There, forced politeness is the name of the game. *This* is Graham's major leagues.

When he leads us several steps from the desk, our backs to the waterfall, he stops smiling. Defensiveness rises up in me. Shacking up in the honeymoon suite, recording my sample in the bathroom while Graham stews in the bedroom, is not the vacation either of us wants.

Graham, however, seems oblivious to this internal struggle of mine. He just looks exasperated. "What would we use the second room for, Eliza?"

"I'll stay there," I say firmly, summoning up every cool, collected character I've ever voiced. "Not the whole trip. Maybe just a night or two."

His expression darkens. "You want to spend our anniversary apart," he clarifies. "We might as well drive back home."

I put a hand on his arm.

He stills, uncertainty and maybe something like yearning painting new streaks into his demeanor. It's been days since I've touched him this way. His expression says he knows.

"No," I say. "I want to be together. But this . . . This isn't together."

The hesitation flattens out of his expression. "And separate rooms is?" he asks archly.

I purse my lips, fighting not to snap. He's not working with me here. I wonder if he even understands how much I'm not enjoying this conversation, how hard it is to voice the problems we're facing instead of letting them ebb into silence like we did in the car. Or how hard it is to reckon with this physical impossibility of love—the way you can grow distant from someone while going to sleep next to them every night.

I think the only reason I'm doing it now is because this is our anniversary. I'm seized with a determined sort of sentimentality—maybe recognizing our commitment to our marriage doesn't need to look like gifts or champagne. Maybe it shouldn't. Maybe it should look like doing something to make our relationship *better*.

I press on. "I just wonder if we should, I don't know, take it slow. Give ourselves space to *want* this."

Graham looks away from me, his eyes clouding. "I do want this," he replies.

I'm glad he said it, but saying it isn't enough. I have to fight down the stubborn indignation this sparks in me. Does he *want* everyone who thought we were too young, too impulsive, too quick in our marriage to be right? "Come on," I say with forced patience. "It's time we acknowledge something is missing here. Let's give ourselves a chance to find it again. I *want* to find it again."

I seek out his eyes, hoping he sees in mine how much I believe in what I'm saying. My husband must know I wouldn't even venture onto this subject if I didn't. I don't *do* this—dig into conversations with fearless vigor. It's the worst sort of uncomfortable for me. Right now, the lobby's perfect temperature feels like punishing heat, my favorite white sweater like coarse wool. Graham must know I'm only insisting on this for him, for us.

Which I am. Fuck the distance. I've never loved anyone like I've loved Graham. We're worth fighting for.

I just need him to fight *with* me instead of fighting *me*.

Graham steps back from me. "I would certainly never make you stay with me when you don't want to," he states flatly. With flippant resignation, he gestures to the reception desk. "Do whatever you want."

His dismissal lodges painfully in my chest. *This* is why I don't expose my sore spots. People I love never seem to resist striking them.

I wilt, but I don't weaken. I know I'm right. Something needs to change.

"We can meet at the bar for dinner in thirty minutes," I say, hiding my hurt under impersonal logistics. "Just enough time to unwind. Apart."

"Fine," Graham says instantly. It's a nothing word. Operational.

Undeterred, I hold my head high and return to the reception desk. "Hi," I say to Rosie. "We want to keep both rooms." I hold up my credit card. "Put the standard room on my card, under my name."

Rosie doesn't blink, even though I'm sure my request is unprecedented. Nevertheless, I feel the need to offer some explanation.

"I have work to finish tonight, and he's had a long drive." While this is, in fact, technically correct, I'm guessing Rosie intuits it's only the tip of the iceberg. Doing me no favors, Graham stays silent be-hind me.

"Of course," the hostess says smoothly. "The suite can be reached down the path outside the doors to your left, the standard room from the elevators to your right." She hands us each key cards. Mine features a picture of pine trees. Graham's has the ocean.

"This will be a good thing," I promise Graham.

I'm expecting no reply, ready for him to leave silently into the night.

Instead, in what I know is the only concession he's capable of offering, he quietly surprises me by nodding only once. He doesn't meet my eyes. Then, sliding his card into his pocket, he walks off toward the honeymoon suite on his own.

4

Graham

SPACE? SEPARATE ROOMS? *On our anniversary?*

Eliza's words clang in my head like a five a.m. alarm I've dourly set for myself. Part of me doesn't want to dwell on how frustrated I am with her. Part of me doesn't want to concede she . . . has a point, even if her solution makes no sense.

But she does. We love each other, but we don't behave like people in love. We don't in our house. We don't in the car. We probably wouldn't in the honeymoon suite. Something *is* missing, like she said. Something she's decided demands exiling us to separate corners of the hotel.

Outside the lobby, I let the eager bellhop escort me to my room. I can tell the guy is baffled to be showing the honeymoon suite to someone undeniably on his own, but I offer no explanations. It takes nearly ten minutes walking the dark path, the hushed rustling of the unseen trees providing the only hints of our surroundings, until finally, out of the forest, we reach the modern private bungalow on the cliff's edge.

I won't lie—it's stunning. Outdoor lighting illuminates the walls of maple wood inset with sweeping curved windows. This place is the essence of private, no faint whispers of nearby guests, no distant flickers of light in the trees. While I wait in front of the sleek entrance, the bellhop unlocks and swings open the door. Every LED inside smoothly comes on, carpeting the pristine room in dim, romantic lighting.

My personal honeymoon suite.

The bellhop clears his throat. "Do you want me to give you a tour?"

I peer down the hallway. "Suite" is too small a word for this place. In front of me is a full living room, complete with built-in furniture in earth tones. Fireplace, curved sofa, the works. "No," I say. "I'm good."

The young man pauses in the doorway, looking like a summer intern who doesn't understand the assignment I've given him and is too nervous to clarify. "Will you be expecting anyone else tonight?" he finally asks.

My stomach turns over. "Not to my knowledge." When the bellhop only nods uncertainly, I hand over a tip. "Thanks so much," I say.

I close the door, ending the line of questioning there. Instantly, I'm aware of the silence. The room is so quiet, my shoes sound sharply on the smooth concrete floor—heated, I would guess. Grudgingly, I explore my accommodations, grimacing at the champagne and rose petals on the bed. The bathroom boasts a sculpted tub with room for two. Outside, the balcony looks over what I'm certain in the morning will be breathtaking views of the cliffs and the water. It wraps around the whole length of the suite and ends in a private Jacuzzi.

In one of my very first cases, one of our big corporate clients was sued in state court in Nebraska. Product liability, hundreds of plaintiffs, the whole nine yards. For three weeks of pre-trial delays, I lived in a shabby hotel outside of downtown Omaha. Just me, my lumpy bed, my rattling mini fridge, and piles and piles of documents.

Right now, I would rather be there.

I stand in the middle of my spacious living room, not knowing what to do with myself for the next thirty minutes before I said I'd meet Eliza at the bar. The truth is, I don't want to spend one unnecessary second in this perfect room. I don't want to be here without my wife. I wish she were with me. I wish we were enjoying this together, not that we know how anymore. The pain of this longing isn't a bruise—it's a splinter. Specific, reminding me of its presence, impossible to ignore.

I unzip my suitcase and change the sneakers I'm wearing for my loafers. I'll just go to the bar early. It beats sitting here, with the rose petals silently imposing. Slinging my favorite navy blazer over my shoulders, I head out the door.

With the chorus of crickets surrounding me, I walk in what I remember is the general direction of the hotel. I'm not looking forward to muscling through one more dinner of small talk with Eliza instead of sweet nothings. I'm just not looking forward to being without her, either. Every day, the same paradox.

I wander in the unhelpful dark for five minutes until I realize I'm on the wrong path. When I glance up from the gravel, I notice I'm not getting closer to the hotel. Disoriented, I turn back the way

I came, continuing until I reach a fork in the road, then uncertainly choose the path on the right.

"The only thing back there is my room," I hear in front of me. The source of the voice is a guy even taller than I am, with stocky shoulders and an enviable spring in his step. "So you're either lost," he continues cheerfully, "or you're presumptuous."

"Shit, sorry. Lost," I say, pausing in the middle of the path. "I meant to head to the bar."

"I'm heading there myself," he says enthusiastically. "I'll walk with you. This place is a maze at night."

I follow him, grateful. Not just for the guidance in these labyrinthine woods, either. While we continue in companiable silence, I work out why. This guy doesn't know me. He doesn't know Eliza. It's an odd relief to recognize. It leaves me craving easy conversation, the kind you can only have with someone you'll never see again.

I seize on the opportunity. "Been here long?"

"This is my second night. I'm here for the dating workshop," my traveling companion replies. His white-blond hair is slicked back, his chin pronounced. He's maybe six foot five. He looks like he smiles a lot. "How about you?"

"I'm here for my anniversary," I answer honestly, even though I know it'll prompt the same conversation I had with the bellhop. But I just don't have the creative energy to come up with some other story.

Sure enough, he looks behind me like he's expecting my partner to materialize from the forest. "Where's your—" he begins.

"*Not* here," I cut him off, sullenly.

From the way his expression softens sympathetically, it's clear he read details I did not intend into my response. Nevertheless, I . . .

don't correct him. It's freeing in the same way the anonymity of this conversation is. He doesn't need to know what's really going on with me.

"Shit, man. I'm sorry," he says. "That's worse than the two hours of online dating photo sessions I sat for today. Let me buy you a drink," he goes on, upbeat once more. "I'm David Berqvist."

I'm on the verge of saying I have plans when I catch myself. For the next thirty minutes, my *plans* consist of scrolling on my work phone, rereading emails while I wait for Eliza. Who is currently recording herself reading a sex scene. In *her* room. Looking up, I find the lights of the main hotel coming into view.

"That sounds great," I say. "I'm Graham."

5

Eliza

I DON'T THINK my producer is going to like this sample. My pacing was fine, my pronunciation clear without stumbling, my inflection sharp. The problem is the note of bitterness in my every word that I couldn't iron out even on my third try. Out of time, I email off the voice memo, then toss my phone onto the crisp white comforter of my queen-size bed.

My room is simple, elegant, but small. My window looks out into the indiscernible black of night. I turn on the sink in the white bathroom and wash my face quickly, then pause, staring into the mirror. I'm not looking forward to dinner with Graham, who I know will be practically wooden. If I'm lucky, he'll charitably try to make succinct conversation. Likelier, we'll prod our food in silence.

Then I'll return here, to my queen-size bed.

Knowing there's no use delaying, I head out toward the elevators. I'm in the main hotel, and other rooms run the length of the hallway. On my way, I pass not one but two canoodling couples fumbling to open their doors. I avert my eyes. Not even my cast-mates backstage during the high school theater productions I was in were this handsy.

I ride the elevator, feeling glum. I know I was the one who suggested Graham and I stay in separate rooms, and I stand by it. Still, I'm not *glad* this is the situation we're in.

Downstairs, I ready myself. Flatbread and hummus and forced pleasantries, here I come.

But when I reach the bar, I don't see Graham at first. Then—*do my eyes deceive me?* He's sitting with a man I don't recognize—laughing, looking convivial. Not wooden in the least.

I stare for a moment, uncomprehending. What pulls me forward isn't obligation or time, but curiosity. I walk up beside the stranger by the bar in time to hear the man finish the story he's telling.

"I swear, my brothers sent me the workshop info as a joke when my ex dumped me," he says emphatically, sounding not even slightly embarrassed to admit the dumping. He grins. "I booked my stay *immediately* and sent them my room confirmation."

Graham, impossibly, is wiping tears from his eyes.

I can't remember the last time I saw him laugh this hard. "Hi," I say, feeling weirdly self-conscious, like I'm the one intruding. "I don't mean to interrupt."

Graham glances up, finally clocking my arrival. While I'm not surprised, I can't fight the pang of sadness when our eyes meet. The light in Graham's doesn't go out, but flickers and fades, like fire in the wind.

The stranger swivels to face me. *His* enthusiasm is unchanged.

"No, not at all," he reassures me. "Have we met? I'm sorry if I'm forgetting. I'm awful with faces, and the seminar today was packed."

"We haven't," I say. "I'm Eliza."

"David." He shoves out his hand, which I shake. I open my mouth to start the small talk, the polite dance of *How long is your stay?* and *Well, I guess we'll see you around.*

Instead, David continues.

"Come join us for a drink. I'm trying to cheer up my new friend, Graham." He gestures casually between us. "Graham, Eliza."

I close my mouth. My eyes dart to my husband's.

"Dude," David prompts. "Shake her hand and stop moping."

Our gazes lock, and I raise an eyebrow, waiting for Graham to clarify. He doesn't.

I don't understand why not, what game Graham's playing. But if he's deliberately not clarifying I'm his wife to his new "buddy" David—I guess I'll follow his lead. I proposed something pretty unusual in the lobby. Could this be Graham's way of doing the same?

I put my hand out in my husband's direction.

"Hi, Graham," I say. "Nice to meet you."

Graham reaches forward slowly, taking my hand in his like he wasn't the one who once slid onto my fourth finger the ring glittering there now. His eyes remain on mine. I see something new unfurling in them. It's something unexpected, something charged, something no less intense for how unreadable it is. Sound without syllables, color without shape.

David chimes in, completely oblivious. He seems like someone who could carry on a conversation for hours. "Are you here for the dating workshop?"

I manage to rip my gaze from whatever is going on in Graham's. "I'm not," I say neutrally, still trying to decipher what just happened.

David throws back the rest of his cocktail. "Neither is Graham," he says, nodding casually to the man whose blood type I know is B negative and who only sleeps in UCLA T-shirts. "I'm trying to convince him to enroll, though," he continues. "Can you believe this—he's here to commemorate his wedding anniversary. Alone. Have you ever heard of something so sad? I told him it's time to get back out there. The workshop is perfect."

I turn to Graham, leveraging years of undergrad drama classes to keep my expression neutral. "Is that so?" I ask lightly. "I'm curious. What exactly happened to your wife? Did she die?" I raise an eyebrow, communicating to Graham that if he told this stranger I passed away, he's going to *need* a dating workshop.

Right on cue, David coughs.

"No, she didn't die," Graham says levelly.

"Where is she, then?"

Graham doesn't back down from my tone. "Beats me," he replies.

Under the low lighting, I feel the pounding of my pulse, like my heart knows something I don't. While I haven't forgotten where my flirtatiousness in the car got me, I guess I'm either foolish or desperate, because I don't overthink my next words. "Well," I venture, "you're too good looking to be sitting here with just David for long. No offense," I note to Graham's new friend.

"None taken." David shrugs. "My guy is handsome, no doubt."

Graham eyes me. I ready myself for his next retreat.

Instead, he sets his drink down. "It sounds like you're offering to join me," he says.

Quietly thrilled, I don't hesitate. I slide onto the stool next to him. "I guess I am."

Graham pauses. I wait. Until—"Can I buy you a drink?" His question comes out uneven, like the first table read of whatever scene we're setting here.

Still, I smile. Not too much, though. "Maybe," I say. "Did you buy one for David?"

Brow furrowing, Graham studies me. "No, but I'm not flirting with David. No offense," he echoes my words to his new friend.

"None taken," David repeats, seeming to really mean it. In truth, this doesn't surprise me. It seems unlikely the golden-haired, volleyball-player-built guy sitting with us is very insecure in his desirability.

"I haven't done this in years, you know," Graham comments.

"What? Celebrated your anniversary with David instead of with your wife—"

"No," Graham cuts in. "Hit on someone."

My cheeks heat pleasantly. It's not just how forward he's being, I realize. I . . . don't know what Graham is going to say next. The anticipation of his every reply sends delicious shivers through me. "Well," I say. "I think it's sort of like riding a bike."

"So risk of injury is high, then? Will I need a helmet to spend time with you, Eliza?"

"No." I fight not to laugh. Graham's quick on his feet, quicker than I remembered. "Easy to learn. Difficult to master."

Graham *hmm*s. Staring past me into the bar, he nods. "Mind giving me a quick refresher course, then?"

I purse my lips in consideration. "How much time do you have tonight?"

"Shit. Sounds like you *don't* need the dating workshop," David comments, sounding impressed. It makes me realize it's the first thing he's said while Graham and I volleyed banter like someone was scripting the dialogue for us. *Banter!* I repeat in my head in wonderment. *We bantered!*

I look at him, eager for the next round of our improvised game. My stomach is fluttering like I really have just hit it off with the cute stranger at the bar. Suddenly, though, the anticipation in Graham's eyes fades as his expression blanks. I know the look well. Stage fright. The actor who has forgotten what comes next.

Graham's reply comes like a slammed door. "No. I do," he says. "I suck at this."

What? Incredulity scatters my delight. How could Graham possibly think that? What conversation was *he* just having?

With stubborn hope, I reach for the spark we were just sharing. Our flirtation hasn't collapsed, I insist to myself. It's just—stumbled. It needs rescuing. "You can't suck that much if you managed to get someone to marry you," I point out.

The effort is futile. Graham's eyes no longer meet mine. He goes on, his familiar angular features seeming to steepen like the impassive walls of his own private fortress. "What I like—*liked* about marriage," he corrects for David's sake, "is *not* having to date anymore."

"Come on," David says genially, no doubt hoping to reinsert some normalcy into the conversation. "Dating isn't that bad."

Graham replies instantly. "It is." His voice is level, neutral. I know he's drawing on years of professional experience debating. Back-and-forth is like breathing for my charming husband. Wiping the perspiration on his glass with his thumb, he goes on. "Endlessly trying to get to know someone—it's exhausting."

"Maybe dating shouldn't end just because you're married," I say, performatively matching his lightness. I might not be a lawyer, but I played Demi Moore's role in *A Few Good Men* in college. "You can still date your spouse, you know."

His eyes flash to mine. "If she were around, that is."

Something jolts through me. "Well," I say, "you're doing a pretty great job of picking me up." Leaving Graham with my honest reply, I find I'm surprised at how quietly significant this exchange of ours is. How unusual for us. Wrapped and veiled in the distance of strangers, this conversation is about our real marriage.

It's not just charged. It's more genuine than anything we've said to each other in months.

David gets up, rolling his shoulders grandly, like he's enjoying relieving tension. "It's time for me to head in, folks. For whatever reason, the online-dating crash course starts at eight in the morning tomorrow. Hey—" He turns to Graham, looking seized by a brilliant idea. "Have you considered online dating? Might be just the low-pressure setting you need to get back out there."

"I met my wife online," Graham replies gruffly.

"Well, shit." David looks unperturbed to have struck out. "Good night, man. Nice meeting you, Eliza." He grabs his jacket from his seat before walking off.

I'm left wrestling with my own mixed-up emotions, maybe even disappointed Graham and I will no longer be keeping up this pretense. Everything I felt in the elevator has come rushing back, but there's something else now, too. I won't just be *not* enjoying dinner. I'll know how different it is from the unexpected charge of the past few minutes.

"Did you order food yet?" I ask.

"No. Not yet." Graham's face is shuttered. It's the gaunt ghost of his expression in the car, the one I can't help summoning. He's reverted to the self-consciousness I never knew to haunt my husband until suddenly, inexplicably, recently.

This time, though, I think I know how to help. "It's not just you," I remark.

He glances up, guarded. "What isn't," he says. Not a question. More like a *No Trespassing* sign.

I trespass. "I feel self-conscious, too," I say simply. When Graham scoffs, I know exactly why. I'm supposed to be this confident actress—free-spirited, charismatic, full of inspiration. *People reject me, too, Graham,* I want to say. *People judge me, too.*

I don't, though. I don't want to open up that conversation, to show Graham how broken I feel. Ready to move on, I reach for the menu, scanning the limited bar-food options. "We should order," I say, hating how much I feel like I'm hiding.

Graham isn't the only one skirting shadows in his head, I recognize. Maybe I retreat too much. Maybe I need to work on fears of my own.

It means something that I want to, though, doesn't it? Especially now, with the tantalizing echoes of the past hour ringing in my head. I'm curious. Not excited, exactly, but I feel it lingering within possibility. While I'm not sure what, we might have stumbled onto something. The truth is, the first few hours of this vacation haven't looked like I expected. We met for dinner from separate rooms. We had a real, raw conversation, if one cloaked in performance. We bantered.

While Graham mulls over the menu, I reach out for one firm thought floating in the electric fog of the evening. Before tonight, I honestly didn't know if banter like that was still possible for us.

Now I know it is.

Graham

I SEEK SHELTER in the menu. Not from Eliza—who never ceases to stun me with how captivating she is. For once, I know exactly what she's thinking. She thought our exchange just now was fun.

I feel exactly the same. It was.

No, I'm hiding in the list of nondescript bar-food items from the conversation she seemed to want to have. *I feel self-conscious, too.* Doesn't she know it's *worse* if I confess to how I'm feeling? Invite it into the room with us? Her sympathy will eventually turn into pity, which will only make me feel lesser.

So instead, I pass my eyes over the menu, once, twice, barely reading. When the bartender comes by, I order something I forget instantaneously. Evading Eliza's gaze, I survey the space, which is crowded. It's peak hours, the place full of people getting ready to enjoy the night. The bar is roomy, with elegant metal light fixtures and furnishings sculpted of deep red wood.

While the minutes pass, we wait in silence for our food. Well, not silence. More precisely, we wait without talking. Consequently, we're left listening to the guy in a well-cut suit next to me hitting on the girl he's with.

Honestly, it's working. The woman's *wow*s seem genuine when he mentions the locations he flies out to for some manner of investment banking—meetings in Singapore, in Rome. She even giggles when he interjects some especially colorful commentary on his coworkers into his story of closing a Wall Street deal. His emphases feel pompous and overdone, but he sounds . . . confident.

It's foreign to me, despite this guy's career not being too far from the years in which I've devoted thousands of billable hours to the CEOs and conglomerates my firm represents. I feel skillful, sure, but not exactly fascinating. It's probably just insecurity whispering in my ear, but it's easy to fear Eliza sees in me something of a cliché. One more gray suit, one more cog in a machine irrelevant to her pursuits. It's a reason I stopped bringing up my work in conversations with her. Like lawyers, finance dudes don't exactly have the greatest reputation in the dating scene, but—the subject of our eavesdropping makes me wonder if maybe it's possible for my kind of profession to seem interesting instead of just irritating.

Finally, our food comes. I dig in, feeling the increasing weight of the pressure to recapture our banter from moments ago. It wasn't easy to keep up with Eliza's wit then. Now, it's even harder. I wish David were still here, his comfortably third-wheeling presence relieving some of the expectation.

"How's your room?" she asks.

I put down my half-finished slider, feeling my hunger subside. The casualness of her question is head-spinning. *Your room?* Like we're colleagues reaching for small talk in between sales presentations. Truthfully, I'm still not very sure of my feelings on our unique lodgings—I'm one part not thrilled to bring our issues out into the open, one part willing to walk into the sun if Eliza wanted me to.

So instead, I reach for pleasantry to match hers. "You could have had the suite, you know. If you wanted."

"I know," Eliza replies. "I was just asking to make conversation."

I blink. More inexplicable nonchalance. But then, we did just have a very weird make-believe session where we got "introduced" to each other. I guess we can pretend chatting about our rooms, *plural*, is normal, too. "The suite is fantastic. Unbelievable," I say, omitting the fact I didn't want to spend one second more than I had to there. "How's *your* room?"

"Very pleasant," Eliza answers.

I finish off my first slider.

"Are we going to talk about how you told that man you didn't have a wife?" she asks calmly.

I choke on my miniature hamburger. Regaining control of my windpipe, I face her. Eliza watches me with emotionless curiosity, the reflected light fixtures twinkling in her gray eyes. I decide not to give her the defensive reply she's no doubt expecting. I've cut apart more complex issues in court. I can certainly find the nuances when I'm litigating for myself. "I didn't tell him that," I say evenly. "I told him my wife wasn't with me. He reasonably drew his own conclusions."

Eliza's expression shades faintly, like a single cloud in an otherwise clear sky. "Right. Well, you could have introduced me at any time."

"You could have introduced yourself," I parry. "You didn't. It's like you want it this way."

I knew she was enjoying the performance we were putting on, pretending we didn't know each other. It wasn't just the actress in her delighting in the exercise, either. It was her. She was enjoying rewriting the rules of us.

While I was, too, this certainly wasn't my plan for the first night of this trip. In fact, tonight has continued to unfold further and further from the evening I'd imagined. I didn't want to be talking to David Berqvist in the first place. I just wanted to have dinner with my wife. I mean, I *really* wanted to have dinner with my wife with whom I have endless topics of engaging conversation, whom I could listen to read explicit content for hours, and with whom I have mutually satisfying sex every night.

But I would've settled for dinner.

"Which way?" Eliza asks. "Us acting like we don't know each other?"

I'm still surprised by how frankly she's handling this entire conversation. I don't show it. "Tell me you didn't like me better when I was pretending to be a stranger," I challenge her.

Her overcast eyes flit from mine for a split second, then return, but it's too late. I know what her answer is.

When she speaks, her voice has softened. More genuine now, less poised. While I'm still pissed, I listen. "It's not about liking you better, Graham," Eliza says. "I love you. But I feel like I don't know you. Not the way I used to." She sighs. "I mean, yeah. You pretending to be a stranger to me felt . . . honest. Like we could say things we couldn't normally. It was *easy* talking to you. Flirting with you. We could be open in ways we haven't been, be comfortable with not knowing each other."

I hide how her conclusion hurts me. "We can be open with each other," I insist, hearing the forced note in my conviction.

Eliza watches me for a long moment like she wants this to be true. It spurs some indignant hope in me. If I can just prove this to her—

"Okay," Eliza finally says. "Let's try it."

My mind fires to life, driven by stubborn insistence. *I prove things to people professionally,* I remind myself. I can do this. Whatever's wrong with us, I can prove we're not so far gone we can't have one dinner conversation. I remember the day, remember its most strained moments—until finally I seize on something. "So, what's this new book you're recording?" I ask.

Eliza's expression dims. "I want to work with you here," she says gently. "But I could email you the pitch for the book I'm performing. I could forward it to you in two seconds. You could read it in ten. You could do the same thing for every book I ever read without really coming closer to knowing *me,*" she explains with pained patience.

Frustrated, yet grudgingly understanding what she means, I retreat into my head, wracking my thoughts some more. *Eliza just doesn't understand the real problem here,* some firm, fatalistic little voice in me says. It's not that I *won't* ask her real questions. I *can't* ask her real questions. I've either asked them already or I can't locate them past veils of not knowing what I don't know.

Suddenly, just like that, quick, shallow desperation cuts into me. Usually, I only feel like I've been treading water for hours. Right now, I feel like I've been treading water for days, with no signs of shore in sight. I need to find something. *Anything, now.*

"Do you want to pick a new show to watch on TV?" I manage wildly.

Eliza doesn't reply. She just looks sad. Unable to keep meeting her eyes, I lower my gaze.

"Graham," she says. Half guarded, half imploring. "Is this what you want? Is *this* how you would prefer this week to look? Honestly?"

"How do *you* want the week to look?" I fire back, looking up sharply. The posture of her question pisses me off, because this—this week, this year, this horrible conversation—isn't *me* failing. It isn't *me* taking wrong turns while Eliza clutches the map. We got to this tense gray place *together*.

"Well," Eliza says, then pauses.

In her silence, I realize she's . . . thinking. I'd meant the question rhetorically, a rejection of sole responsibility for our issue. But in the midst of my flourish, Eliza is starting to form an answer. There's some decision here, some idea forming secretly in her. The entire room narrows down to her hesitation.

"Maybe we *should* be strangers," she says.

I know I don't hide the dubious shock on my face. I'd begun to wonder whether she wanted to go home or maybe go to counseling. Not even years of high-stakes litigation have prepared me for *this*.

"For a couple days," she clarifies hastily. "Just like we did tonight. Play this game, see where it takes us. Because"—she swallows—"I want to have more conversations like the one we just had."

I want to object to her. I'm good at finding argumentative angles, supplying facts or twisting words to support my claims. Here, though, it's harder. Part of me knows she's right—or right in some regards. Our relationship *has* lost something, and our discussion of dating had substance in ways our conversations never do.

"Why don't you want to?" Eliza presses gently. There's no misreading her tone. She isn't pushing or judging. She's inviting. In my silence, she reaches out, her hand finding my arm.

The featherlight contact of her fingers is instantly reassuring. I stare into the slate swirl of her eyes. I want to reach for easy dismissals, to say we don't live in a make-believe world.

Still, part of me is drawn to the idea, even though it's unexpected. But then, recently I've begun to believe *expecting* how your marriage will look is like trying to trace the unknowable. It's their beauty and their terror. Every marriage is its own dance, every step revealed only in the moment of its creation. Invisible to everyone except its two participants, unpredictable even to them.

Is this our next step?

Maybe.

"I'm . . . not saying I don't want to," I manage. In some distant corner of my head, I'm quietly stunned at how hard this conversation is. Part of my career is literally negotiating, parsing complexities into one-way-or-the-other conversations. I've never once found it this difficult. "I'm just . . . not saying it would work," I go on.

When Eliza shrugs, the easy grace of it seems superhuman. "Sure," she says, "but why not try? Unless there's some other reason you don't want to."

I hesitate. I could employ those familiar muscles, could supply rebuttals and counters until the cows come home.

But—this is Eliza. If I'm going to resist, I owe her the real reason why.

"I don't know that I can," I confess, thinking of how I choked just minutes ago. "I don't know if I'm good enough at this sort of thing."

My wife watches me. "What sort of thing?"

I pull my eyes from hers, gazing off into the open, dark bar. "Being . . . charming. Interesting," I say. "Fun."

When Eliza laughs, it's my worst fears confirmed. Of course my chorus of insecurities is ridiculous to her. Why couldn't I escape into stilted small talk over ordinary hotel food? It's not long now before this moment of truth—this moment of weakness—turns into one more deficiency in me. No longer hungry, I start to get up.

Eliza moves to interlace her fingers with mine, stopping me. I dare to meet her gaze. "I think you are," she says. "Look at the conversation we just had while we were pretending to meet. It was—let's see." She pauses like she's concentrating hard. "*Hm.* Charming. Interesting. Fun. Three for three, I think."

It's not quite enough to reassure me. But it is enough to return me to my seat. Eliza waits like she understands I have more reservations to unpack, more to say.

Which I do. "What if it doesn't work?" Behind my question hide doubts I think she hears. I'm not one of her thespian friends. I'm not spontaneous or inspired. I can't just *riff* with her like they would.

"Then we'll stop," Eliza says. "We'll figure something else out. But I want us back, Graham." The ease in her voice splits down the middle into something raw. "Don't you?"

It is the only easy question of the night.

I grip her hand tighter. "More than anything."

"Then try this for me," Eliza implores me gently. "Please."

On our first night in the one-bedroom in Westwood we moved into when I was finishing law school, we were determined to complete our unpacking in one go. In hindsight, this was ridiculous. Taking the bar was easier. But there we were, methodically moving through suitcases, wordlessly organizing sheets, soap, silverware, while our eyes started to sting from exhaustion. Finally, Eliza set to putting her shoes on the flimsy shoe rack I'd built earlier in the day. I guess I missed one or two screws, because the moment she placed her favorite sneakers on the top rack, the whole thing collapsed.

Eliza just stopped. She moved to our new couch, where she sat down, staring into space, strands of her hair gorgeously out of place. She was done.

I don't know why—moved by her tenacity or by the idea that if we could unpack from 1 p.m. to 1 a.m., there was nothing we couldn't do—but right then, in front of the couch, I proposed to her. She said yes.

It's sort of how I feel now. There's nothing in common with the time or place, obviously. We're six years older, surrounded by this swanky hotel bar, no shoe racks in sight. The connection is in how, despite the rest of the world continuing on in its easy nighttime rhythm, I feel like we're on the edge of something.

I take a deep breath. "What are the rules?"

Ingenuity leaps into my wife's expression like a scratched match hissing into flame. Releasing my hand, she pushes her plate to the side. She reaches brazenly over the bar and grabs a pen, then unfolds her cocktail napkin.

"We pretend we're strangers," she offers. I nod. No surprises there. This was the premise, this unlikely idea starting to seize me more with its wild wonder with each passing moment. "For, let's say, two days?" Eliza goes on.

I swallow. "The whole trip," I say, before I lose my nerve.

Eliza's eyes widen. I keep my expression neutral. I guess, if we're going to do this, I want to give it everything. Like unpacking until one in the morning. Like getting engaged because you just know you can't imagine life without the woman sitting on the couch in your new living room. Besides, getting this game right in two days is too much pressure.

Eliza doesn't question me. *Whole trip*, she jots onto the napkin. "And we have to commit. We stay in character except for emergencies," she goes on, half in her head, inspiration ushering her on now. "I also think we should do something together at least once every day."

"At least," I repeat, privately glad, although I never figured she would use the game to avoid me. "And just because we're pretending to be single doesn't mean we're opening up our relationship," I go on. It's a firm line for me. This is for *us*.

"Of course," Eliza agrees. *Monogamous*, she writes. When she glances up, I can't overlook the fresh excitement in her features. It is wonderful to witness. "Anything else?" she asks. "We can continue to discuss the rules anytime, you know."

I hesitate. Past Eliza, Finance Guy has maintained his stride, captivating his female companion. *Interesting you should mention fashion design. Fascinating world. Fascinating market. Ever stayed in Rome?* "Are we . . ." I start, then stumble. I don't know how to voice what's on my mind. How to confess I'm . . . tired of myself. "We're strangers, but are we us?" I finally manage. "Am I a lawyer from San Diego?"

While I read surprise in Eliza's eyes, her reply comes out evenly. Like my question is interesting, not embarrassing. "I suppose we can be whoever we want," she says. It's reassuring how quickly she embraces my proposal. The fire in my cheeks starts to subside while she dashes one final point onto our napkin list.

When she writes, her penmanship doesn't falter.

Whoever we want to be.

Like she knows neither of us has more to contribute, Eliza clicks the pen. Much more than the handwritten outline of the coming week sits within the space separating us. I don't know what this week will bring. I don't know who we'll be when we drive home. But I'm ready to find out.

Eliza smiles coyly. "It's nice to meet you," she says.

I can't help catching the mirror of her smirk. "Very," I reply.

Noticing our plates pushed to the side, the bartender pauses in front of us. "Ready?" she asks, starting to stack our plates when we nod. "One check or two?"

I don't speak. Eliza reaches for her purse.

"Two," she says.

Eliza

THE RESORT SERVES breakfast outdoors on the expansive stone-paved patio overlooking the cliffs. With the gentle breeze off the ocean playing with my hair while I walk out, I sweep my eyes over the patio tables, searching for Graham. It's midmorning, and the space is crowded with everyone from athleisure-clad guests our age to older couples simultaneously reading on their phones, seemingly oblivious to the beauty of the view past the thin metal balcony railing next to them.

I head to the tasteful buffet, where I fill my plate with breakfast potatoes and a spinach omelet. Returning outside to choose my table, I note the weirdness of coming to breakfast separately from my husband.

Not bad-weird, though. I feel like I'm coming to the summit of some towering roller coaster I've never ridden before. I'm pretty sure I'm going to enjoy myself, but I know I'm going to get thrown for some loops in the process. When I filled Nikki in this morning, lying in my bed with my phone practically under the comforter, she replied with strings of emojis I didn't realize they'd invented yet, then proceeded to heap some very welcome encouragement on me. I'm not certain this will work and end the stiff spell binding me and Graham recently, but this charge, right now, feels good.

Instead of routine expectation, I indulge in the tingling possibility that Graham will sit near me or with me. Strike up conversation. *You can still date your spouse.*

On the picturesque patio, I find myself remembering the first time Graham and I met in person, our first real date following weeks of messaging online. I was running late, per usual. Graham was right on time, per usual. I hustled into the coffee shop on Melrose and spotted him. When I saw his face, I remember feeling like I knew him. The details, the emotions, the impressions I'd developed of this person over our digital conversations suddenly mapped perfectly onto the man in front of me, inscribed on his strong yet boyish features in a way I found inexplicably natural.

I wonder how it's possible I could forget how to read the signs in those ever-so-familiar features.

Picking up my fork, I find I'm completely unable to think about anything except when Graham will arrive. Left to his own devices, I don't really know when he would get up. He goes into the office early on weekdays, sometimes even on weekends. We're no longer the lying-in-bed-together-every-morning type of couple. We were— one more faded detail I haven't bothered to bring back into focus.

It's not until I'm nearly finished with my eggs that I glance up and—Graham. He's walked onto the patio with David.

Our gazes lock, and he deliberately veers in the other direction, choosing a table far from me. I feel my eyebrows rise. *He's taking this seriously.* He's putting the ball in my court, practically inviting me to be the one to approach him. If I want to, of course.

Which I do.

I'm not going to rush right over, though, looking desperate. Instead, I sip my grapefruit juice, indulgently fanning my flicker of resentment. *Oh, he doesn't want to talk to me this morning?*

I wait five minutes, then casually saunter over to Graham's table. To strike up a conversation with David, of course.

As I come nearer to them, I see they're hunched over David's phone. Graham's voice is encouraging. I catch the end of his reassurance to David, who's eyeing his phone nervously. "The hair looks great, dude. Really," Graham promises. "The undercut really stands out."

David slants his head. "I don't know, man," he says somberly. "With the blazer and T-shirt, don't I just look too hipster?"

"It's a clean look. I promise." Graham is emphatic. "You look great. Women seeing this will know you take care with that kind of thing."

I can't help smiling. *Is Graham . . . pumping David up on his dating profile photo?* It's sweet enough for me to consider eavesdropping instead of cutting in.

Except—my heart is pushing me not to hesitate. One night in my solitary room and . . . I miss Graham.

So I sidle up to them. "How was the online-dating crash course?" I ask David, inserting myself in their conversation.

His concentration pulled from his photo, he looks up, grinning. "Eliza, hey," he says genially. "Join us." He pulls out their table's spare chair.

I cut my husband a loaded glance as I sit. Graham's performance is perfect. He looks politely interested, nothing more.

"It was fine," David answers my question. "I'm now set up on more dating apps than I care to enumerate." He looks to Graham. "Which one did you meet your wife on?"

"Hinge." We answer at the same time—me without thinking. David notices, obviously, his eyes flitting to me in confusion. I flush, ignoring how smug Graham looks in the corner of my vision. Yes, the improv classes I took in college focused more on comedy and less on extricating yourself from strange blunders you've made while pretending you and your husband have never met, but skill is skill. I find my cover fast. "I knew it," I say, pleased how confident I sound. How normal. "It's the only one I've ever had luck on as well."

"Oh yeah?" Graham speaks up, a note of challenge in his question. "What kind of luck?" His stare fixes on me.

"I met someone really great," I reply. This time, though, improv classes haven't given me what I need to come off detached. Staining my voice is wistfulness—I remember the first messages we exchanged, how we went from *hello*s and *how are you*s to *what's your favorite book?* and *who are your childhood nemeses?*

"Did it work out?" David's question pulls me from my recollection. He looks at my hand, but I stow it in my lap too quickly for him to clock the ring on my ring finger. I haven't taken my ring off—it's one practical point we overlooked in our napkin negotiation last night. Standing over my nightstand earlier this morning, feeling some insistent, fond instinct squeezing my heart, I slid the ring on—my reminder of why we're doing this.

However, I don't know how I'd explain a wedding band to David. Graham has the plausible reason he's supplied David for acting single despite wearing his wedding ring. Me, not so much.

Unable to come up with a good reply to David's question, I change the subject. "David, where are you from?"

"San Luis Obispo." David's voice is light, easily letting me grab the conversational steering wheel. "You?" He reaches for his coffee on his saucer. He seems interested, like he's not just making chit-chat. I wonder if his chattiness is a product of the dating workshop or just how he is. My reply is on my lips when David continues, looking to Graham. "Wait, where are *you* from?"

Catching myself, I close my mouth. *La Jolla* dries up on my tongue. My eyes lock with Graham's. I remember how, last night, he didn't just want to be strangers. He wanted to be someone new. I don't know why, but the reason doesn't matter now. In everything else, he's committed to what *I've* suggested, what I've proposed.

I can commit to what he wants, too.

"Boston," I blurt.

Graham watches me curiously, head cocked. There's something genuine in his gaze, like he just wants to know why I picked Boston out of nowhere. Honestly, I don't know why I did. I haven't been to Boston in years. One summer right out of college I interned at the American Repertory Theater there before moving to LA. I hardly ever think of the Charles River and the redbrick buildings.

Slowly, Graham turns back to David. "Santa Fe," he says in answer to David's question. While he shifts in his seat, his hand finding his gold sunglasses hanging from his collar, his voice sounds solid. Sure.

The surprise of his choice pulls me from my summer recollection. "Santa Fe?" I repeat. Graham has never once mentioned Santa Fe. We've never taken a trip there or even talked about taking a trip there. I'm pretty certain he's never been there before in his life.

His eyes swivel to me. "Yeah. Why? You're surprised?" Wind gusts off the ocean, shifting his hair, the only movement on his otherwise unreadable face.

Of course I'm surprised, I want to say. In fact, I'm full of questions. Why did he choose this southwestern city we've never once considered visiting? It's not a question I can ask here, though, with David drinking his coffee between us.

"You just don't strike me as a New Mexico guy," I say, forcing myself with more effort now into the role of vacationing stranger.

"Well, we don't know each other," Graham replies pleasantly. "Yet."

I study him. What he's said floats lightly over the sounds of clinking silverware and the redwoods rustling in the distance. Once more, we've wandered out onto the ledge of the truth. It's a little frightening, in the way of high places. Like last night, I'm not certain what waits over the edge, but I'm still glad we're here.

Then the moment vanishes into the morning. I nod, resuming our performance. "True," I say.

Hope flickers in me suddenly. Because, it occurs to me, this morning we've pretended we've only just met, we've invented other selves, or the start of them—most of what was on our list planned out last night. The next piece to be played is obvious.

A first date.

I guess I'm expecting Graham to make the next move. I was the one to walk over to his table. Now, though, would be the natural time for me to get up. This would be Graham's window. His opportunity.

But Graham says nothing.

It dampens my mood like the wispy clouds on our street filter the sun—still bright, but not the same. Finally, I stand, then push in my chair. "Enjoy your breakfast. It's past time I hit the pool," I say breezily, to the table, not to Graham. He can take the time he needs to ask out his own wife.

It's David who speaks up. "Maybe the three of us can get dinner sometime?"

I wrestle down disappointment. Somehow *David* is the one up-holding Graham's and my promise to see each other every day.

"I'm in," Graham says. "Eliza?"

His green eyes linger on me. "Of course." The short sentence echoes with unspoken questions.

It's day one, I remind myself, making my case to the whispers in my heart. I wanted to plan our "first date"—not dinner with David. *We'll get there,* I insist. *We'll get to dating.*

I turn to leave, feeling my husband's gaze on my back.

Graham

I STARE AT my wedding ring, the sun reflected in the metal searing my eyes.

If I'm going to mope without my wife, I'm going to do so on my private balcony, lounging on my deck chair under the crystalline California sky. The view is stunning. I can follow the rolling hills endlessly, the greenery decorated with sun-dappled ripples of tree branches.

I've spent the day out here, finishing off the room service I ordered for lunch. I don't plan on leaving, either, despite how David has texted me several times, trying to get me to go to a happy hour mixer tonight in the hotel's lobby.

I've replied vaguely, knowing introductions with complete strangers—real ones, not Eliza—are the furthest things from what I want out of tonight. I'd rather soak in my private Jacuzzi, then respond to work emails on my phone, hiding from the worry—the regret—with which breakfast left me.

Why couldn't I ask out my own wife?

I know she wanted me to. I'm not completely vacant in my faculties for reading her wishes. Yet when the moment presented itself, I just—couldn't.

I face the frustrated jury in my head, presenting my case. *Isn't it true that asking out Eliza Kelly was hard enough the first time? Isn't it true that you've loved her more with every passing day, grown even fonder, even more dazzled by her wit, her beauty, her everything?*

Then, jury persons, would you have no choice but to conclude asking her out now would be exponentially, immeasurably harder?

Just because it makes sense doesn't mean it's comforting.

I flop onto my cloudlike bed, gazing up into the white expanse of the ceiling. Heaven may be a place on earth, but purgatory is a luxurious hotel room without your wife. *I just—need everything to be perfect,* I rationalize. The invitation, the date itself. Part of the point here is giving Eliza what she deserves. Offhandedly mentioning grabbing coffee isn't enough.

The breeze picks up over the hills, chilling me on my bed. *Time for the Jacuzzi,* I decide. Barefoot, I cross the room to the steaming tub, where I pull off my shirt. When I get in, I sigh with the sensation, the heat so shocking it nearly hurts until my body acclimates. Leaning my head back, I close my eyes. With the dull warmth of the sunset on my face, my limbs soaking under the water, it's bliss.

I'll figure out how to contact Eliza later, I comfort myself. It'll take ingenuity—I don't think I can text her because we're committing to our performances. Our "characters" don't have each other's numbers yet. I'll think of something, though.

Right then, my room's doorbell rings.

My eyes flit open. I didn't order more room service and I *did* put up the do-not-disturb sign. If this is the hotel surprising me with some honeymoon-suite, romantic-sunset champagne bullshit, I won't be thrilled. I ignore the chime, hoping whoever it is takes the hint.

The doorbell rings again.

Exasperated, I haul myself out of the Jacuzzi and head, dripping wet, to the bedroom. When the bell rings for the third time, I conclude it must be David, tired of my evasive replies to his texts and here to drag me to the mixer. Hustling into my pristine hallway, I fight down my irritation. He's just being friendly. I reach for the handle and reluctantly swing the door open.

It's not David.

Eliza stands outside wrapped in a hotel robe. Her hair is up and lightly wet from either the shower or the pool. The sight works on me profoundly—not just how the gauzy fabric hugs her willowy curves or how her lithe legs peek out from the hem, or the faintly freckled skin of her chest exposed by the front. I'm caught up, too, in the way the light over my door casts on her features, breathtakingly beautiful in their combination of shadow and illumination, familiarity and surprise.

I realize how much I missed her in just the last couple hours.

Shaking myself from my stupor, I blink. "Eliza."

"Hi," she says, hurried, businesslike.

"You shouldn't—" I stumble, sorting myself out. "You wouldn't know where my room is. Aren't you breaking character?"

"It's an emergency," she says. "So it's allowed. Per our rules."

"Are you okay?" I look her over, instantly concerned. She doesn't seem upset or hurt. "What's the emergency?"

"My heels are in your suitcase," she informs me.

I smother my laughter. *Emergency. Right.* Even if this is breaking the rules, I don't care. I won't question this quest for her shoes. Not when it's led her to my door.

"Wait, how *did* you know this was my room?" I ask.

"I asked the front desk," she says. "My name is still on it."

I nod. "Right."

We stand on either side of the doorway for a moment, until Eliza raises her eyebrows indicatively. "So can I get my shoes?"

Impatience hints in her demeanor like fire licking the edges of dry wood. The joy I felt seeing her sags, because I know why. She wishes I'd invited her out instead of David doing it. *Makes two of us,* I want to say. Instead, I swing the door wider. "Your name *is* on the room."

Eliza walks in. I see her pause for a split second, taking in the suite. Part of me wonders if she's regretting spurning the room. She doesn't comment, instead only heading into my bedroom, where she flips down the lid of my suitcase to reach the top zipper.

"So . . ." she says. "Santa Fe."

I'm not certain which Eliza the question is coming from. *Does the shoe "emergency" extend to this conversation?* I don't want Eliza to feel like I'm giving up, looking to ignore the game I committed to, so I match her vagueness. "Why not? Santa Fe is lovely." In truth, the city choice sprang easily from my lips. When work is demanding and I need to decompress, sometimes I'll pull up Airbnb and search wherever inspiration carries me. I've found myself drawn to Santa Fe's Southwestern architecture, the rich scenery of the desert, the art scene. I've never mentioned it to Eliza.

She starts rummaging in the compartment and looks at me, raising an eyebrow. "Fair enough," she says. "So what is it you do in Santa Fe?"

I consider for a moment. Part of me wants to invent something wild. Maybe I could make her laugh. I write bestselling legal thrillers, or I breed corgis. Or I've inherited untold fortunes from my mysterious great-uncle.

I settle for something closer to the truth—something closer to why I suggested new personas in the first place. I want the freedom to be someone else, but I want to prove something maybe just to myself—that this professional world of business and finance can be fun, even interesting. I remember the guy charming his date at the bar, his confidence unwavering.

"I'm an investment banker," I say.

Eliza blinks. Then she frowns. "You're an investment banker in Santa Fe?" she asks skeptically.

I deflate. Fine, my story has inaccuracies. I don't care. I bluster forward, projecting Wall Street confidence. "Yes, I close Santa Fe's hugest deals," I declare. While this, regrettably, only increases Eliza's confusion, it can't be helped. This is exactly what worried me yesterday—I don't have her or her improv friends' readiness for this type of fabrication. Hastily, I change course. "I fly to New York plenty, of course," I concede.

"Interesting," my wife remarks, giving up none of her interrogative poise. "Do you . . . like it?"

I'm in this now, I tell myself. It's everything or nothing. "Oh yeah," I say, summoning the conversation we overheard. "It's electric. Chasing the high of every million we move. I thrive on it."

Eliza nods, and I feel like maybe I'm starting to sell my story.

"What do you do in Boston?" I ask pleasantly.

"Oh, so much. Some theater, some teaching." While she speaks with poise, I'm satisfied to note she seems to be groping for something to say. I see the moment inspiration flickers into her eyes. "But mainly, I run a business with my three sisters."

I frown. Eliza only has one sister, and they're estranged, or something close. Eliza hasn't spoken to Michelle in months. She never mentions it to me, and the one time I tried to bring it up, she swiftly shut down the conversation. "What kind of business?" I ask.

"Vacation planning," she replies. "I specialize in cruises."

Vacation planning—it hits me in the next split second she's playing the same game I just was. The profession sounds familiar because the character she was narrating in the car was a vacation planner. The one who was wet with— I close off the memory of the drive. Eliza knows exactly what she's doing.

She smiles winningly, suddenly looking fresh faced, whatever strain of ideation I saw a second ago completely gone. It looks easy for her, which it probably is. She's a compelling actress.

In fact, despite my confidence at the bar, I've found myself with no choice but to concede she's better than me. She handled the Hinge hiccup during brunch seamlessly. Now she's snared me hook, line, and sinker with this vacation-planner line. While I'm not sure if this game of ours has a score, if it does, I'm losing.

It's impressive—and strangely motivating. I went into today wanting to cooperate with her, to honor the terms of her unconventional proposal. Whether out of courtroom competitiveness or the playful spark of something deeper, I suddenly want more. I want to show her I can go toe-to-toe. And I want to show myself, too.

Eliza pulls from my bag black stilettos I've never seen before, and I can't help myself. Curiosity steals my voice. "Going somewhere?" I ask.

She stands up, gripping her shoes in her hand. "There's a happy hour tonight. Figured I would check it out. Since I don't have any other plans," she adds with a loaded look.

I don't let my reaction steal onto my face. There's a mask I put on in court, for my clients, for the judge, for the jury watching. I need the mask now, to hide how directly the hit landed, how cleanly she's called out what I've wrestled with this whole morning. "Maybe you can get some new clients," I get out calmly. "For your vacation-planning business."

Eliza's grin spreads slowly. "Maybe," she repeats. She heads for the door, then turns back, giving me a final once-over. For the first time in this exchange, I'm conscious that I'm currently shirtless, my trunks wet and sticking to my thighs. "I'd say I'd see you there, but you seem really busy," she finishes.

As she stands by the door, I feel like I'm watching the end of sunset waver on the horizon, miragelike, before day cedes to twilight. It grabs hold of me.

"Eliza," I say before I can restrain myself.

She spins, heartbreakingly hopeful.

I need to rewrite my failure this morning. Instead, questions begin to pile up in my head. *To do what? Is now the right time? Will it be enough?*

"Our—our rings," I say, changing course. Swerving from oncoming collision. "David keeps telling me I have to take it off. To get out there, you know," I go on, cringing inwardly from my own cowardice. "Obviously I don't want to, but if we're really doing this . . ."

When Eliza's eyes widen, it occurs to me there are plenty of ways to betray people while being faithful to them. "No, you're right," she finally says with put-on pragmatism. "It's just for a couple days."

With those final words, she walks past me, out the door of the honeymoon suite, her shoes dangling in her hand. My wife, on her way to the hotel's happy hour.

The moment the lock on the door clicks, I march miserably to the Jacuzzi. I immerse myself in the tub, grimacing from the too-hot water.

I slide my wedding ring off my finger, placing the platinum band on the side table.

Five minutes later, I feel weird with the ring off entirely. I know we're playing parts, but not even this joint performance of ours will make me ditch my wedding ring. I don't want to be *that* in-character. In private surrender, I pick up the ring, compromising by putting it on my right hand instead of my left.

Leaning back in the Jacuzzi, I exhale, trying to lose myself in my spectacular scenery. But this time, my body refuses to get used to the temperature. The heat feels wrong. I know it's because of the images jammed into my head, impossible to dislodge.

Eliza in her dress and heels.

Me, here, in my Jacuzzi.

Mustering my resolve, I get out of the water. I head for the shower, deciding I *do* have plans tonight.

9

Eliza

I PULL OUT the flowy red bohemian dress I wore to one of Graham's work events last year, stubbornly set on the plan I envisioned for the night.

It's such a me dress. With its bell sleeves and plunging neckline, I stood out like a sore thumb in the midst of the professionally sleek lawyers and preppy spouses. I'd wondered if Graham minded, if he wished I fit in more, made more sense in his world. But I decided it didn't matter when later that night Graham took the dress off me slowly, untying the wrap and letting the fabric fall.

In front of my room's narrow mirror, I put on the dress, inspecting my reflection. If I were me, I'd let my hair dry in loose curls I'd wear over my shoulders. Instead, however, I remember one thing. Tonight, I'm not me.

I consider the character I'm playing, the one I invented in Graham's neatly organized honeymoon suite. Eliza, the travel planner from Boston. I pulled from the book I'm recording, put on the spot by questions I should've expected from my husband. Yet the more I spoke, the more I found myself weaving in my own details spontaneously, not knowing entirely where from.

Staring into the mirror, I imagine those details on the image of the woman in front of me, like an existential Instagram filter. Eliza from Boston is harried, running her own business with her family. She juggles so many obligations, pursuing everything that catches her interest while spending most of her time with three women. She probably has no patience for air-drying.

So neither do I.

Decisively, I move for my suitcase, where I ferret into my toiletries bag for the bobby pins from when I was a bridesmaid in my college roommate Mara's wedding a few months ago. One YouTube tutorial later, I've pulled off a messy bun, with one asymmetrical strand of hair framing the right side of my face.

It looks good. Not great.

I don't care, because it looks like Eliza from Boston.

Feeling inspired now, I dig into my makeup bag. Normally, I gravitate toward lighter lipsticks, but this Eliza spends her days bundled in sweaters and scarves. I pull out the darkest shade I have, enjoying myself now. Having fun dressing up in character. Brown eyeshadow comes next—not my normal palette either, but I don't hate the effect. When I step into the stilettos I brought for this trip but haven't yet worn, I look back into the mirror to take in the full effect.

It's exhilarating. I almost look like a different person, even while I'm wearing my own dress.

My eyes snag on my wedding ring, still sparkling on my left hand. Graham was right, but I don't want to leave it behind. I unclasp my necklace and slide my rings onto the chain, then return the necklace to my neck. The rings rest over my heart, the platinum cool on my skin.

In the mirror, my bare hand completes the strangeness of the sight in front of me. The parallel Eliza, leaving her hotel room on her own.

I'm not even sure why I'm going to this mixer—it's not like I want to meet anyone. I just got out of the pool earlier this evening restless, deciding I couldn't sit around waiting for my own husband to ask me out. I have to do *something*.

The sign on the hotel patio for the mixer caught my eye while I was heading up here in my bathing suit and robe. David, I figured, would be going, and possibly my husband with him. I'd turned in the opposite direction—needing my stilettos, yes, but figuring my visit might not be the worst way of spurring Graham to ask me out. But he seemed content spending the night in.

Still, my hopeful heart whispers, maybe he'll be curious enough to come see me.

Despite this one hitch in the day, I won't deny how much I enjoy this game we're playing. There's something freeing in our pretense. I feel like I can ask him questions and I'm allowed to not already know what he'll say. Like I have permission to not know him. To not expect him to know me. If he comes tonight, I don't know if he'll like my look—my hair up, my darker makeup. I want to find out, though. It's exciting, provoking reactions out of him, uncovering new details of the man I married in his responses to the unexpected. Sifting for gold on shores I thought I'd wrung clean of fortune.

I want him to get to know Eliza from Boston. I want to get to know Graham, the investment banker from Santa Fe. I wonder, if we really were strangers, if I'd be intrigued by him.

I think I would.

It's not entirely unfounded speculation, of course. Hand on my necklace, I remember the eager-yet-playing-it-cool twenty-three-year-old Eliza who walked into Verve coffee on Melrose in white denim shorts, looking for the guy she met online. I was attracted to Graham the moment I laid eyes on him. Even when he was a young law student, I could feel how his golden hair and Midwesternish charm weren't the whole story. There's an intensity to him, a precision magnetic to me from the very start. If anything, in our past few interactions here, it's only gotten sharper, seductively so.

I wonder if he would feel the same way. Would he be attracted to this me? It's a question hiding other, more immediate ones. If he found out the woman he ran into a couple times in this hotel was going to the mixer, would he go to meet her? Would he dress to impress the way she is?

I smile at myself in the mirror. There's only one way to find out.

Graham

I WALK INTO the lobby in my favorite fitted dress shirt, my hair still damp from my quick shower. I feel pulled in opposite directions. Half of me remembers my idyllic Jacuzzi, the quiet of the California cliffs surrounding me.

Half of me would rather be nowhere else but here.

The lobby is packed with people in cocktail attire. Groups stand and converse at the high tables next to the bar set up by the registration desk. While this is officially a welcome event for the dating workshop, no one is checking in guests. It's easy for me to wander into the room like I belong.

My pulse is quick. I spent the walk over—on paths I navigated successfully this time—wondering when Eliza would get here, or whether she'd reconsider even coming.

I've never found knowing myself to be challenging. I knew from the beginning of law school I would find being a lawyer fulfilling, and I was right. When I met Eliza, I recognized the spark of *rightness* in me from our first conversations. I know what I want.

But immersed in this game of Eliza's, I feel the pull of questions I'm genuinely confused by. In flashes over only the past day, I've found the guy I used to be. His charisma, his quickness. I just can't manage to hold on to him, like how the image of lightning burns in the sky for split seconds following the strike, then disappears into the night. But if I could hold on, would he even be me? When does pretending to be myself become . . . living?

I'm distracted from these questions when I walk into the room to notice I . . . don't find Eliza. My first thought is to hope she bailed, which would give me time to retreat to my room, to work myself out to do this right.

Then I see a familiar dress. The billowy red one I love that I haven't seen in a year. It's draped almost delicately on her frame, and I remember in vivid detail how easily it comes off to pool at her feet.

Despite the familiar dress, Eliza is . . . transformed. My eyes rove over every little change hungrily. Her hair, worn up tonight, leaves the pale line of her neck bare, while her dark red lipstick draws my eyes directly to her mouth. She's standing at one of the tables, looking entirely comfortable conversing with a group of four strangers.

When she reaches for her drink with her left hand, though, I notice the biggest change she's made.

Her ring is gone. Of course it is. Still, the sight provokes something like possessiveness in me. I want to see the ring I gave her on her finger. I want to turn around, find the hostess tucked somewhere near the makeshift bar, demand Eliza's room key, and storm upstairs to find where exactly she's hidden the diamond ring I gave her the day after I proposed to her in the middle of the night.

It hadn't been the plan, of course. I'd had the ring picked out. I'd paid for it. I'd intended to wait until we'd known each other longer, not because I felt I needed more time to be sure—I *was* sure. But because I knew it was fast. I was going to give it to her in the coffee shop where we first met. Then our shoe rack collapsed in the middle of our night of unpacking. Somehow, I'd known I couldn't wait.

Seeing her bare finger now, I'm struck by how that spontaneity clashes with every opportunity I've let pass me today. It strips whatever streaks of confidence I'd managed to hold on to clean out of my grasp. Maybe the old me is fundamentally too far to reach, despite flashes of feeling otherwise. Losing my nerve, I turn to walk in the opposite direction.

Threading through tables, I feel my pulse slow with every step I take. The questions stacked high in my heart and head start to shift in one direction.

I don't want to leave. But I feel like I need to warm up before the main event tonight. I just need some distance. Distance, and a drink.

When I reach the bar, I spot David in a navy sport coat standing on his own. He sips a beer, sizing up the room. It surprises me how much relief I feel finding him. I barely know the man, but already he's becoming a friend. Even though he doesn't know the real me, doesn't even know who my wife is, he's the only person aware of a small piece of what I'm going through.

He grins when he sees me heading for him. "You came! I thought for sure you'd hide in your room." He claps me on the shoulder in a good-natured bro greeting. I don't know what he does for a living, but I'd guess it's something in finance. Maybe I can parrot his language next time I talk to my non-wife.

"I still might." I feel my eyes pulled to Eliza, dragged like she has her own mystical gravity. Defiant, I turn to face the bar, keeping her entirely out of my view.

David looks genuinely crestfallen. "You can't leave," he says. "I have to tell you how I fell in love today."

My eyebrows shoot up. Sufficiently distracted even from my simmering thoughts of Eliza, I face him. "You—what? With who?"

"I didn't catch her name," David replies.

Now I start to smile. David's begun mulling this over earnestly, like the inconvenience of the fact is just occurring to him.

"Well," I say patiently, and not unthankful for the distraction, "what happened?"

David instantly looks renewed. "I was on a hike and I got a tad turned around and this woman—this *goddess*—pointed me back to the trail."

I wait for the end of the story, until I realize that *is* the end of the story. "Let me understand this," I start. "You're saying a woman gave you directions and now you're in love with her?"

"Yes." David nods once, like I've finally caught up. "Exactly."

I blink. Without hesitating, I flag the bartender and order a drink, knowing I'm going to be here awhile.

David looks sincere. It'd be comical if he didn't seem genuinely nervous. He runs one hand through his hair, his eyes pinging over the room. It's obvious he's looking for someone. He has the lovestruck intensity of a high schooler waiting for his crush to get to class. "I was hoping she'd be here," he says, sounding like his hope is flagging. "But I haven't seen her yet."

"You're *sure* you're in love?" I press him when the bartender hands me my drink. I sort of know what he's going to say, but in depositions, some questions function just to double-check unlikely truths. "You've only met her once," I point out, holding in the fact that *met* is a strong word for their encounter.

"That's all it takes!" David replies exuberantly. His eyes go distant. "You should have seen her. She has these dark eyes and she was covered in dirt like she'd been hiking for miles."

I consider what he's said. Not the *dark eyes* or the *covered in dirt* parts—the premise. *That's all it takes.* Frustrated by how poorly I'm managing my marriage, I want to scoff. But I did feel something in my first conversation with Eliza. I remember the singe of heat lightning when she first walked into the coffee shop where I would eventually intend to propose to her.

Deciding to give David the benefit of the doubt, I swallow the first sip of my drink. "Are you going to look for her?"

"I shouldn't," he says contemplatively. "I'm still on the rebound. I should work on myself right now. That's why I'm here, doing the workshop. I'm not sure if I'm emotionally ready for love right now, you know?" He leans back, with both elbows on the bar, facing the room. Romeo in a sport coat. "But on the other hand—it's love."

Mirroring his posture, I turn to look out into the crowd. I find my eyes drawn to Eliza again, unconsciously, unwaveringly.

"But of course, *you* get it," David goes on.

It takes me a second to realize this statement doesn't fit with the divorced version of me David knows. "What do you mean?" I ask.

"You're already in love with Eliza." He grins knowingly.

In law school cold calls, professors interrogate you in class on the details of cases and statutory codes until you stumble or, less likely, remember everything correctly. While I was one of sharpest students in my class, even I would sometimes hit the wall on sections of the SCC regulations or nineteenth-century evidentiary rulings. It's how I feel now. I have to give David credit for his perceptiveness, even though what he said was jarringly confusing.

"No, I'm—not," I fumble to say. "I've barely even spoken to her."

"Like I said. It's all it takes," David replies smugly. He cuts me a look, like *don't even try to deny it*. "Besides, you two had mad sparks last night at the bar. I should have been wearing sunscreen for the heat you were throwing off. Then this morning—it's all over your face when you look at her," he says. "Don't be embarrassed of your heart, man. You should have gotten her number yesterday. Or this morning. This morning would have worked, too. It could be true love," he finishes with utter sincerity.

"I don't even know her," I manage. But my mind is stuck on his words. Our energy last night was intense, but not for the reasons David thinks.

David shrugs. "So ask for her number tonight. *Get* to know her." His large, friendly hand descending on my shoulder once more, he pushes me in the direction of the crowd, the direction of my costumed wife. Downing his drink, he places his bottle on the bar. "I'm going to search for the woman from the hike."

Fortifying my resolve, I force myself to step into the crowd. While I want to go back to my room, I also don't want to admit this defeat. I'm not close to Eliza, which gives me time to consider while I slide past shoulders and elbows and the echo of small talk. *Even David knew I blew two chances with Eliza.* Tonight, I counsel myself, only feet from her now, I cannot go zero for three.

I stride up to her table, stepping into the open space across from her, summoning swagger. It's us and four others. They're swapping stories of what led them to the workshop. The woman speaking now is recounting with humor the three times in the past year she was stood up.

I say nothing, sipping my drink.

Then Eliza speaks. "I'd argue there are worse dates than a no-show. Haven't you ever wished your date stood you up? I know I have."

I nearly spill my drink when I hear her voice. Because it's *not* her voice.

It's the one she was using to record on the road, her normal pitch and cadence shifted ever so slightly. The words I last heard her speak in this voice ricochet in my head, and I nearly involuntarily kick the table.

It's sort of genius, I grudgingly concede. Eliza's here in subtle costume. Why wouldn't my voice-actor wife put the final flourish on the reinvention in the way only someone with her skills can?

The guy next to me speaks up. "Okay, you sound like you have a good story," he says to her. "Spill." His honeyed cheer makes me wince.

For the first time, Eliza's eyes flit to me. It's a loaded look, the place where a promise meets a warning. Then she smiles winningly at the crowd, her audience. "Well," she says, pausing to revel in every syllable and second of the performance. "The date itself was a dud. No chemistry. It's always a risk when meeting people online. I was in such a rush to get home I pretended my sister was having an emergency."

I watch her, fascination winning over frustration. Nothing she's saying is true. Eliza and Michelle haven't lived in the same city since high school, and Eliza certainly wasn't online dating as a minor. I recognize what she's doing here—early in our relationship, when Eliza would land new roles, I would sometimes listen or "help" her while she developed her understanding of her character. She would flesh out family relationships, childhood traumas, friendships, and fussy habits. Stuff she would use to evoke her character's complete personality. It's similar to what she's doing now. Creating this new Eliza.

She goes on with gusto. "So I *finally* make it out to the parking lot where I get into my car. Except I live in Boston. The pavement was frozen. I was in such a rush to leave that I backed up too fast and couldn't brake on the ice. I ran right into the car behind me. Guess who it belonged to?"

While everyone groans with sympathy, I fix my stare on her, ignoring the fact it's—okay, a pretty funny story to have concocted on the spot. However, I've watched enough depositions to know most fabricated stories crumble under scrutiny. "What happened next?" I ask.

"We got in a screaming match in the parking lot," Eliza replies. She smiles, coy and self-deprecating and loving this. "Then I went home with him."

Everyone roars with laughter. Except me.

"Sounds made up," I say.

She raises an eyebrow. "Does it? I guess it would to you," she replies lightly. "You're probably too busy pulling long nights in the office to have wild dating stories of your own."

I keep my cool, taking a sip of my drink. "It's hardly prohibitive," I say.

"Oh?" Now both Eliza's eyebrows rise. I know what she's going to say before she says it. "Well, tell us."

While I shrug noncommittally, my brain fires into creativity. This isn't the first time I've had to engineer a fast rebuttal or counter an unexpected request. I do the same in courtrooms or settlement negotiations, don't I? It's harder here, facing the high stakes of my marriage, but surely I can find some of the same finesse now. "When you leave the office at four in the morning but you're too wired from closing a deal to sleep, and you go on Tinder to start swiping, you can meet some pretty interesting people."

The moment the words leave my mouth, Eliza's eyes sparkle, like stars made of fog. It is, for a distracting moment, stunning.

"Who'd you meet?" she asks.

Using years of story-spinning for juries, and the episodes of *Succession* I devoured over the summer, I start inventing on the spot. I register, distantly, how I'm, maybe, arguably, starting to hit my stride in this game. Not just the creativity—I like how it keeps Eliza asking me questions. How much more she wants to know about this version of me. "Once," I venture, "it was the same woman I'd just spent the past four hours negotiating with. We closed out the final deal points, left our respective offices, and both happened to hop on Tinder . . . only to swipe right on each other."

I let my demeanor shift, let myself occupy this new character more and more while he becomes someone less and less like myself. Louder, more comfortable living his life on the edge.

"We ended up pulling a different sort of all-nighter than the one I'd expected," I boast. The group laughs in unison. I'm vaguely gratified, noting with curious pride how quickly Investment Banker Graham drew the table in. Even so, I can't resist refocusing on Eliza, watching her reaction with interest I'm certain betrays me.

Her smile splits wide.

Caught in the rush of seeing her expression, I laugh with the group. Suddenly, the pressure I've placed on myself since I got into the Jacuzzi this morning melts off of me.

I can't deny it—this performance is starting to be fun.

Eliza

I EXCUSE MYSELF from the group to refill my drink, privately surprised. Whatever's come over my husband, this was *not* the insecure Graham I left in his room when I went to fetch my shoes. I've seen plenty of uncomfortable, reluctant performers over the years—Investment Banker Graham from Santa Fe is *not* one of them.

Reaching the bar, I pass my glass over. I haven't waited long when I feel Graham come up beside me. "Didn't think I'd see you tonight," I say, keeping the way my pulse picks up out of my voice.

"Disappointed?" he asks, and *dear god*, did he just wink?

I study him, the way he leans on the bar, the slant of his shoulders. He's carrying himself differently. It's slight, but it's there, the way he takes up just a little more space. It would be a truism to say, *No, I'm definitely* not *disappointed*. "You sound like you lead a pretty interesting life," I reply instead, still using the voice I put on for most of the romance novels I perform, which I knew Graham would notice. Right now, it secures this conversation within our game, the next scene in our intricate performance.

"You could say that." Graham smirks. He knows exactly what he's doing—leaving *me* to make conversation if I want to keep talking to him.

Which I do.

"What about the investment banker clichés?" I ask, in the way *this* Eliza would, half judgmentally amused and half innocently courageous. "Snorting illicit substances off of scantily clad women in limos? You've done that, I'm guessing?"

He forces out his next words. "Oh, yeah. I've definitely done that. Bunch of times."

He's fire-engine red. I laugh into my drink.

It is, I notice immediately, exactly the window Graham needed to recover. His posture somehow straightens while relaxing, and his lips flicker with a smile. "What about you?" he asks.

"What *about* me?"

The smile forms. "Are you the type of woman who'd take a total stranger to bed?" His voice is confident, calm, and even.

Now it's my turn to fight my blush. My turn to lose. I square my shoulders to his, and his gaze dips for a moment to my chest.

Watching him war with the impulse, I let myself hope what I wouldn't before. Graham *is* enjoying this game, even if he's not eager to show it.

The subtext of his question is hot between us. It's enough to hold us apart from the rest of the room, from the sea of singles making conversation over cocktails. The high tables, the warm hotel lighting, the well-dressed clamor—they cease to exist. The world becomes me and Graham and the strip of bar between us.

I set my drink down. "Not a total stranger," I say.

Graham's jaw tightens at my double meaning. Of course, he's not a total stranger. Not at all. When his eyes dip once more, he's no longer in a rush. If my blush was heat before, now it's flame. Nevertheless, I keep my posture straight, my chin haughtily high.

"Good to know," he says.

I hide the new current of confusion joining with everything else coursing through me. Which Graham is the one saying he's a total stranger to me—the charming caricature in front of me, or the man whose bed I share? Or, normally share.

The question suddenly seems burningly important. I wet my lips, working out how to formulate it within our veils of pretend.

Before I can, David walks up, interrupting us.

"Eliza, hi. Sorry," he says hurriedly. He leans closer to my husband. "Graham, I have an emergency. I need your help."

Graham blinks, the moment between us disrupted. He shifts his focus to David, not quite keeping the bewilderment out of his expression. "Are you . . . okay?" His eyes rove over David, like he's searching for visible wounds or other dire issues.

"Physically, yes. Existentially, no. I'm horrible," David declares. "I'm sorry to interrupt, but this is serious. Graham, just get Eliza's number so you can continue this conversation later."

I fold my lips to hide my smile. Neither Graham nor I could explain to David the unintentional humor in his order, or how David is the most unnecessary wingman in dating history. I've had Graham's number since I plugged it into an iPhone 6.

But my smile vanishes in earnest when Graham's eyes return to me. Insecurity steals the fun out of the moment. What if Graham *wants* to keep his distance? In practical terms, it's silly of me to worry. Graham can text me whenever he wants. Even so, if *this* Graham coolly says he's sure he'll run into me some other time, it would be a brush-off. I wouldn't be sure if it was for real or for show.

When he grins instead, my relief is a little embarrassing.

"Sure, I'd like that," my husband says. "Can I get your number?"

I reach for the pen I used to sign for my drink and scrawl my number on my napkin. My heart is beating hard, and I'm not even sure why. This isn't a new step for us, but it feels like one. I have to fight to remind myself this already happened—the last time he got my number, it was on Hinge, before we'd ever met. But despite the repetition of the exchange, it's somehow just as exciting the second time.

I hand him the napkin, the corners of my lips upturned slightly as our fingers brush.

Graham receives the soft paper carefully, his eyes remaining on me while he does. He folds and then slides the napkin into his pocket like he really needs the ten black numbers written on one side. Like I'm not already a favorite in his phone, the only contact with no last name, the number on the in-case-of-emergency form he filled out for his job.

"Talk later, then," I say lightly.

Graham only nods. The moment passes, the connection between us going quiet when he straightens up. When the impatient David immediately starts for the door, Graham follows one step behind him.

I watch his receding back. While he leaves, it settles on me what just happened. Graham just played the game for real. He spent the entire night in character with flair, earnest effort, and, frankly, seductive confidence. Whatever self-consciousness my husband had is gone, replaced with the guy who just got his wife's number like she's the hot stranger he met on vacation.

Objectively, I know what we're doing is ridiculous. I know it is. But—I feel it working. I proposed this idea because the personas take the pressure off us, letting us get to know each other again.

Tonight was something different, though, something hiding in the way my pulse pounded when I gave him my number despite having already done so years ago. Re-creating those feelings with Graham might be part of reigniting them for good.

I cap the pen and place it on the bar, wondering just how far we'll take our game of pretend.

12

Graham

I FOLLOW DAVID back to his room. The night is even deeper now. David is uncharacteristically withdrawn, leaving our walk silent except for the rustle of trees, the faint whir of insects, and our shoes on the gravel path.

Entering his room, I feel my eyebrows rise. The place is chaos. Housekeeping couldn't have come more than a few hours ago, yet already David has managed to litter the floor with towels, clothes, and room service dishes. It reminds me of the houses on UCLA's fraternity row, the hooked street curving down one side of campus, their windows lined with beer bottles and lawns boasting speckled mattresses. Honestly, it fits. I suspect if I asked, David could recite a sizable portion of the Greek alphabet.

Taking no notice of the mess, David gestures for me to sit on the couch, which I do. His room is a suite, not honeymoon-sized, but it's expansive. Very seriously, he perches on the chair across from me.

"I found her," he says, "and she's my soul mate."

I fight down my laugh, picking up that David is very much not joking. "Okay," I say gently. "Who is she? Was she at the happy hour?"

"No, she just got back from a run. I saw her walk through the lobby when I went to the bathroom," he replies, conveying this information with excitement verging on reverence. "I know the timing isn't right, but I don't think I can let this go. What if she's the one?"

He looks harried, like he's been struck by lightning. He drops his head into his hands, which is when the truth reveals itself to me fully. While David's sport coat, groomed hair, and messy room suggest a certain level of bro-ishness, it's not the entire story.

David, I realize, is a huge romantic.

"So, random question," I start genially, "but, uh, how many times have you been in love, David?"

David looks up, unperturbed. "Twenty times."

My eyes widen. I haven't even been on dates with twenty different women. I keep my voice even while David presses his palms together, looking tense. "This is twenty-one, then. Blackjack," I joke weakly. When David seems unamused, I go on seriously. "That's a lot of heartbreak, man."

His expression drawn, David nods solemnly. "Yeah, it hurts every time a relationship falls apart. But . . ." He regains his boyish enthusiasm. "I'm pumped for the next one no matter what."

I smile. I can't help being charmed by David's love of love, even if it sounds exhausting to me. "Okay, then," I venture. "Let's figure out how you can get to know this woman—your soul mate—better. You said you saw her on a hike this afternoon and now a run. So, she's outdoorsy?" I reach for the Treeline Resort schedule on the nightstand. "Maybe we can find her at one of tomorrow's outdoor events." I remember the brochures from the receptionist and posters in the lobby—guided hikes, wildlife experiences.

David looks once more struck by lightning. "Yes! You're a genius." Before I can start reading the schedule, David speaks again. "How many times have *you* been in love?"

I pause. I know what I would say if I were playing my usual part, how the investment banker David knows would boast of his expansive romantic history. I could cleave to my playboy-ish part the way I've done this entire night.

But I can't. Not on this. "Only once," I say. "My wife." I can't help sounding sad, remembering how she won't even spend our anniversary in the same bed with me at the end of the week.

"Seems like Eliza might change that, though?" David says encouragingly.

I blink, trying to reconcile reality with performance. It's confusing, remembering how the Eliza David's referring to isn't the wife he thinks I mean—or she is, but not to him.

When I look up from the floor, guilt hits me. David's watching me with such earnestness, right on the heels of having bared the secrets of his heart to me. In fact, in the twenty-four hours we've known each other, David's been nothing but honest, openhearted, and generous with his friendship.

Folding the brochure in my hands, I decide right then— I can't keep deceiving him. Even if it's harmless, I don't want to lie to David. I like the guy. What's more, I'm starting to realize how nice it might be to have one real, uncomplicated friend here. I breathe in slowly, meeting his inquisitive gaze.

"Eliza *is* my wife," I say.

David's brows understandably furrow in confusion. "Eliza . . ." he repeats. "The woman you met yesterday?"

Part of me wishes we hadn't left the bar. A drink would very much help me divulge what I need to. "Yes," I say. "We've been married for five years, but things haven't been great between us recently. When we got here, one thing led to another, and now we're staying in separate rooms and pretending we're different people who've never met." I rush the ending, knowing the confession is ridiculous, like I'm telling him I time-traveled from the future.

Despite my expectations, David only grins. "Oh, I get it," he replies, not goading, but genuinely enthusiastic. "This is like role-playing, right? Spicing things up in the bedroom?"

"We'd have to share a bedroom for that," I mutter miserably. I shift in my seat, suddenly feeling like my every muscle is pulled tight. "Eliza thinks it'll get us out of our rut, help us reconnect. Maybe it will, I don't know." I stare out the window of David's suite, into the formless dark. "I still feel in way over my head."

Reclining on the chair, one leg crossed over his knee, David nods. He's really considering this, pensive like the senior partners when I bring them my questions on case strategy. I have to recognize what a good guy he is for rolling with the reveal I just dropped on him without laughing or judging me.

His eyes return to me, clear and decisive. "*I* know what you have to do." My hopes lift, even while I half expect David to pitch some rom-com-ready grand gesture. He goes on. "You love her, right? You want to fix your marriage?"

"Yes, and more than anything," I say. Finally, easy questions.

"Then it's simple." He stands, looking renewed. Pulling the brochure deftly out of my hands, he unfolds the pages and nods once. "We're going to go on tomorrow's hike down to the beach, where we will hopefully encounter my soul mate," he informs me, decisively, like a general giving out battle plans. "And *you* need to ask your wife out on a date."

13

Eliza

I LIE UNDER the crisp sheets of my bed, trying to position my feet somewhere cool. Usually, I love hotel beds. The heavy plush of the comforter, the calming uniformity of the white sheets, the piles of pillows. Tonight, however, everything is wrong. I've turned over three times, stuck my elbows out in strange directions, shifted my feet like I'm treading water. Nothing works. I'm hopelessly uncomfortable for one very frustrating reason.

I can't believe I'm honestly obsessing over whether my own husband will text me tonight.

It's not that late, I reassure myself. I saw no point in staying at the happy hour after Graham left. I figured I'd make it an early night. Instead, I've lain here, expectant, sweating into my tank top, *wondering.* Thus far it's been a lose-lose. I haven't slept, and Graham hasn't texted.

I turn over once more, frustratedly trying to put my phone from my mind. This is ridiculous. I know I could just text him. His number is in my phone, attached to hundreds of thousands of texts. And yet, here I am, waiting for him like I have to.

While I'm tired of waiting for Graham to make every move on this, the rules of our game demand I do. If I were to text him, to pull up the thread where we've discussed drive times and errands and what we're having for dinner, I would be breaking character. Once in the name of rescuing my heels is permissible, but twice is pretty much throwing out the whole premise. I'd never know if Graham the investment banker is interested in Eliza the vacation planner. I wouldn't know how far the rules of this game extend.

As the minutes drag on, I remind myself he showed up tonight. He came to the happy hour when he wasn't planning to, just because I mentioned I was going. He *flirted* with me.

Remembering his posture, his smile—his familiar yet unrecognizable eyes lingering on my dress's open neck—I become more and more sure. It has to mean something. It has to mean this is working.

The thought comforts me enough that I start to feel the heaviness of sleep settle onto me. My eyes droop, my breath evens out. My thoughts turn light, cloudlike, on the verge of dreams.

Then my phone buzzes loudly on the nightstand. The effect is immediate, like downing a triple-shot of espresso before going into the studio too early in the morning. I turn over, and in the darkness, Graham's name is illuminated on my screen. My breath catches, my head filling with possibilities.

> Hey. This is Graham. The guy from
> the bar.

I laugh. We're still playing. The realization is comforting in a way I didn't expect. I feel safe, confident. I've been nestled in layers of down pillows and high-thread-count sheets for more than an hour, and only now do I feel truly comfortable.

I see he's typing something else, so I settle deeper into my mattress, chewing my lip as I wait. Finally, his next message comes. I don't keep my eyes from racing over the text, consuming his words hungrily.

> David and I are going on the hotel's
> hike to the beach tomorrow morning.
> Do you have plans?

The flame in me flickers, then quietly goes out. I read over his message once, twice, making sure I'm not missing something. Because this question . . . is an invitation, but it's not a date. It couldn't be more friendly, more intentionally buffered. *Come hang out with me and David?*

I type back, noticing how the sheets have started to feel smothering once more.

> I think I can make that tomorrow.
> Thanks.

I lock my phone screen, not wanting to see the conversation. I feel foolish, and more disappointed than when I was waiting for him to reach out. Here I was thinking we were getting somewhere, reconnecting. Now I feel like Graham is back to restraint, to the least venturesome version of doing strictly what we said we would.

When my phone buzzes in my hand, the screen lighting up my ceiling in icy blue, I consider not checking it. Irritatingly, though, I know the question will keep me up. I relent, lifting the screen.

> This is not a date, by the way.

I frown. *Quite a way with words, he's got. A regular iMessage Cyrano.* I'm moments from flipping my phone over when it vibrates with Graham's follow-up.

> When—not if—I ask you out, it will be
> an activity without David.

I pause. Then, decisively, I take the opening he's offered me.

> Without David? Interesting. What could
> we get up to without David around?

Pleased Graham is finally pointing this exchange in the right direction, I jab the blue Send button with my thumb without letting myself hesitate. Off my message goes, leaving me huddled in the dark with my phone illuminating my face.

> I can think of a few things.

> Feel free to describe them.

> Actions speak louder than words.

> Certain words speak pretty loudly.

DO I KNOW YOU?

> You don't know me very well yet, Eliza,
> so I understand your wanting some
> proof of concept. Let me assure you,
> however, what I have in mind will be
> very enjoyable.

I smile into my phone. We haven't texted like this in years. It reminds me of the Graham I matched with on our dating app, when we were just getting to know each other through flirtatious messages.

> Give me three guesses.

> I'll give you one guess.

> You're not very generous, Graham.

> I can be plenty generous in other ways.

I shift under the covers. My legs feel hot under the hotel sheets.

> You'll just do whatever date I guess,
> won't you? Pretend it was your idea the
> whole time.

> Come on, how boring would I be if I
> did? Of course not. You can't blame me
> for wanting to know what's first on your
> mind, though. Where does Eliza from
> Boston like to be spoiled?

I know he means "where" like restaurants or nightclubs. Right now, though, the flutter in my stomach is making me think of different sorts of places where I like to be spoiled. I reposition my legs again under the covers.

> No way, Graham from Santa Fe. Now,
> I'm going to make YOU guess.

> There are so many options. So many
> possibilities.

My fingers hesitate over my phone. What's sprung to my head to reply to Graham is—well, it's even more unlike how Graham and I have texted recently. It's not how we messaged when we first met, either. Much too bold for us when we were really strangers. But right now, we're strangers and more.

I go for it.

> Hard, isn't it?

While my heart pounds, Graham doesn't reply.

It's head-spinning how quickly the racing of my pulse switches from feeling like excitement to feeling like mortification. This conversation couldn't possibly be so casual that he got distracted by what's on TV, could it? The other possibility, which is worse, is I've suddenly scared him off, like my audiobook reading in the car.

When my phone vibrates, I snatch it up hungrily.

Extremely hard, Eliza. I think I need a
hand.

My muscles clench deliciously at his words. I linger over my response, the way Graham did.

But I thought investment bankers loved
hard work.

Fair point. We do. All night, sometimes.

I'll put it on the list of what I know
about you. Generous (sometimes),
loves hard work (all the time). With
enough intel, maybe I'll figure your
date out in one guess.

Doubt it. Here's something else for
your list:

Unexpected.

I smile. He's not wrong there.

Consider me eagerly awaiting, then.

I will.

Figuring our exchange is over for the night, I'm starting to put my phone down on the nightstand when it buzzes insistently. I lift the glowing screen, where Graham's new message displays.

> You looked beautiful tonight.

I soften, glad he's chosen to shift from flying sparks to this deeper, sweeter level. I don't know in whose voice he's sent this text, but I don't really care. Seeing those words on my phone from my own husband thrills me. It's not that Graham hasn't told me I'm beautiful. He does, often. Our problems don't come from him not appreciating me, or me him. But you can admire the northern lights without understanding them.

No, what's thrilling isn't him telling me I'm beautiful. It's him *texting* it, which never happens because we live together. When we're talking, we're usually physically in each other's company, in the same room. The newness of his message—the intentionality of typing every letter into his phone—heightens the compliment.

It emboldens me enough to send what I do next.

> I'm glad you used my number. Part of
> me wondered if you only asked for it
> to be polite.

There's a long pause, one in which I recognize my anticipation mounting. I know it's because, for the first time in years, we're not on opposite sides of the same bed. I can't predict what Graham will do or say, can't read his body language or try to decode every flicker of his expression.

I can only wait.

Wait and wonder. Wonder whether he'll be coy or brash, wonder how long he'll leave me hoping. Wonder if this exchange will feel vain, like fishing for compliments. I grip my phone until, finally, Graham replies.

I asked because I wanted it.

14

Graham

I WAIT WITH David where the hike is going to begin, right in front of the hotel. Outside, in the crisp morning, I have the opportunity to take in the scenery. We're high up on the cliffs, with the ocean sparkling past the hotel. It's not just us here—groups of twos and threes hang out together, talking.

There's no sign of Eliza, though.

I'm jittery, flexing my feet in my shoes, distractedly tugging on my windbreaker. I wonder if my wife knows how long I worked over in my mind the question of when, exactly, to text her last night. There were factors to consider, ones I found myself weighing with the sensitivity of only the tensest of settlement negotiations. There was the realism of what her flirtatious, new acquaintance Graham would do, the eternal struggle of wanting to flatter her while not seeming desperate, the question of how strong to come on.

"What the workshop emphasizes is *active curiosity*," David says next to me. He's been strategizing for this walk for the past ten minutes, eager to put his workshop knowledge to use. "Which basically just means asking questions. So that's what I'll do. I think you should, too."

I frown, skeptical. "What kind of questions?"

"Anything!" David replies enthusiastically. "From small stuff like *What did you have for breakfast?* to the bigger things. The important things. Like, you know. *What makes you happy? What do you want out of life?*"

"David, she's my wife," I say, half patient and half discouraged. "I already know her answers." Well, I guess I don't know what she had for breakfast. But I know the bigger stuff. We're not *that* disconnected—just out of touch.

David gives me a dry look. "Aren't you pretending *not* to know her? Ask the questions you would if you really were meeting her for the first time." The logic of this suggestion earns him nothing except a scowl. Satisfied, he goes on. "Here, we'll do it together. It'll be fun. We'll each ask ten questions, then report back to each other. Buddy system."

"You sound like a kindergarten teacher," I grumble.

"I am a kindergarten teacher," David says.

Surprised out of my sourness, I pause, mapping this new information onto David. "Really? How do you like it?"

David grins excitedly. "That was great," he says, like I just flushed the potty on my own for the first time. "See how you asked me questions? Do that with Eliza."

I have to fight down my smile. Honestly, while I first guessed finance for David, his real career is starting to make more and more sense. His kindergarteners probably love him.

Right then, Eliza walks out, looking like the sunlight should be glad to shine on her. It's the way she holds herself, something I noticed in just our first few weeks of dating—her chin tilted up, posture somehow straight yet loose, poise in her lips and her sharp gaze. I can't help the thrill I feel the instant I see her.

David nudges me. "Remember," he says softly. When I look over, he holds up ten fingers. "Buddy system," he whispers.

I roll my eyes. Next he'll be having us make hand turkeys.

My gaze returns to my wife, and I find she's noticed us. She walks over, smiling. Watching her, I'm struck with the strangest sensation. I've seen her lightweight workout wear dozens of times—deep purple leggings, jacket slung over her gray sports bra—when I'm stuffing them unceremoniously into the washing machine, or when she walks past me while I'm working in the kitchen on weekend mornings. Yet somehow, right now, they look like they belong to someone else. It's hard to explain, even to myself. This game is definitely getting into my head.

"Hey," she says, reaching us.

David's ten fingers flash in my head. "How"—I start, sounding forced and formal, like I just landed on this planet yesterday—"was your breakfast?"

Eliza blinks, taken aback by my awkward delivery. "Um. Good. How was yours?"

"Also good," I reply, once more with unevenness I know comes out weird. *Why couldn't we be texting this conversation?*

Eliza smiles politely, obviously knowing I'm not throwing strikes here. I glance at David, who sends me a subtle thumbs-up. While well intentioned, it only manages to stress me out more. Banter is one thing, but there has to be more than banter in a romance. It's great for the beginning of a relationship, but getting to more substance is where connections so often stumble. Not that I'm beginning my relationship with Eliza—but in this game, I very much am.

I must look like I'm floundering, because what pulls me from my spiral is David. "Eliza! *Fancy* meeting you here," he practically cheers. "So wait, I feel like you haven't said. What do you do?" David goes on—no doubt trying to lead by example.

Eliza spins answers about her fake career, sliding easily into character, recounting details of her fictional workplace, fictional clients, and fictional day-to-day with ease and specificity.

I listen carefully, searching her words for ways of understanding the Eliza who is my wife. Instead, I start to feel like I'm studying astrophysics by memorizing the constellations—none of the celestial creatures I can imagine will help me understand how the sky really works. While Eliza's fabricated New England life is fun, I can't find real insight into her or us.

Eliza eventually returns David's questions, not pretending her surprise when he reveals the details of his own employment and shares some admittedly adorable details about lesson planning. The conversation is cut short when the group leader joins us. "Hello, everyone. Here for the guided nature walk?" she calls out welcomingly. "My name is Zoey, and I'm the hotel's naturalist. Unless anyone has to run to the bathroom, I think we'll get going."

When I notice David's gaze roaming the group worriedly, I know who he's looking for. "She didn't come?" I ask him.

"What if she checked out?" David speculates with plain panic. "What if I never see her again?"

"See who again?" Eliza cuts in.

"No one important. Just my *soul mate*," David practically whines. While Eliza is left in bewildered silence, the group starts to move forward, down the winding dry-brush trail leading to the ocean. David reluctantly moves with us, visibly fighting his flagging enthusiasm.

Until we're just stepping onto the trailhead. With incredible timing, one last woman dashes from the hotel entrance over to our group, clad in activewear perfect for hiking, clearly relieved she didn't miss the excursion.

David turns. His eyes latch on to our new guest. Relief crashes over him like a wave.

I can't help grinning when he straightens up, invigorated. "I'm going in," he declares, then promptly falls to the back of the group to join her.

Zoey walks backward, leading the group down the trail right outside the hotel. Behind me, I hear David waste no time in cheerfully inquiring where our latecomer is from.

While I'm honestly rooting for him, his predictable departure leaves me alone with Eliza—and with the pressure of this conversation. We follow the group, unspeaking. Even having spent the past couple of days surrounded by the glorious scenery, it's striking to me how quickly the chic campus of the resort cedes to outright wilderness.

I like the outdoors, though I don't often have the time or the opportunity to get off the grid. Despite my inexperience with the "active curiosity" approach, I let myself relish the scent of the ocean drifting up the hillside, the swish of the pine trees, and the dirt under my shoes. The coastal cliffs where we're walking really do steal my breath, with the turquoise mouth of the Pacific opening up suddenly past the lichen-laced rocks clad in rolling green foliage.

The scenery—the openness, the extraordinary natural wonder—makes me feel freer, enough that I decide I'll keep going with the questions David recommended. While we head under low brush and Zoey begins giving the ecological history of Big Sur, I psych myself up, remembering who I'm pretending to be. Investment Banker Graham would have questions ready for the beautiful woman he met on vacation.

"So, you . . . like nature?" The moment the question passes my lips, I wince. I consider flinging myself off the nearest cliff. I wouldn't die, but I might break my leg and need to be airlifted to the nearest hospital. "I mean, uh. Do you like the outdoors?" I continue hastily. "Hiking? Camping? That stuff?"

Of course, I know what the real Eliza would say. She enjoys the occasional hike—it's hard to live in San Diego and not want to hike *sometimes*—but once, early in our relationship, I suggested we camp for the weekend in Joshua Tree.

From the chore of cooking on the portable stove to the bone-deep chill seeping into our tent past sundown, not to mention the unyieldingly hard surface on which we unrolled our sleeping bags or the unfortunate reality of peeing outside, Eliza was miserable. In six months of dating, I'd never seen her so displeased. Waking up to her forced smiles and dark-ringed eyes on our second morning, I proposed we end the trip early and go to a hotel. This went over *much* better.

Eliza strides forward on the trail, her running shoes snapping twigs on the ground. "I love the outdoors," she says, full of enthusiasm. "Have you ever been to Joshua Tree? I went camping there last year. I can't wait to return."

I can't help myself—I frown. Somehow her chipper reply turns the morning cold, the sunlight brittle. Coming up with new careers or texting flirtatiously is one thing. Rewriting the details of our real relationship seems like something else.

"Yeah. I have," I say haltingly, not sure I like or understand the direction she's leading us. Unlike her, I'm not faking this conversation well. I know because she reacts to the tone in my voice the way one would to sipping day-old coffee. The silence between us turns stony. We step over rocks on the path while Zoey in front leads us down the trail, the sand where we're headed coming into view below the verdant cliffs.

It's several minutes before I snap the silence.

"I took my wife to Joshua Tree," I say. "She hated it."

I feel Eliza's breathing hitch. "I'm sure she didn't," she replies lightly, making sure her words don't strictly step out of the bounds of character. There's something different in her tone, though, something not even her modulated voice hides. She's speaking like she doesn't want to wake something up.

It's one step too far onto this uncertain ground she's charted for us. "You know"—I start, knowing intuitively that Eliza will understand it's the real me speaking—"I like this game. But please don't use it to hide from hard or unpleasant things, or pretend they never happened. You need to be open with me."

Whatever hope I harbored that Eliza would understand dissipates quickly. Storm clouds gather over her mood, her eyes flashing like lightning.

"What's the emergency, Graham," she says icily.

"What?"

"You broke character. It's against the rules of our agreement," she declares. Then, unhesitating, she walks off into the group of hikers.

I don't follow her, sticking to the back of the crowd while the trail slopes toward the shore in the cool shade of the mountains. Remorse wrestles with righteousness in me. Watching the wind gust over the ocean, I wonder if I said the wrong thing.

I don't think I did. Having fun for a week pretending we're getting to know each other is fine, but what happens when vacation ends? When we have to return to our real lives without having solved any of our issues? While I'm enjoying what pretending is doing for us, we can't *just* pretend. Five years into our marriage, problems can't be solved by packing up a tent and checking into a hotel. If this is going to work—really work—we can't conceal issues under rose-colored paint. We have to surprise each other *and* be real.

I'm just not sure how to strike the balance yet.

15

Eliza

IF I COULD, I would turn around and head back to the hotel.

Unfortunately, though, I'm not the experienced outdoorswoman I was pretending to be with Graham. *Graham*, whose break from our conversation frustrated me in ways I can't fully explain. I settle for moving forward into the group of hikers, feeling confined by the cliffs. I'm certain if I were to venture back to the resort, I would end up getting promptly devoured by the local bear population our hike leader just described.

Focusing on the scenery, I pointedly ignore the feeling of Graham's stare on the back of my head. But it's not easy. Honestly, I wish I'd stayed in my room instead of taking Graham up on his invitation. I only got myself out of bed for *a beach hike* because I thought we would be like we were last night. I don't know how we went from having so much fun to this—to him out of nowhere accusing me of hiding from our issues.

"Hey," a stranger's voice—a real stranger—says next to me. I look over to find a woman has fallen into step with my stride. It's the latecomer, the girl David enthusiastically joined—the one he insinuated was his soul mate. She's tall, broadly built, with dark hair and a perfectly put-together hiking outfit. She's not smiling, but the expression doesn't look unfriendly on her. She nods behind us. "Is that guy bothering you? I can't help noticing him staring at you. I'm guessing husband?"

I startle, not needing to follow her gaze to know she means Graham. "No—not my husband," I say, sliding on instinct into character. The words still sound odd.

The woman's severe expression deepens into a frown. "Do you know him? I can alert hotel staff if he's harassing you."

"No," I say hastily. While I'm pissed at Graham, the last thing I want is for him to end up in hotel jail. Recovering my cool, I recognize what she's trying to do. "No, he's not harassing me. That's really thoughtful of you, though. Thanks."

"Of course." The woman still doesn't smile, but there's warmth in her matter-of-factness. "Being a woman traveling on my own, I've learned to keep an eye out. I'm Lindsey."

"Eliza. Nice to meet you."

Despite myself, I glance over my shoulder, finding Graham's eyes on me. Promptly, he shifts his gaze to David, who is now walking beside him.

"So what's the deal, then?" Lindsey asks. Having watched this whole wordless exchange, she's eyeing me curiously. "Boyfriend?"

"Not yet," I say, hearing the strange echo of myself from six and a half years ago. I was talking to my sister, Michelle, on the phone, describing what Graham and I had done for our second date. He'd

103

taken me to a play at the Geffen and we'd made out on my couch after. *Are you official?* my sister asked me. *Not yet. Soon, I hope,* I told her giddily.

Lindsey's eyes sparkle. "Playing hard to get. I like it."

I can't help laughing. "Something like that." *You have no idea,* I think to myself.

We follow the group, descending the gentle incline of the trail. The foliage is not heavy, only small bushes carpeting the rocks in swaths of green. The day smells nothing like even our seaside neighborhood in La Jolla. Right now, we're *really* out here, where the crisp scent of plants and water is everywhere. It's perfectly clear out, the pale sky cloudless. The morning is still cold, but the sunlight is beginning to warm through. The ocean whispers down below, the gentle sound of the tides scribbling white foam on the stunning crystal blue.

Fifteen more minutes of hiking in companionable silence with the rest of our pack leads us onto the sand, where the group stops. The small beach is pristine, the sand smooth, the water rippling softly. I stand with Lindsey while the guide hands out granola bars and water to whoever wants them.

"Are you here for the workshop?" I ask her.

"Yeah, a gift from my mom, who thinks I'm lonely." She shrugs with what looks like wry humor. "I'm not lonely. But I *do* love dating, so I figured, why not up my game? Worse comes to worst, I just meet some more singles at a stunning hotel."

I smile, getting used to the way Lindsey speaks fast and frankly. Noticing David eyeing her from the sand, I wonder where their conversation ended up—David seemed hopeful.

Lindsey nods in my direction. "How about you?"

"I'm not here for the workshop. I'm a vacation planner," I say, noticing once more how quickly I slip into my story. "So I'm sort of on the clock." I search the shoreline, now wishing I hadn't taken the guide up on the water bottle. "Where do you think the bathroom is?"

When Lindsey laughs, I turn back to her, not having meant to be funny. "The ocean?" When I make a face, she continues more earnestly. "I don't think you'll find restrooms here on the beach."

Ugh, I think. Hiking down here was fine, I guess. Being trapped out here with nowhere to pee except *the ocean*—I honestly don't know if Lindsey was being serious—is not my favorite, though. Neither, now that I think of it, is this dry granola bar, when knots of hunger have me imagining the hotel omelet station. I wish I'd—

My train of thought crashes sharply. Because, goddamn it, Graham was right.

It's easy to pretend I only resent him for violating our rules when he broke character. Deep down, though, I think part of me knew he was calling me on something I *do* need to do less of.

I don't know why I pretended I'd loved our Joshua Tree trip, except out of some instinct to pretend problems never come up in our relationship. To use these imagined selves to rewrite reality instead of just venturing outside it. I'm *not* a person who wants to go camping in Joshua Tree, and pretending I am, even in this game, isn't going to help us. We're putting on pretenses, but on some level, we still have to be us—even when the truth is hard or frustrating.

"Don't look now," Lindsey says, distracting me, "but that guy is totally checking you out." I follow her gaze to Graham. "He's hella hot," she continues. "You sure you want to hold out on him?"

I blink, not sure how to respond. It's not like I'm threatened—it was just an offhand comment from Lindsey. But I'm not used to people checking out my husband around me, because of course I'm not.

Honestly, I guess I don't really check him out much myself, either. It's not because he isn't desirable. I know he is. It's just not top of my mind every minute of every day of our marriage. I couldn't get anything done if it was.

"No," I say. "I definitely don't want to hold out on him."

16

Graham

I TAKE THE hint.

Eliza doesn't want to talk right now. She needs room to collect herself, which I don't begrudge her, though I haven't wavered in feeling right to say what I did. The Eliza I've known for our whole relationship doesn't dwell on the negative. I love her for how well she puts problems into perspective if I'm viewing them out of proportion, or even pushes past them entirely.

The issue is, on occasion, she ends up stifling feelings of hurt or conflict so deeply they end up spilling out of her in painful ways. The poisonous by-products of the fuel of hope on which she runs. While she is a great actress, she's also human, and I wish she could be real with me—even while we're playing this game.

I walk the length of the secluded beach with David, who has kept up nearly incessant conversation describing the interaction he had with his "soul mate" before she joined Eliza. He's learned her name—Lindsey—how often she travels, and where she's from. I have to hand it to him, his inquisitiveness is impressive.

Eventually, though, even David runs out of rapport. He retreats to grab more water from the guide—understandable, with all the talking he's been doing—leaving me with nothing to do except ruminate. The more the minutes stretch, swept off by the breeze buffeting us from the ocean, the more demoralized this sudden new distance between me and Eliza makes me feel. I walk to the edge of the blue water, where I linger, taking in the vastness of everything.

It feels unexpectedly profound, painfully metaphorical. My marriage feels full of infinite space, endless distance. Every day I reach for Eliza over lengths I can't cross, or I quietly give in to their intractable hugeness. I don't enjoy doing either, but for too long, those distances have felt like the ocean in front of me. Too vast to build bridges over. Too eternal to close up.

I'm so deeply in these thoughts that I didn't notice the other hikers have started up toward the trail. I no longer hear the sounds of their conversations, and David has certainly abandoned me to chase after Lindsey. Eliza, I figure, is heading into the hotel with her new friend, planning for an hours-long brunch on the patio, or poolside drinks, or side-by-side pedicures.

I don't move. I just feel the wind rustling over me, the sunlight on my skin.

But when it's silent, when I feel like the last person out here, someone comes up next to me. I don't have to look—I can sense it's her. I don't know how. I just do.

For a moment, Eliza and I say nothing, listening to the crashing waves. They're a restless contradiction, the violence of water striking stone carrying up into the gentle, whispering echoes surrounding us. I feel on the edge of something myself, unsure yet whether the jump is safe or not.

When Eliza finally speaks, her words couldn't be further from what I expected. "Lindsey thinks you're hot."

It's so unexpected, the verdict so dryly delivered, I can't help laughing. I look over, finding for the second time today a smile pulling Eliza's mouth. It's like a second sunrise, somehow. Like despite the cloudless sky we've hiked under this entire morning, only now is real, brilliant light finally spilling into the world.

I shake my head humorously. "I won't tell David," I say. "Is that what you two were discussing? How hot I am?"

Eliza raises an eyebrow, clearly wanting to say something. I start to grin, a little daring. Whatever was on her tongue, I watch her bend it like a cherry stem into something new.

"Would Graham the investment banker be interested in someone like Lindsey?" she asks. "Maybe she's exactly his type."

I make sure now to look her directly in the eyes. They're like the water in front of us, the dark depths of the ocean glittering in the sunlight. They make it hard to concentrate, but I do, putting everything into what I reply. "He's too hung up on someone else to know."

We're quiet once more. I search her expression, wishing, wondering. If I hope hard enough, I can halfway convince myself she's starting to build bridges over the ocean.

I contemplate returning to my room, to the day I'm facing. It's not difficult to envision—spending another afternoon alone with my Jacuzzi and my room service and my spectacular, solitary view. My perfect isolation. The prospect is not a happy one, not today.

"Is this ever lonely for you?" I ask. I mean this trip, this pretense.

I just need some indication it's not pure fun for her. Some indication it's hard for her like it is for me.

Eliza looks out over the water. "In some ways, this year has been the loneliest of my life," she says, her voice stripped bare.

It's not the answer to the question I asked. Nevertheless, I know her response is real. Whether it's part of the role-play doesn't even matter. While we stand in silence for a few more minutes, I realize I was wrong. David was right. I did learn something new about my wife—something it only took asking to uncover.

"I hate outdoorsy stuff," she goes on suddenly. I look over, a little startled by the subject change. "You were right. I hate it. Especially Joshua Tree."

Despite the bite in her tone, I laugh. "I figured." It's what Investment Banker Graham would say, with no nod to our own very real camping trip.

The shadow of humor plays over Eliza's lips. "You don't know everything about me, though," she replies.

I smile. "I'm looking forward to finding out more," I promise her.

17

Eliza

I TAKE THE script I need to read for work out to the pool. I was right—my producer was, politely, uninterested in the sample I recorded of the romantic scene I was working on while Graham and I drove up. She gave me literally dozens of notes I'll have to incorporate when I record in the studio for real. In the meantime, I wound up with this video game's intergalactic military officer role after I emailed my agent yesterday morning requesting something completely different.

Now I have Brigadier General Jett Hathaway to keep me company while I stretch out on the lounge chair in my swimsuit cover-up and, underneath, my white bikini. The day remains crystal clear, so uninterruptedly blue it looks like someone colored it in with the paint bucket on Photoshop. Unlike on the hike, it's gotten warmer thanks to the sun rising higher in the sky. I'll go in the water when I reach that perfect level of slightly too hot.

I read for half an hour. It's the ideal environment for my work—

early enough in the day that the pool is scarcely occupied, no one shouting or splashing in the water. The deck is serene, sunny, and mine.

The jangle of the gate distracts me from Hathaway's explanation of battle strategy.

I look over and falter, finding Graham entering the pool yard. Frankly, I'm surprised to see him out. We haven't made our next plan yet. I didn't mention I was coming here, so him showing up seems like coincidence. *Happy coincidence,* I can't help feeling.

I gaze through my sunglasses, vaguely and entirely preoccupied with the question of whether he'll come over here. I feel like there's a good chance. Our stranger-selves have hit it off—there's no other way to say it. It would be entirely normal for Investment Banker Graham to swing over and say a casual hello to Vacation Planner Eliza.

But he doesn't. His stride unhesitating, he kicks off his sandals on the other side of the pool. Then he takes off his shirt and jumps into the water.

I try to return to reading. I really do. I have missions to elucidate to the young cadets under my command.

Instead, I'm too distracted. By my own husband, shirtless in front of me.

By his water-slicked hair, wet gold in the sun. His broad shoulders with their spattering of freckles. The flat line of his stomach. None of these details are new to me. I've traced my fingers down his chest, put my mouth on those freckles, tangled my fingers in his hair. Obviously, I'm attracted to Graham.

I guess I forgot just *how* attracted I am to him. Lindsey was right. My husband is hot.

As I'm watching him swim laps, my phone rings. I check the

screen and see it's my dad. Distractedly, I pick up, nearly fumbling my phone onto the flagstones of the pool deck. "Hey, Dad."

"How's your trip?" he asks.

"Really . . ." The pause draws out while I watch Graham. "Good," I finish, hearing how disjointed my reply is. It's just, Graham has great freestyle form. It's a very shoulders-focused stroke.

"What have you and Graham been up to?" There's trademark enthusiasm in his voice. Not enthusiasm for everything—in fact, my father is the opposite of enthusiastic when it comes to his work, software engineering in Oklahoma. My dad is, however, enthusiastic when it comes to family. He only calls, never texts, and treats every conversation like we're old friends sitting down to dinner for the first time in years in the fanciest restaurant in town.

I blink, tearing my eyes from Graham, aware I need to be coherent for this. "We went on a beach hike this morning, and now we're at the pool. How're things with you?" It's not a lie, but it's not a very accurate portrayal of the trip, either. I realize that pretending things are fine is how Graham and I ended up in this mess. But—I'm not about to tell my father that my husband and I are role-playing as perfect strangers. He'd take it the wrong way.

Not that it's totally the wrong way, I have to concede. My eyes have, unfortunately, strayed back to Graham, who's lifting himself out of the pool, water running down his shoulder blades and back.

I turn to face the opposite direction. Desperate times call for desperate measures.

Dad regales me with his thoughts on the new restaurant in town he and my mom tried last night. While I enjoy my dad's phone calls—I really do—I nevertheless have to force myself to focus this time, consciously concentrating on the details of the tastefully understated menu, the swift service, the lovely patio garden.

"I was thinking it could be a good place for the rehearsal dinner," my dad says offhandedly.

This yanks my concentration to the phone. I stiffen, instantly uncomfortable. "Oh, that's nice," I say. This turn in the conversation has somehow changed the entire tenor of the perfect day. The sunlight is suddenly prickling, the frame of the lounge chair hard where I'm sitting. I dread conversations about my sister's wedding because I know exactly where they'll lead.

"Speaking of," my dad goes on genially, "we haven't gotten your RSVP yet." He wasn't this convincingly casual the first time he brought the topic up. But he's had practice.

I feel my whole body cringe. It's not that I don't want to go to my sister's wedding. It's that I know Michelle doesn't want me there. Different words from a different conversation echo harshly in my head. *Of course this is exactly what you'd do.* Sweat unrelated to the poolside sun gathers in the creases of my cover-up.

"That's because I never got an invitation, Dad."

"So?" I practically hear the grandiose shrug in my father's voice. "You're family. Obviously, you're invited—it's assumed."

"No, actually, it's not," I reply, my patience fraying. Past my frustration, it's kind of heartbreaking how unwavering my dad's conviction is. I've felt on occasion—recent occasions, certainly—like he's a TV dad, Craig T. Nelson or Ty Burrell or someone, and he's struggling with events not conforming to the script's happy ending. "Why don't you ask Michelle instead of me?" I go on.

"You're being ridiculous. It's your sister's wedding. She wants you there," he insists quickly. From his phrasing and switch of strategy, I realize what he's not saying. He *did* ask Michelle, who didn't give him the assurance he's giving me. Now he's come to his other daughter in hopes of getting the answer he wants.

I've entertained this conversation long enough. It's starting to hurt. "She doesn't. You know she doesn't," I say more quietly. I know, logically, my and Michelle's fight has gotten out of control. It's deepened, dark and ugly, into a crevasse in my life I prefer to ignore. I just—can't be the one to end it. It's not my place.

Or, I'm pretty sure it's not. It's *definitely* not my place to show up to a wedding I wasn't invited to. Even if it's my only sister's.

We haven't spoken since Michelle's engagement party. I helped her plan the whole event, perused slideshows of restaurant photos on the Instagram links she sent me, helped her pick out party favors, came up with the name for the specialty cocktail. I was even supposed to give the toast, which I'd had written weeks earlier.

I missed it. Not just the toast. The entire party. My sister's engagement party.

The day of, I was in the studio, recording for hours. The job was really important, and a lot of other people were depending on me to meet this deadline. I couldn't skip it. When I rushed out of the studio, I had fifteen minutes to get to the airport. I pushed past lines and crowds, raced to my gate, and it didn't matter. My plane was gone.

Despite my every effort to book a new flight that would get me to Oklahoma in time, I couldn't. When I finally reached Oklahoma City the next morning, it . . . was for nothing. Michelle was furious. I don't enjoy these conversations with my dad because every one brings wounding reminders of my little sister's flushed cheeks, of the waver in her voice like I'd never heard. *Of course this is exactly what you'd do. Just another episode of the Eliza show, huh?* She said I was a failed actress who didn't like ceding the spotlight. She said I wanted to make her night about me and my job.

Of course, we haven't spoken since.

I never even explained *why* I couldn't make it. Never said how hard I honestly worked to reschedule my flight, or how it wasn't about my job, but about the people depending on me. I would have if Michelle had asked. Which she didn't, not even once. She should have known I would never do something like this on purpose.

Instead, she just assumed. It stung enough that I didn't even want to correct her. If I'm the negligent sister, the selfish sister, the unkind sister to her, fine. The least I could do is be those things out of her life.

With the pungent whiff of chlorine in my nose, I fix my gaze past the flagstones. The gorgeous view of grasses and sky is incongruous with the very not-tranquil pounding in my temples. My dad huffs into the phone. "Well, it doesn't matter. I'm paying for half of this wedding, so I say you're invited. Do you and Graham want fish or chicken?"

I wince. His bluster poorly conceals the fact that he's feeling the way I do. For some reason, he just insists on fighting it.

"Dad," I say softly. "I can't just show up at her wedding. It would ruin her big day."

"No, what would ruin her big day is not having her big sister there for her," Dad charges on. "You don't want this little tiff to get in the way of one of the most important events of Michelle's life. You'll regret it forever if you do. You both will."

My stomach twists. This is what he doesn't understand. I *know* I'll regret it. I've envisioned the regretting, tossed and turned in bed over the regretting. I can see how the day will go with painful precision, like the Greek prophetess Cassandra in the Aeschylus play we read in my college Classical Drama class. I'll see the posts come up on the hashtag I still follow, ignore the notifications from the now mostly silent family group text. It will be wrenching.

But I know if I come uninvited to the wedding, Michelle will think I'm doing exactly what she accused me of. She won't recognize sisterly support in my presence. She'll only see narcissistic Eliza stealing the spotlight again.

It's hard enough to think, much less to say. I've had enough. "You know what, we'll have to talk about this later," I say. "Graham and I are—walking into a couple's massage," I invent wildly, "and we're running late. Love you."

"Eliza—" my dad starts.

I cut him off. "Bye now."

I hang up, my heart pounding. Clenching my phone in my hand, I sit there, fighting to collect myself. I know I can't put off this conversation or the question of Michelle's wedding forever. But some self-destructive little part of my mind whispers . . . what if I could? Couldn't I just let the days pass, let my dad's focus return to Michelle while I slip out of familial sight, where Michelle wants me? If I'm selfish, mean Eliza, wouldn't it be better if she just forgot me?

At the very least I can give myself one week of vacation to ignore this. The questions will keep until I get home. It's the only fortifying thought I find, and I hold on to it. I have room to relax in the carefree coming days here, not to mention things to look forward to. The sunlight starts to feel warmer and more welcoming, the gentle poolside breeze more calming.

But when I face the pool, my heart sinks. Graham is gone.

18

Graham

I'VE GONE TO the pool, walked the entire hotel grounds, gotten coffee twice, read the magazines in my room, soaked in my private Jacuzzi, watched TV, and tried to nap.

And it's only four p.m.

I couldn't keep swimming luxurious laps in front of Eliza, no matter how much I wanted to. I'd gone to the pool knowing she would be there—Eliza loves the water—riding on confidence I hardly recognized. The eyeful of me I'd fully intended to give her was nothing other than shameless flirting. However, I'm playing by the rules of our game. We've only just met, and texting her so soon after we hung out would be coming on too strong. Hence, gliding through the water in front of her instead.

I'm presently lying flat on my bed, having utterly failed to sleep. I'm bored, bordering on edgy. Staring at the ceiling, I'm coming to terms with the fact that I don't really understand vacation. Even in this modern masterpiece of a room, with cliffside sunlight and the sounds of the waves surrounding me, I have no finesse for doing nothing.

Of course, this trip wasn't supposed to be me doing nothing. It was supposed to be *us* celebrating our anniversary. I couldn't have known I would be carefully planning my texts to Eliza like I did when we first matched online.

I wish I'd packed my work computer, which I instead deliberately left on its charger in our living room, not wanting to give myself the excuse to bury these days in briefs. Without work or Eliza, however, I have no idea what to do with my time. Reflecting on my life—the way one does when lying on one's back on the bed of one's empty hotel room—I realize this makes some sense. Inspired by my parents' high-flying careers and lifestyle, I went to college planning to go to law school. I got good grades. I went to law school to go into corporate litigation, which I did. Every step of the way I've packed hours with studying, with writing papers, with networking events, with the late nights needed to go from promising first-year lawyer to partner track.

Only one significant change ever really entered this plan—a beautiful woman who is right now pretending she's a vacation planner from Boston.

I could text her. Shit, I *want* to text her. Only in the interest of adhering to the rules of first dates—not calling too soon or too late—have I committed to holding off texting her until 5 p.m. I should be able to distract myself until 5 p.m., shouldn't I? I'm an adult man, not one of David's kindergartners.

Unlocking my phone, I pull up my new friend's number. I text him, wondering what he's up to.

David replies immediately, which I'm coming to realize is a character trait of his.

> Creating Intimacy workshop. You want
> to come crash it?

The title makes me cringe, not out of judgment for the workshop—out of judgment for myself. I'm pretty sure one thing *not* being taught in Creating Intimacy is constructing an elaborate role-playing game where you pretend not to know your spouse.

I reply to David.

> I'm good man. Catch up with you later.

I stare up, counting the light fixtures on the ceiling. I'm completely out of ideas.

Dismally, I reach for the hotel schedule on my bedside table. The staff slides one under my door every morning, freshly printed with new events for each day. I start to scan the short list with flickers of hope. Maybe I could . . . go bird-watching. I would imagine the California coastline has birds interesting enough for the bored and lonely.

But there's nothing except Creating Intimacy until tonight, when a couples' cooking class is happening. *Nothing.*

Devoid of my own inclinations, I open up a grudging new line of questioning. What would Investment Banker Graham do? When he's not working or having wild nights with random women from the internet, how does he occupy his hours?

I push myself to call on my creativity, to cultivate my character the way I imagine Eliza would. First, I need inspiration. I draw from memories of my corporate clients, especially the finance people we've counseled on lending gone wrong, broken bank financings, insolvency situations. Like I'm pulling something heavy out of storage, I reconstruct conversations, render details, replay chitchat . . .

Finally, it comes to me.

I haven't had time to exercise seriously since law school, when I would hit UCLA's Wooden Center on my way home from contracts or torts. I did everything—weights, rowing, running. I enjoyed it, how the physical balanced out the mental work in my days. Okay, I enjoyed the confidence of being in shape, too.

Work got overwhelming when I joined my firm, leaving barely enough time for grocery shopping or sleep, not to mention serious fitness. Investment Banker Graham, however, probably goes to Equinox at six in the morning before the office. It would be good to reconnect with the Graham who got in regular workouts. Flush with the momentum of my first real idea since my ingenious second coffee trip, I spring from the white comforter. I grab my tennis shoes from the floor and pull on a T-shirt.

Time to hit the gym.

19

Eliza

I LOVE THE water. Graham, not so much. On our honeymoon in Greece, despite the crystalline waters of Santorini, I could only keep him at the beach for an hour before he would get restless and want to wander into town for gyros or sightseeing. Not that I really minded. Our honeymoon was perfect.

Nevertheless, without Graham checking his watch next to me, I stayed at the pool until it closed. The hours were serene. I floated in the water, swam lazy strokes to exercise the stress from my muscles, read my script while I sunned on the lounge chair—in short, I vacationed.

Finally, though, with my feet in my sandals, hearing the gate clang closed behind me, I could no longer ignore the faint tug I'd felt since I'd gotten there earlier. I hadn't seen Graham since he left the pool hours ago, hadn't even heard from him. The couple times I checked my phone, pretending to myself I wasn't wondering whether he'd texted, I found only my background photo—sand dollars I found washed up on the shore in La Jolla.

How is Graham spending his time? For the past fifteen minutes, I've nonchalantly strolled the hotel grounds, searching for some sign of him instead of returning to my room. Maybe he's been holed up in his Jacuzzi, but I figure, honeymoon suite notwithstanding, he would have to be bored by now.

I walk by the bar. Graham's six feet and two inches would put him over the heads of the other patrons, but his golden hair is nowhere to be found. I continue to the business center, convincing myself quite reasonably I'll find him logging into his work email or printing out hundreds of pages of case documents. But the space is empty, orderly with disuse, the two computer screens showing only photographic slideshow screensavers. I even walk the winding path down to his room and ring the bell on the pretense of wanting to check his bag for something I can't find. He's not there.

In fact, he's nowhere to be found.

Finally, I give up. My curiosity feels like a hangnail. I pretend it's no problem and I'll forget it in five minutes, knowing the whole while it's going to distract and irritate me *every* five minutes. But I'm not going to keep up my one-woman search party for my own husband late into the night, scouring every inch of the Treeline Resort.

Instead, I'll head back to my room, where I'll shower, then casually text Graham, just like I would if we really were just starting our relationship. Like I did *when* we were just starting our relationship. I like these echoes, these reprises. It's like when the chorus repeats in your favorite song.

On my way back to my room, I walk past the gym.

Then I stop.

I double back to peer in the windows.

Because there is Graham, sitting at the *bench press*, out of breath. His white T-shirt stretches over the drool-worthy shoulders I ogled in the pool earlier. He's doing biceps curls, focused on each rep with grimacing intensity. The sheen of sweat on his brow, his forearms, the collar of his shirt, shows me he's been here for some time. It's extremely distracting in the best way.

I watch him. For the second time today, I just stare, lost in the sight of him in front of me.

Until he catches me looking. We make eye contact through the window while he lowers the dumbbell slowly. His green eyes linger on me for a second before he raises an eyebrow, like he's asking, *Been there long?*

Despite the new flirtatious charge between us, I will *not* have him thinking I was just out here gazing in wonderment for the past five minutes. In fairness, it's been more like three minutes. Quickly, I school my features into impassivity and waltz into the gym like I'm unembarrassed.

While I walk up to him, he doesn't change what he's doing— just picks up the dumbbell with his other hand. I reach him, and I can't help myself. I ask the question in my head even though it's not in character. "What are you doing here?"

He looks up, grinning when he sees me. "Getting my workout in. Normally, I'm a morning-gym guy," he replies, despite this being nowhere in the vicinity of the truth. Graham is a morning-coffee guy. Sometimes a morning-reading guy, though I have no idea what's on his Kindle. A morning-*gym* guy? He hasn't gone to the gym since law school.

Yet there's nothing except casual conviction in his voice. I stare, my reason different this time. For once, Graham is undeniably, un-questionably playing our game better than me.

He deposits the dumbbell on the floor. "I'm only out here now because, well," he goes on, starting to smile, "when I'm not in a re-lationship, I find working out before bed helps me burn off my extra . . . energy."

I swallow, trying to get back on track. When did he get so *good* at this? Despite myself, it's making me a little competitive. I fix my eyes on him, cocking my hip slightly. "Having a nice workout, then?" I ask.

"Yes, actually. It was great."

I falter because of the light shift in his voice. While his reply is character-consistent, what's showing through is honesty. He really is enjoying himself.

He straightens up, eyeing me with his hands resting on his knees. In his expression, I can practically feel his coming question. "Did you come here to work out or just to watch me?" He takes in my wet swimsuit, visible through my pool wrap, like he knows I couldn't possibly be here to work out. Still, something in his eyes says that's not the only reason he's looking.

I won't flub my lines just because he's checking me out, though. "I came to . . . see what classes they have tomorrow."

"Did you." His eyes dance. "Well"—he gestures to the white-board behind the desk listing tomorrow's classes.

Chewing my lip, I read. They all sound intense. Cardio and Core, HIIT, CrossFit. I'm not even 100 percent certain what some of the words mean. I scan them several times, my eyes glazing while I ask myself how he caught me in my bluff.

"Anything look good?"

I startle a little at hearing his voice closer, just over my shoulder. "So much," I say. Facing him, I find he's stood up and stepped toward me. "Boxing looks fun," I lie. Actually, it looks painful, but I don't say that.

He gazes past me, leaning forward ever so slightly. "It says for non-beginners," he observes.

"Perfect." I square my shoulders. "Because I'm not a beginner. I guess you are, though, which means I won't be seeing you there." This works out great, I realize. I don't have to go boxing. I can bail on this plan without him knowing.

"Wrong again." He grins. "See you at nine a.m., Eliza."

Shock snaps into me, and I sort of love it. Whatever the holes and inconsistencies in my knowledge of my husband, of one reality I feel pretty certain. He's no intermediate-to-advanced *boxer*.

I don't know how or why he's pretending to be one, but I know what the fib I've backed myself into means. If he's pretending he knows his way around a punching bag—at nine a.m. tomorrow—then so am I, for one very good reason. The chance to see him.

Lifting my chin, I smile determinedly.

"See you then," I say.

I walk out, frantically typing "differences between beginner and intermediate boxing" into Google.

20

Graham

I CAN HARDLY move.

While this wasn't my first time *ever* going to the gym, I'll admit it's been a while. Furthermore, though, when I used to do this, it did not leave me feeling like my arms were rubber bands made of pain. Maybe I went for more ambitious weights today, I reason with myself. Or maybe I'm just nearly thirty years old.

Either way, every physical activity is now transmuted into torture. This includes lifting forkfuls of chicken piccata from my room-service tray.

Present consequences notwithstanding, I enjoyed the workout. I *really* enjoyed Eliza's surprise visit, but even the pleasantest surprises can have consequences. Before I knew it, I'd somehow roped myself into boxing tomorrow morning. Or, likelier, making a fool of myself while *trying* to box.

I've spent the hour since I left the gym searching boxing class videos on YouTube, studying the basics. Swallowing my last bite of chicken, I recognize I now have no excuse to keep my coursework to the couch. I stand up. My shoulders screaming, I try to imitate the motions the instructor makes look so easy. Quickly, however, I realize even the simplest combinations of coordination—walking while punching, for instance—surpass my capabilities.

As desperate as I am to quit, to drop onto the bed with one of the hotel movies playing, I don't. While I have no real interest in boxing, I don't want to embarrass myself, not with Eliza watching. Not when our connection is this, dare I say . . . good. Deliberately *not* facing the mirror in my room, I patiently copy the instructor's stance, once, then twice, then twenty times. I have no idea if the practice is working. Despite the excruciating minutes, the motions definitely don't feel more natural.

I keep going dismally until my phone buzzes. Wishing powerfully for it to be Eliza coming up with some excuse for why she has to cancel tomorrow's class and forfeit this unspoken challenge, I fumble for my phone.

It's not Eliza. David's name displays on my screen.

> Just got back from my seminar. What
> are you up to?

Disheartened, I fire off a reply.

> Know anything about boxing?

> I take a class every week. Why?

I pause, phone in hand. To put it mildly, this was *not* the response I was expecting. The stroke of fortune is honestly impossibly lucky, but I'm not going to protest.

Instead, I weigh my options. I could confine myself to YouTube and, more important, to the privacy my god-awful boxing form no doubt requires. Or . . .

I remind myself how handily Eliza's risen to every complication of this game of ours. She's going to manage this one somehow, while I'm going to look ridiculously incompetent. The furthest thing from the Graham whose presence she's now enjoying.

Packing up my self-respect, I shut my computer screen. Not leaving myself time to hesitate, I step out the door and head down the path to David's room.

When I reach his suite, the lights are on. I can hear the TV through the door. It's chilly out, and dusk colors the sky gold past the trees. Huddled on the porch where the woodchip path meets the concrete of his entryway, I knock gently.

David answers a moment later, then laughs at what he sees. I'm standing on his bungalow's small patio in my gym clothes, which I didn't change out of when I returned to my room, wrapped up in my focus on the boxing dilemma. Furthermore, I know I must look miserable.

I cut to the chase. "Eliza challenged me to a boxing class tomorrow, and I was so busy pretending to be someone else that I forgot I'm going to be a disaster and she'll see me fall over myself and never want to go out with me again."

David, still grinning, doesn't seem disturbed by the panic in my run-on sentence. He opens his door wider. "Come on in."

Morosely, I trudge into the chaos of his room. It's worsened since my previous visit, I notice. The piled clothes and detritus look like the product of nothing short of a Category 4 hurricane.

David faces me from the entryway. "Do you know any of the basics?" he asks.

"I've been watching videos, but I can't replicate it very well," I reply, catching the note of urgency in my own voice. Why did boxing need to be tomorrow *morning*? With twenty-four hours, maybe I could've prepared. Instead, I've got twelve, of which I'll spend seven sleeping. Nine, if the exhaustion of my workout wins out.

David gestures to the small space of floor not occupied by furniture or laundry. "Show me your boxing stance."

I drop into the posture I've cobbled together from two hours of YouTube. Embarrassment rolls over me in waves. Most days I feel tall—now I just feel gangly. I'm a collection of elbows, half-hunched in the middle of this hotel room.

David's gaze sharpens. It's sort of interesting to see, how suddenly he's not just happy-go-lucky but concentrated, even studious. "Weight evenly distributed," he counsels, nodding his head in one direction. Following, I lean to center myself. "That's better," David says. "Okay, take a step forward."

I do. One awkward, searching step.

David moves quickly to my side, correcting me. I jettison my pride right into the small wooden wastebasket next to the minibar. "Just keep walking," he goes on. "Four steps forward, four steps back. We'll worry about hands later."

Following his instructions, I continue to pace the floor in this plodding, silent dance. Eventually I graduate on to side-to-side, which leaves me questioning how I even had the coordination to learn to walk in the first place, but David remains encouraging.

"You're going to be fine," he tells me, words I get the distinct impression he's repeated to legions of five-year-olds with skinned knees. "A couple hours of practice with me and you'll be looking like a person with beginning-to-moderate boxing experience."

"That's the dream," I reply. Daring to introduce talking into my side-stepping routine, I go on. "I've taken this too far, and if you can get me through it, I'll seriously owe you."

The truth is, I don't want to look goofy in front of Eliza because nobody likes to fall flat in front of their wife, obviously—but for me, the fear that brought me to David's doorstep is something more. I admitted it to myself on the walk over, under the silent trees. I wouldn't worry about losing luster in Eliza's eyes so much if I didn't think I'd only just gotten it back. With every one of my ungainly punches, I feel like I'm fighting for my relationship, literally.

David hands me one of the complimentary water bottles on the tray near the ice bucket. "It must be kind of freeing, though," he speculates encouragingly, "pretending to be someone else, with the only stakes being a boxing class."

Cracking open the cap on the water bottle, I really consider. "Maybe," I concede. "It's definitely getting me to try things I wouldn't otherwise. Letting us have fun together. I don't constantly *feel* my marriage hanging in the balance. Even if it still is." It's not easy to say, and I probably would have kept silent if I weren't exhausted from the gym and hours of YouTube tutorials. With my inhibitions down, I've voiced out loud thoughts I usually don't even let cross my mind.

David grins, leaning against the closet. "Oh, it's not."

I glance up. "What?"

"It's not hanging in the balance," he clarifies with confidence. "Eliza is into you."

I laugh, too sheepish to betray how much this outsider's conclusion pleases me. Not being completely clueless, I got the impression Eliza was drawn into the weight room this evening by *something* other than spontaneity, but while I know I'm in decent shape—not to mention six foot two—the feeling she's out of my league and knows it hovers over me like a dark cloud. David's conviction is nice to hear, even if I can't quite believe it.

"I hope so," I say earnestly. "How're things going with Lindsey?"

"Put your hands up, do some jabs," he instructs.

I resume my stance, then start swinging as David offers helpful corrections, raising my fists, pushing my elbows in. I stay silent, knowing he can't resist a direct invitation to talk about Lindsey. Sure enough, when I'm punching more fluidly, he elaborates.

"I think the beach hike was huge progress. I haven't gotten her number yet or anything, but I learned she works in conservation, with a focus on marine life. She likes this hotel because the developers didn't cut down any trees when they built the place. I'm trying to learn about nature and environmentalism to impress her before I get back into the ring." He grins at the cheesy boxing idiom, and I roll my eyes. "You know, I don't think dating is all that different from the role-playing you two are doing," he goes on. "We're all trying to impress each other, trying to play smarter, cooler versions of ourselves."

I drop my hands, struck by David's words. They're . . . enormously reassuring. I've felt like this game of pretend we're playing is evidence Eliza and I are broken. What if it's not? I mean, obviously it's out of the ordinary, unconventional to say the least. But what if, fundamentally, it's nothing but one week's much-needed refresher course on dating? Even once you've passed the bar, you're required to earn credits of continuing legal education every few years. How is this much different?

It's suddenly invigorating, this conclusion. Continuing romantic education.

Full of renewed energy, I put my hands back up. This time, I attempt to throw a hook. Instead of recharging my newfound confidence further, I instantly feel how awkward my movement is.

David frowns, not improving matters. "Okay, maybe this will take more work than I thought." He claps his hands together. "But all in the service of love, right?"

I square up.

"Love," I say. "Right."

21

Eliza

I WALK INTO the boxing class, fighting the nervous twist in my stomach. *It'll be fine,* I reassure myself. Okay, I don't know if it'll be fine. But I'll probably be better at this than Graham. In college, I took some dance and stage combat classes and did pretty well. I've always been coordinated, even if I haven't been putting miles onto the treadmill lately. It'll be . . . well, in the vicinity of fine.

The class is being held in the open multiuse room off the main gym, with rubbery black floors and mirrors on two walls. Punching bags have been strung up on chains from the ceiling, ready for their beatings. I hold my head high, hoping to look like this is just one of the boxing gyms I've had the pleasure of frequenting in my pugilistic life. It's almost funny how I'm doing more acting on this "vacation" than I do in some workweeks.

I take a spot at the back of the class. No way am I letting Graham stand behind me, able to watch me fail while I can't see him.

Everyone else here, I'm *delighted* to find, looks completely comfortable. In large part, they are the classmates I expected. Guys in black sleeveless hoodies, wiry women who look exported straight off the magical island in *Wonder Woman*. It is possible each one of them is a nervous imposter like me, playing their roles with fragile confidence, but I doubt it.

I mimic their stances. When the instructor comes by, offering to wrap anyone's hands, I quickly and gratefully accept, glad I won't have to contrive some explanation to Graham for why Vacation Planner Eliza, the intermediate boxer, does not know how to do this herself.

When Graham walks in, I'm not surprised to find David with him. What does surprise me is the pair of very legitimate-looking boxing gloves David's holding.

My stomach sinks. Of course David, frat-boy kindergarten teacher and gentle giant, is a fucking boxing aficionado. Which means, if I know Graham, they've been up until two in the morning practicing.

They both have their wrists wrapped.

I grit my teeth, feeling grateful for my spot in the back of the room. When Graham sees me, he flashes me a smile. I send one right back.

David's eyes flit between us. Then, clapping Graham on the shoulder, he moves to the front of the room. Either he doesn't want to cockblock his friend or he's picked up on some simmering energy between Graham and me with which he does not want to engage. I honestly don't know which.

Graham struts over to me, gym bag on his shoulder. It's new, the white strap still spotless. I have to hand it to him, I'm momentarily impressed by the prop. With unexpected and complete conviction, I know if I questioned him on its newness, Investment Banker Graham would produce details of how he'd just worn out the old one he'd had since his college basketball days or whatever.

"Hello," Graham says, two playful roller-coaster syllables. "Glad you decided to come."

"I wouldn't miss it."

He drops his bag and bends down to take out— *Oh my god, he* bought *boxing gloves?* Where did he even get those? I guess this gym might sell them. Or maybe he got the car from the valet first thing this morning and drove to the nearest sporting goods store. He grins, looking relaxed, while I immediately start searching for some way I can match him.

The nervous pickup of my heartbeat isn't unpleasant, though. I'd be lying if I said this petty war wasn't fun. The game of pretend we're playing this week isn't a competition—it's a dance—but this boxing class has lit the first fire of friendly rivalry.

Right now, Graham's got me off guard. In my head, I note his little victory. *Nicely done, husband.* In my heart, though, I'm pushing myself to figure out my next move.

Until I notice a hitch in his movements.

I smile indulgently. "You okay? You seem a little sore. Maybe you pushed it too hard yesterday."

Graham loses some of his relaxed charisma, and I know I'm right. It's perfect—at least we're on even footing. While I lack preparation granted by a kindly, bro-y hotel friend, I have an advantage in my muscles not aching. When Graham zips up his bag in one swift pull, like he's out to prove his mobility, he winces in a wonderful backfire. I smirk.

The instructor walks to the front of the room. "Good morning, everyone," he calls out. "Let's get to it. Warm up with some laps."

The group falls into pairs, starting to jog the perimeter of the room. I hold my arm out, an *after you*. Graham looks less than pleased. When he picks up his pace into a jog, he grimaces.

I fall into step behind him, feeling smug for about two minutes, which is when my extreme lack of cardio catches up to me. My heart pounds in my chest, my windpipe stinging. It's not long before we're firmly in the back of the group. David laps us twice. Pretty soon, I'm wishing for whatever will end this torture.

"Burpees!" the instructor calls out. I promptly realize how unwise my wish was.

Dropping into my first plank, I pretty much dissociate. I fully leave my body for the entire set of burpees, until the instructor finally tells us to stop.

"Take one minute to rest," he says. "Then pair up on a punching bag. You're going to alternate thirty seconds of jab, cross with your partner."

Graham is wheezing. I couldn't hide my own exhaustion if I tried. In fact, I do try. There's no escaping my ragged breathing or the sweat on my brow. My husband picks himself up off the floor, then trudges over to the nearest punching bag, looking like someone spent the past fifteen minutes kicking him in the thighs. I'd laugh if I didn't feel exactly the same.

Putting his hands on the bag, he turns to me and raises an eyebrow.

Exhausted, panting like I just ran a marathon, I nonetheless find the will to peel myself off the floor. I walk over to join him. Graham's regained some measure of control over his breathing, which is irritating. He gives me an enthusiastic smile.

"Last chance to ditch and get coffee with me instead," he offers, effortfully keeping himself from breathing hard. "Pastries could be involved."

While the idea of coffee cake is nearly enough for me to unwrap my hands, the fun of not giving in wins out. "Are you asking me on a date *now*?" I reply with dry incredulity.

Graham shrugs. "Maybe."

I pout skeptically. "Not very convincing. *I* think you're just trying to get out of this boxing class you chose to come to."

"I'm perfectly happy in this boxing class," Graham replies. He pushes the bag to me, which I catch when the heavy cylinder swings over.

"I want to see what you've got," I say. "*Then* you can ask me on a date."

"Go ahead and start," the instructor calls out.

Graham does. I feel my expression morph into one of unhidden surprise when he shifts readily into the boxer's stance he's mysteriously learned since yesterday. Or maybe not yesterday. I don't know, maybe Ruddington & Roeper has an underground fight club beneath its law offices.

The bag shakes with the rhythmic thumps of Graham throwing jabs and crosses. His skill is, I have to concede, impressive. It's funny, over the past few days, I've seen Graham in new lights, heard him pretend to be a different person. This is the first time I almost don't recognize the man in front of me.

The instructor walks by, nodding in approval. When Graham just keeps punching, leaning into the fast, measured movements, the questions slips out of me. *"How?"*

Thump. Graham's fist strikes the bag. "I told you," he replies without stopping. "I take lessons." *Thump.*

My face heats. But not with embarrassment. Graham's upper body rotates, his hand flying forward. *Thump.* His competency is incredibly attractive. I'm so distracted by the sheer spectacle in front of me that I forget I'll have to take a turn—that is, until the instructor starts a countdown to switch.

I wait until Graham's done, feeling panic setting in. Starting the class in the back didn't help—if I'm not boxing competently in the next thirty seconds, I *will* be embarrassed. Why can't there just be an audience for boxing classes? Why do I have to participate in order to stare at Graham? I start watching everyone else, memorizing their movements, fighting to bolster my confidence. Graham might've taken the rehearsal route, which I didn't expect. I'm just going to have to play this like improv instead.

"Switch!" the instructor shouts.

Showtime.

I unwrap my hands and pull on the gloves I borrowed from the gym. They're stiff, heavy, and I can feel the foam flaking inside. I pretend they're familiar sensations, remembering professors who instructed me that convincing *myself* I was the character I was portraying was half the fight. Eliza, vacation planner, Bostonian, boxer.

With this mantra running in my head, I lash out for my first punch. *Thump.*

I only barely manage not to wince in surprise. Not pain—part of my surprise is how well the shiny black glove cushions my knuckles when they strike the bag, which is startlingly solid. The chains rattle. I notice Graham past the wobbling gray bag, wiping his forehead with his shirt, exposing his stomach. He's projecting inconspicuousness, but I feel his eyes on me.

I throw out my next punch, quickly realizing Vacation Planner Eliza's flagging confidence will be a constant battle. Something's wrong with the way I'm holding my elbows, I just know it. From the barely perceptible narrowing of his gaze, I get the feeling Graham does, too.

Maybe I'm not going to be as good at this as he is. But that doesn't mean my turn at the bag has to be a complete waste. "From the way you're staring," I say, "you're either *ridiculously* into me, or I'm doing something wrong."

Graham says nothing. Which is fine. Perfect, even.

"Isn't this the part where you use 'helping me with my form' as an excuse to stand close behind me?" I ask.

He doesn't hesitate. "Absolutely it is."

While Graham walks over, I square up my stance, anticipating—I've seen every movie where this happens. Nothing prepares me for the warm chill I feel when Graham lines his body up with mine. His hands slide up my forearms, positioning and caressing at once. His chin is close to the shell of my ear.

"There," he murmurs, his breath warm on my neck.

Yes, I want to say. *Right there.*

"Mhm," I manage instead.

"Okay. You're looking perfect," he says.

Graham crafts eloquent casework every day—he knows words well enough to intend the double meaning in what he's saying. The one that refers not to the position of my hips but to how they look in my leggings. I can't handle the new heat spreading through me. My head is short-circuiting, my body a live wire, leaving me ready to send every flicker of the electricity filling me squarely into my next swing.

Graham steps back, nodding in satisfaction before returning to the other side of the bag. "Great. Now, when you punch, just picture your ex-boyfriend's face."

I smile. Then I unleash.

Wham.

Graham, on the other side of the bag, widens his eyes, impressed. "What did the poor man do to you?"

The instructor calls for us to switch. "Now jab, cross, then hook," he continues. I drop my gloved fists to my thighs, my arms searing in pain. Squaring up to the bag, Graham starts in. *Wham.* I frown. *He's practiced hooks, too? How long did they do this last night?* Maybe David should be leading this class.

"It's more what he didn't do," I answer Graham's question. "I don't think he saw me. Or . . . I don't think he saw the changes in me."

Graham misses a punch. His eyes find mine.

I hold his gaze. I didn't expect to be this truthful today. Granted, I was pretty preoccupied with being this class's clumsiest intermediate boxer. But Graham's question was the first time he's ever asked me what was wrong in our relationship. I wasn't going to waste it.

I keep going, finding bravery in the remove of this charade to speak the fear I try to hide from even myself. "I sometimes wondered if we got together too young," I say, my voice not my own. It's not the sort of thing I would usually let myself acknowledge. But I'm remembering our conversation at the beach. We have to be real about the hard stuff.

Graham grabs the punching bag, stilling it. The whole room feels still. Sweat drips down my chin while I wait.

"No." He looks me in the eye. "No, I don't believe that."

He resumes punching, his punches now looking a little more like mine. Better, honestly. But rougher. Harder. Like he's not just punching, but punching something.

His unequivocal answer, succinct as it was, fills my heart. Now I feel like I could run dozens more laps around the gym. "What about you?" I ask. "You look like you're working something out yourself. Let me guess." I purse my lips in pretend speculation, kneading one glove into my leg. "Big *deal* closing?"

Graham throws one more hook before the instructor calls for us to switch again. My smugness disappears when I realize, *Shit, I have to figure out hooks in the next five seconds*. I gamely, semi-successfully copy Graham's form, grateful I haven't popped my shoulder out of its socket. Yet, when I glance to Graham, expecting to find him looking delightedly dubious, I notice he instead seems lost in thought.

"Yes, exactly," he says softly. I switch to my cross with a little more confidence, waiting for him to continue, which he does. "Just like last month's. Just like next month's will be."

I don't know what to say to the fragile note in his voice. It's left me wondering if this is Graham following what he told me on the beach. Being real, even while he's speaking in the voice of his character.

Reflecting on his response, I swing my next punch. *Whack*. I don't know where this reservation is coming from. Graham enjoys his work. He's genuinely interested in what he does. I remember how he would light up describing to me his Moot Court competitions in law school, or the first cases he was put on when he joined his firm.

I find my path up to the line in the sand we've drawn separating our new selves from our real ones. "You seem like someone who would enjoy his job." I punctuate the suggestion with my next swing, which feels more natural.

Graham nods slowly. "I do," he replies with earnestness I know is coming from the real him. "I love my job. It's just—well, it's the same thing, every day, every month. Which I don't mind. Never too much of a good thing," he continues. "I just wonder if doing the same thing for my entire professional career will . . . do something to me. Monotonize me. If I'll wake up one day unable to recognize the world past the work routines I've put so much care into. Won't recognize I've happily painted my entire self in the same shade of gray."

His speech startles me. I never knew he even had this worry. I struggle to quiet the part of my mind looking for fault—mine for not asking? His for not saying something? It doesn't matter. The last couple days have dislodged the truth.

"Well, I think—I *know* that if you're fulfilled in what you're doing, everyone in your life will feel it," I say. "It will make them happy, too."

Instead of waiting for him to reply, I hammer out my next punch. While the chains ring, I notice Graham's expression has softened slightly.

"It's easy to talk to you," he says, and I'm caught off guard by the undercurrent of gratitude running within his casual words. "I like that. I haven't felt that in . . ." He pauses. "A while."

I place one glove on the bag, steadying its swing while I face him. Now I hear not only honesty in his voice. There's admission, too. It's achingly gratifying to hear, because it means he understands. He knows *this*, this levity, this comfort, this fun, is how things should be. I hold my husband's hesitant gaze, steady, unsure, hopeful.

"Jumping jacks!" the instructor shouts out.

I roll my eyes grandly. Graham closes his in suffering silence. We separate and remove our gloves, officially unable to keep talking during this portion of the workout. Flinging my hands up into the exercise, I'm sad the moment was interrupted, but much, much gladder it happened.

The room echoes with the soles of shoes tapping and thumping on the rubber floor for what feels like eternity. I lose count of my jumping jacks. I hear myself wheezing, hear Graham doing so next to me. When the instructor calls for us to return to the bags, my eyes lock with Graham's as he holds ours in place for me.

We fall into a rhythm, punching, alternating, sometimes speaking, sometimes not. Finally, after what feels like forever, the workout ends. Graham and I aren't the only ones who collapse on the floor, too tired even to rub the fire from our arms. My chest heaving with Graham laid out flat next to me, it drops onto me how incongruous this moment is, how unexpected—how freeing.

I can't help laughing. The truths we shared weren't necessarily happy ones, but I feel lighter regardless. I'm glad they're out in the open. Over genuinely respectable intermediate boxing, Graham and I managed to flirt *and* be honest with each other, have fun *and* admit complicated truths. It's proof I didn't know I was looking for—not only that it's possible, but how good it feels.

Beside me, Graham catches my eyes. He isn't laughing, but when he smiles, somehow I know it's him. The real him. I smile back, a stolen, shared moment. Like performers meeting backstage in the theater of our own lives.

"Oh, it wasn't that bad, was it?" I hear David's voice and look up to find him standing over us, impossibly chipper. "Who's up for brunch?"

22

Graham

BRUNCH IS MUCH needed following the intensity of the work-out. We head for the buffet, where I go for one of everything. I have a hard time fitting onto my plate the quantity of sweets and savories my boxing-worn body is demanding.

Eliza seems to be doing the same. What this results in, I'm de-lighted to find, is us repeatedly bumping into each other. First when I'm going for the French toast tongs while she's craning to examine the potatoes past me and our shoulders connect. Once more when I step back from the omelet bar and there she is, waiting for hers. Finally, over the parfaits, when our hands cross reaching for the yogurt cups. Each innocuous collision is its own exhilarating jolt.

There's only one strawberry left in the whole tray of parfaits. I go for the yogurt *next* to it, leaving the berry for my wife. They're her favorite.

She notices. The misty gray color of her eyes warms, like the sun behind clouds. When she shoots me a smile, I forget for a second we're playing a part. It feels like we're just here celebrating our anniversary as we planned.

But I'm grateful for the role-playing. Boxing was surprising. When Eliza pitched the whole idea of stranger-selves, I was willing to try it, but I wasn't sure it would work. But there's no denying we're getting closer. Some of what she said hurt, not like insults, just painful confessions. Knife wounds I don't want to forget. I hadn't known she didn't feel seen—it's sometimes how I felt at home, too. Like we kept expecting each other to be who we'd always been, and whenever something didn't fit those preconceptions, it created distance.

Here, I'm seeing her. I have to, with how attuned I've become to her, parsing what's real and what's pretend. She's seeing me, too. Her reassurance about my professional insecurity, veiled though it was, felt good.

Now we just have to figure out how to bring this back home with us.

We settle into our seats with our plates heaping. Today we're inside, swapping the sunlight for the restaurant's modern wood interior. Eliza and I, ravenous, don't speak for stuffing our faces. David doesn't seem to mind, happily keeping up a steady stream of local marine-life facts.

"Did you know"—he holds up his pancake-laden fork with professorial emphasis—"the Sur Ridge is an underwater mountain range, home to over two hundred and sixty different species of animals?"

Eliza and I shake our heads. I hold in laughter. His question presupposes there was a chance we *did* know the Sur Ridge is an underwater mountain range, home to over two hundred and sixty different species of animals. *No, David, I'm sorry to say they passed this subject over in first-year Civil Procedure.*

"Well," he goes on with mounting enthusiasm. "They have comb jellies and bubblegum coral and *vampire squids*. How great are those names?" Leaning back in his chair, he shakes his head in rapture. "I have to do a marine-life unit with the kids. Maybe we can take a trip to an aquarium."

"Are you sure those animals are real?" I ask, unable to restrain myself. "You're not mixing up picture books with two a.m. Wikipedia research?"

David holds up his phone, displaying photos of what is, indeed, captioned a vampire squid. While I inspect the small, orange, umbrella-shaped creature with growing curiosity, David squares his shoulders proudly. "I'm sure Lindsey knows all of this already, of course, but I'm *ready* to impress," he says.

Eliza speaks up, spooning, I note with satisfaction, the strawberry off the top of her parfait. "I met Lindsey," she says, completely casual. "She seems cool."

"Yes, she's my soul mate," David replies. Eliza swallows her strawberry. "I told her I was into nature conservation and learning about the local ecosystems," he continues cheerfully.

"You're sure this isn't going to backfire on you?" I prod gently. "I mean, how much could you learn in one night?"

David frowns, looking deeply disappointed in me. But he's cut off from defending his honor by none other than Lindsey herself, heading from the patio inside toward the exit. I elbow David's forearm resting on the edge of the table. "Dude," I say, nodding my gaze in the brunette's direction. "Now's your shot. Show her the vampire squid."

"You jest, my friend, but I absolutely will," David replies. He's entranced. "Eliza," he says urgently, eyes never leaving Lindsey. "Can you wave her over?"

Eliza smiles. "Why don't *you* just talk to her? You're clearly great at making vacation friends," she points out.

"Eliza," David repeats, shifting in his seat. Lindsey's nearly reached the exit. David manages to yank his eyes from her diminishing shape. "Please," he implores. "True love is in your hands!"

Eliza laughs—but when Lindsey is reaching for the door, with David sweating rivers next to me, my wife stands up. "Hey, Lindsey!" she calls out, nonchalant and spontaneous, like the greeting wasn't just demanded by our friend who decided he couldn't handle saying hello to his crush this morning.

When Lindsey finds the source of the hello, her eyes light with recognition. She heads in our direction, sidling past tables with brisk efficiency. "I'm going to do it," David murmurs to himself. "I'm going to ask her out. Now is the moment legends are made."

I clap my hand on his shoulder, earnestly encouraging. "You got this, man."

Lindsey reaches us. "Hey, how's it going?" Her voice is sharply upbeat, like someone flipping the lights on while you're sleeping.

"Pretty good," Eliza says. "How about you?"

"We should go on a double date," David says suddenly.

Understandably, this silences everyone. Lindsey looks to Eliza, then to David, then to me, like she's struggling to figure out the pairings. David's gone linen-white, clenching his phone, unmoving, like he's handcuffed to the table.

I decide to step in. David's been the perfect wingman to me this whole trip. "That sounds like fun," I say. Then I meet the eyes of my wife, who still looks startled from David's outburst. "If Eliza will go out with me, that is."

What crosses Eliza's expression is like sunlight warming ocean water. "I suppose so," she says, her gorgeous gray eyes smiling.

Past the utter happiness this instills in me, I notice it's worked the desired effect. With the organization of this double-date clear, Lindsey has started unsubtly checking David out. Like he's realized the same, David straightens his posture. When he sets his phone on the table, Lindsey's gaze catches the screen. "Cool squid photo," she says.

"V—vampire squid," David elaborates.

I fight not to laugh. It's nice to know every guy is capable of being reduced to a bumbling mess in front of his crush.

"Sure," Lindsey replies, taking the vampire squid comment in stride. "A double date could be fun. Could be terrible, but hey, we're on vacation and we'll never see each other again, so why the hell not?" I can't help catching Eliza's eye when this remark lands. Lindsey glances to my wife. "Eliza, you'll text me?"

"For sure," Eliza promises.

When Lindsey leaves, quiet falls over us. I watch David, the recognition of triumph dawning over him, until his eyes rove slowly to Eliza.

"You've had her number," he says, "this *whole time*?"

My wife just shrugs. "Better brush up on your squid facts," she replies. "It's game time."

23

Eliza

I **REALLY WISH** we'd figured out some system for trading the honeymoon suite, because right now, my sore body desperately needs Graham's private Jacuzzi.

No interpretation of our characters' places in each other's lives convinces me Vacation Planner Eliza could invite herself over to the hot tub she doesn't even know her sparring partner has, however. Not without becoming *incredibly* forward, which wouldn't be consistent with the will-we-or-won't-we flirtation I've been very much enjoying. *Sigh.* For the rest of the day before our double date, which I coordinate with Lindsey for this evening, I settle for the next best thing, which is relaxing in the hotel Jacuzzi.

It's perfect—the midday sun on my face, the steam rising faintly from the water, the wind lifting the herbal scent of dry plants down from the mountains. Perfect except for no Graham, of course, but I'm guessing he's giving us space on purpose, not wanting to look desperate. Letting us miss each other.

Unwinding in the hot water of the Jacuzzi on the wide flagstone pool deck, I let calm come over me. I'm happy. Hopeful. The space we're giving each other is working. Our conversations feel freer, less scripted, less freighted with expectation or disappointment. We've started uncovering surprising truths within this shared fiction. What I've felt the past few days, I recognize, isn't that I'm meeting some new Graham, despite this being the premise of our game. Never in recent months have I forgotten his quick wit, his poise, his charm. No, what I've felt nestled in the Treeline's splendor, wrapped in our layers of pretend, is like I'm *rediscovering* Graham.

In the years before I met him, I dated plenty of people. I spent those relationships bombarding myself with the same questions— *Was this working? Was he into me? Was I into* him? *What would our future look like? Did we want the same things?* With every musician, aspiring novelist, and psychology major who ironically needed therapy himself, those questions would surface, and I would cut and run.

When I met Graham, the first things I appreciated were his humor, his kind and patient conversational demeanor, his height, and his boyish charm. What made me fall in love with him was none of those things. I just realized one day, with Graham, I didn't have any of those questions.

It's what's been so hard about the recent months. It hasn't made me worry I've married the wrong person. It's made me worry I've messed everything up with the *right* person. Which is so, so much worse. I can't cut and run with him—there would be nowhere to run to.

When the sun starts to set, I get out of the Jacuzzi and go back to my room. I shower, return my wedding rings to my neck on their necklace chain, and take the elevator down to the restaurant. I'm dressed casually, in black jeans paired with white sneakers, the comfortable Converse I impulse-bought myself two birthdays ago. Checking my phone in the hallway, I notice I'm seven minutes early, having slightly overestimated the walk from the elevator bank to the restaurant entrance.

I'm excited for my double date with Graham. It feels like the perfect way for Vacation Planner Eliza and Investment Banker Graham to take the next step. It's not the first time we've double-dated—when we were still getting to know each other, Graham introduced me to Nikki, and we went out with her and Nikki's boyfriend at the time. Graham and I hit it off so well it was embarrassing, and Nikki broke up with her boyfriend a week later because she could feel how stark the contrast was.

I remember those early feelings of trying on the idea of an "us." Of seeing how Graham was around his friends and not just me. He was more relaxed, more himself. Graham is wonderful at working a room—almost better than he is one-on-one, where insecurities more easily surface. Nowadays, the only chance I get to see that Graham is at his firm's holiday party.

The only chance, that is, except for tonight.

Reaching the patio entrance, under the stunning blue-pink gradient of twilight, I decide I'll wait outside, not wanting to be the first one in. I'm certain I have emails to delete or reply to.

Except, when I walk up to the restaurant, Graham is already there. Waiting for me, I know from the soft smile on his face and the way his eyes watch the archway from which I just emerged.

He walks over to me. I walk over to him. We meet in the middle.

"Permission to break character for a moment?" he asks.

His question surprises me. So does the magnitude of the almost-teenage excitement I feel meeting him out here, like I just got out of sixth period to find him leaning on the hood of his car in the parking lot. "Permission granted," I reply, heart fluttering.

"Okay," Graham says seriously. "David has been talking about this for, like, the entire day. He can't wait. Obviously, this is huge for him."

I smile, remembering brunch. "Yeah, I gathered."

Graham nods. "Well—" He pauses delicately. I wait, becoming curious, until he continues. "You know how double dates can get . . . awkward, in certain circumstances."

From the indication in his gaze, I know he's remembering the same thing I was. Sushi in Westwood, Nikki's favorite place, where Graham had me in tears of laughter while Nikki's boyfriend did nothing except inquire whether she thought this was better than Nobu. Nikki texted me the next day, complete with shrugging-girl emoji, saying she'd dumped Garrett because our Sugarfish double date put into perspective just how un-fun he was.

"You're worried we have an unfair advantage," I say, realizing Graham's point. We had only just gotten together when the Garrett episode happened. We have years of marriage to our name now. "You don't want to ruin this for David by being so great together that Lindsey will feel like they have no spark in comparison."

"Well, we are hugely compatible," Graham notes.

"Hugely."

"I just don't want to outshine them *too* badly, you know?"

I tilt my head in resignation. "Guess we'll have to turn down the chemistry then."

"Unfortunately," Graham replies, matching my pretend dismay.

"You simply must be less charming then," I instruct him.

He smiles. "I'm sorry to say you are also a potential liability."

"It'll be tough, but I'll try to be duller." Graham laughs, and I feel my heart swell. I gesture to the door. When I speak, it's in Vacation Planner Eliza's voice. "Shall we?"

We head in together. The clamor of the restaurant is inviting, energetic, lively with the sounds of silverware and conversation. This is the hotel's casual eatery, full of families and people in from the pool, dining under the bright lighting and upbeat music.

It turns out we're somehow not the first ones here. Immediately, I spot David and Lindsey already seated at a table in the center of the room, chatting.

"Graham, Eliza, hey!" David scoots to fit Graham next to his massive frame. I slide in next to Lindsey. "We were discussing the seminar we just got out of."

I pick up the menu, scanning it briefly before deciding I'll get the burger. "Oh yeah? Tell me the key to long-lasting love."

Graham's gaze cuts to me. I feel a pang of guilt, not having meant to cast the question onto our own marriage. Except . . . figuring out long-lasting love sort of *is* what we've been trying to do here.

Lindsey grins. "I'm not sure we've gotten that far yet," she replies. She, I notice, is not wearing jeans. Her dress is low-cut and frankly enviable. "Tonight, though," she continues, "we were told to decide what we consider the most important characteristics in a partner. Too often, people try to make it work with someone who can't or won't fulfill their fundamental needs."

Graham stretches in his seat, grinning with good humor. "Okay, David," he says. "Let's hear it. I'm sure you *loved* this."

David straightens, his face lighting up. "Okay, well, she has to like kids, obviously. I'm a kindergarten teacher," he adds to Lindsey. "Other than that, I really want her to be passionate about something . . . like, nature. For example," he qualifies with nonchalance performed heavily enough it reminds me of my freshman-year acting courses. "Someone who loves to travel, who likes hotel-led beach walks, hikes on the trails surrounding the Treeline Resort. You know, brown hair, brown eyes."

Lindsey looks to him, visibly fighting down flattery. "You didn't actually write that."

"I did," David insists. "I can get my notebook." Lindsey laughs, charmed, pink painting her cheeks. David goes on, his eyes sparkling from the unique victory of making one's crush laugh. "But the real question is, what did you put on *your* list?"

"Oh, the only thing I need is someone who shares my interests," Lindsey replies lightly.

David grins. "I showed you the vampire squid photo already, didn't I?"

"It was quite impressive," Lindsey says. "I made a mental note."

David leans forward. "Just wait until I roll out my Sur Ridge facts."

Lindsey giggles. "On a first date? *David!*" she says, faux-scandalized.

I look to Graham. When our gazes lock, I know he's realized what I have. We didn't need to worry. David and Lindsey are absolutely hitting it off.

The waiter comes over then, ready to take our orders. We go around the table, giving our choices. Realizing I'm famished, I go for the extra fries option with my burger. David manages to talk Graham into splitting their meals. It's cute, I concede. I've never seen Graham have such a good guy friend. His closest friend in college was Nikki, and since then his male friendships haven't progressed past the level of work buddies. The warmth in my chest lingers. I like seeing this side of him.

When the waiter leaves, David and Lindsey fall into easy conversation. I sip my water while they enthusiastically discuss how they'd love to get out hiking in the nearby state park. With nothing to contribute on this point, I shoot Graham a smile.

He returns it.

I open my mouth, ready to start a conversation, when laughter from Lindsey cuts me off. Startled into silence, I reach once more for my water.

Graham repositions himself in his seat like he's entering conversation mode. I straighten up, matching him. "Did—" he gets out, until, without warning, David jostles his elbow exuberantly, wanting the understandably confused Graham to chime in on something.

"*Right*, Graham?" he asks.

"Uh—right." Graham looks back to me, but I can see in his eyes he's lost whatever he was going to say. Leaving us still without speaking to each other since we sat down.

Beside me, Lindsey and David are sharing the details of where they grew up, finding out that they're both from the Midwest. This flows quickly into their families, their first jobs, their pets. Topics lead one into the other, each a mutual discovery, like uncharted islands.

I try to focus on Graham—it's just that David and Lindsey are throwing me off. Slowly, I realize I . . . don't know how to pretend to get to know Graham while the real thing is happening right next to us. From the pinned-on pressure in Graham's expression, I can sense he's starting to feel the same.

While I'm working the conundrum over, he speaks up. "How was your afternoon?"

"Great. I went to the Jacuzzi," I say with overeager cheer. Just having something to say is like the relief of sliding into the heated water. "You?"

He smiles. "Oh, you know. Replied to some work emails. I know I shouldn't while on vacation, but I couldn't resist."

Out of the corner of my eye, I notice Lindsey's gaze flit to me. Sparks of concern flicker in the brown eyes I do not doubt David cited on his dating checklist. It's quietly a little mortifying. Is our conversation so obviously stilted? *What's going on here?*

"Napped some, too," Graham goes on, reminding me I just sat there, not replying.

"Oh, yeah, um," I flail. "Nice. Love to . . . nap."

Graham nods, head bobbing like shipwreck driftwood on open ocean. Sweat springs to my hands. I feel like I've forgotten my lines on stage—which only ever happened to me once.

Until it hits me suddenly, sunlight streaming from parted clouds. *We don't need to stay.* We can escape this stifling double date, do something—anything else. Leave David and Lindsey to enjoy their evening.

Quickly I text Graham under the table.

SOS. Meet me by the bathrooms.

I follow Graham's eyes, which drift down to his smartwatch. It's fortunately *not* on the wrist closest to David. He scans my message, and relief floods his features. When his gaze snaps to mine, it's the reply I needed.

I stand up. "I'm going to hit the restroom before our food comes," I say. My mind leaps forward—to strategies, well-worded excuses, clean getaways from this evening. We won't end tonight like Nikki and the ill-fated Garrett. I refuse.

"Oh, great. I'll come with," Lindsey says.

Graham frowns. I only just manage not to do the same. This complicates our strategic moment of privacy.

Lindsey, oblivious, gathers up her phone. *This isn't her fault,* I remind myself while Graham purses his lips, looking peeved. *She's just enjoying her date.*

I shoot Graham a pained glance over my shoulder while Lindsey and I leave the table. We continue through the restaurant to the dark hallway in the back. I hold the bathroom door for her, and she walks right up to the mirrors, pulling out her lipstick.

"I'm so glad we're doing this," she says. She scrutinizes her reflection, then starts touching up her makeup, which doesn't really need retouching. I head into a stall despite not having to pee. Really, I'm just hoping Lindsey will leave before I'm finished—before Graham comes back here. "David is *great*," she goes on. "I mean, I knew he was friendly but, like, wow. I haven't had this much fun on a first date in years."

I can't help smiling. "You have really great chemistry," I say, meaning it. I flush the toilet, having no good excuse for sitting in here this long. While Lindsey's fluffing her hair, I go to stand next to her in front of the mirror.

"I'm sorry your date's a dud, though," she goes on matter-of-factly. Like she's offering me traffic tips. "But you could totally just bang him for his body before leaving, despite the lack of long-term potential."

I freeze, the cold water of the sink rushing over my hands. Not only what she's said, but the offhand way she said it, clashes with my reality. The idea that Graham doesn't have *long-term potential* is impossible to comprehend when I've pledged myself to him eternally, while the very notion of a stranger writing him off so quickly feels like the warped manifestation of some parallel universe I've stumbled into.

I fight to return to the moment. When I do, I find I'm offended on Graham's behalf.

"Why doesn't he have long-term potential?" I keep the question casual, reaching robotically for the hand soap pump. Of course, it doesn't matter what Lindsey thinks, except that her conclusion is so ridiculous that I can't let it stand.

Lindsey frowns through her fresh lipstick. "Come on—the only conversation he could muster was about his work emails? You know what I mean. Suits can be fun for a night, and then they're boring," she says, like the word tastes salty.

My heart pounds with hidden anger, my breathing thin in my constricted chest. I slam the button for the dryer next to me, and the howl fills the room. Lindsey's evaluation revolts me. It's snide, superficial, dismissive, and unfair.

While my hands dry, however, I realize there's something else beneath my disgust. It's fear, quiet and insidious. Does Graham think I think that about him? Under the restroom's low lighting, I face the harsh facts here. I should show more interest in Graham's career because he *is* interesting. This trip has more than proven that.

"He doesn't seem boring to me," I say softly.

Lindsey shrugs, clearly unaware of this little internal struggle I've waged. "Well, he could be fun, I guess." She straightens her dress and turns to me. "How do I look?"

"Oh," I muster. "Great."

Lindsey grins. "See you back out there." Winking, she walks out the door.

I wait for it to swing shut before I let my face fall. Graham is going to rendezvous with me in a few minutes and—then what? I came in here ready to strategize. To put my theatrical skills to the task of whatever excuse would extricate me and Graham from the worst, weirdest double date imaginable. But . . .

No, I decide. Despite my intentions when I came in here, I'm not leaving this dinner. I'm full of the indignant urge to prove to Lindsey, to myself—to whatever part of Graham that might believe her—just how wrong she is.

24

Graham

I APPROACH THE restrooms hoping to avoid Lindsey. When I left David, he was ready to jog through the restaurant with fists raised in triumph like Rocky, thrilled with how his date is going. I'm genuinely happy for him, though I do not share his delight on my own behalf. This isn't exactly the best first date I've been on with Eliza.

Reaching the hallway, I find it empty. I'm in the clear. With Lindsey still in the women's room, I duck into the men's, where I text Eliza. I'm guessing we're on the same page—we both want to get out of here.

Eliza walks in minutes later, looking frustrated. Carefully, she closes the door behind her. Her eyes snap to mine. "This is an emergency," she tells me in her own voice.

"Proceed," I say, the way I've heard judges do.

"Graham, we're being upstaged."

Just being near her, with no conversational cross-traffic from

Lindsey and David, is intoxicating, even under the harsh lights of the restroom with the plastic-floral smell of hand soap surrounding us. I scoff lightly. "It's not *that* dire," I say.

"Lindsey just told me she feels bad for me for being on a dud date." I wince. "Ouch."

I'm expecting my self-deprecation to light a spark of humor in her eyes. Instead, she folds her arms imperiously. "You are *not* a dud date," my wife declares. "You are the best date I've ever had, and I don't want anyone, not even Lindsey, to think otherwise."

Moved, I say nothing. Words like those from Eliza hold value for me like nothing else in the world. It's one of love's fundamentals, I think. Kindness slips from her tongue to my heart like starlight compared to the flashbulb shine of other compliments.

I'm opening my mouth to reply when we hear footsteps approaching the bathroom door. Eliza's eyes widen with panic. She pulls me into one of the stalls right as a man enters the restroom.

We're not exactly inconspicuous, I know. If he were to glance at the floor to check which stalls are occupied—which he's certainly doing—he'd see two pairs of legs facing each other. The assumption is obvious.

The reality is . . . not far off. Within the cramped confines of the stall, I'm pressed precariously to Eliza, her breath warm through the fabric of my shirt. Her scent, like jasmine, sunshine, and something indescribable, fills the inches separating her face from mine.

Her head is tipped downward until she looks up, through her lashes. I'm not prepared for the swift kick of desire I feel, or for the inescapable charge of the moment, despite our efforts to dodge each other's eyes. We might be pretending not to know each other, but our senses remember. Our bodies remember. Mine wakes up when we breathe in simultaneously, our chests touching for the barest second.

Our unwelcome guest washes his hands. Then uses the dryer. Then leaves the bathroom—the door thudding closed behind him.

Neither Eliza nor I move to leave the cramped stall. Finally, our eyes meet, and from the electricity humming in the gray of her irises, I know how well she remembers me, too.

Images wash over me, searing into my skin. The thought of stepping into her, pressing her against the stall door. Of putting my hands on her, on the base of her hips or the curve of her cheeks, with our mouths desperately close—the taste of her the second our lips meet, the little hitch of breath I hope I would feel from her chest—

Except I don't know if I can do those things, I realize. How *does* she see me right now? Do I have permission to be her husband, or do I have to stay the guy she met on vacation?

She offers me no clues. I search the gray of her eyes, but just like the fog their color so resembles, I can't see through the haze. I have no idea what she wants. She doesn't step toward me. Doesn't bring her lips to mine, doesn't lift her hand to my chest the way I can't help imagining.

So I wait.

Eliza clears her throat, centering herself like she's about to go on stage. The slight movement shifts her hair, sending one strand down her forehead. It lures my gaze—then my fingertips, which move to her face in the quiet under the conjoined rhythm of our heartbeats.

When I reach her forehead, she draws in her breath, then stills, her chest rising up to mine in our confines. Her irises flit indecisively from my eyes to my lips, then back. It feels like fire in pure oxygen. Empty one moment, engulfed in flame the next.

Slowly, I sweep the strand over the curve of her ear.

When I lower my hand, I think I read the faintest tremble in her mouth.

"See," she whispers. "We have chemistry."

I need no convincing, not with my pulse raging in me everywhere. I *want* more convincing, though, in every form I'm capable of imagining. Because when it comes to Eliza, I have a very, *very* good imagination. I rake my eyes over her body, envisioning every curve of her skin I want to caress. I don't need her to speak to know she's walking with me into this dream, this dual fantasy.

"You feel it, too?" I finally ask. Partly because I want the answer. Partly because I think I know and want to hear her say it.

Her eyes find mine, close enough I can discern their flecks shining like diamonds. "Always, Graham," she says.

Suddenly I want nothing more than to finish this date, to live up to the me I am in Eliza's eyes. "Let's prove Lindsey wrong," I say, reaching for the door.

Her fingers clasping my wrist, Eliza stills my hand. "Or we could wait fifteen minutes," she suggests. "Or twenty."

Temptation licks the edges of my mind like fire. I raise a leading eyebrow. "Here? Now?" I get out, then shift my voice just slightly. Similar to how Eliza does, if less pronounced. "But we hardly know each other."

Eliza shoves me lightly, her wry smile urging my pulse on even faster. Leaning in, I lower my lips to within inches of hers. She smells incredible. Like *her*. I decide it's reductive to say she smells like flowers or sunshine or whatever. She smells indefinable, her own heavenly fingerprint left on my senses.

I lower my chin just a little, like I'm going to kiss her, enjoying dragging this out. We never get to tease this way anymore. I don't want it to end now. Not yet.

"Let's have our date first," I say to her lips. "Then we'll see what comes next."

While my words roll over Eliza, I slide open the stall's latch.

Eliza doesn't move for several moments, her perfect mouth upturned like she wants me to want to kiss her. Which, *fuck*, I do. Then, snapping the electric tether holding us, she swings the stall door open.

"I'm going to make you regret that," she says before stepping out.

I grin. "I look forward to it."

She walks to the bathroom exit. But when I follow, she stops me with her hand on my chest.

The flash of my fantasy from the bathroom stall stills me in place. It's riveting, the charge of remembering everything I wanted. Everything I was perilously close to doing. The place I envisioned my hands on her hips. How I could practically *hear* the rattle of the latch when I imagined pressing her up to the door to kiss her.

"We can't go out there together unless you want them to think we were doing something we weren't," she says. Her whisper is low enough I dare to wonder whether she's envisioning hints of what I was. "Wait two minutes."

I nod, my mouth dry.

She takes her hand off my chest and walks out. I watch her—or, "watch" isn't the right word. It implies this is voluntary. But I couldn't take my eyes off the way her jeans and T-shirt hug her shape if someone offered me the world.

She glances ever so slightly over her shoulder. Her small smile just for me hits like a jolt to my heart right before the door swings closed between us.

25

Eliza

I RETURN FROM the restroom newly confident. I'm going to enjoy my second first date with my husband.

Even by the time our entrees get here, my heartbeat hasn't fully reset from the hurried pace it hit when pressed up to Graham in our wonderfully cramped stall. Graham's glances—his quick smiles, the undercurrent of promise in them—say he feels the same.

It carries me with new ease into the conversation with David and Lindsey, who we get to know. Lindsey, who works for one of Oregon's many environmental nonprofits, is impressed when David explains the unique difficulties of corralling five-year-olds into essentially everything. David is visibly delighted when he recognizes the names of several of the national parks Lindsey mentions, complete with details he can levy into informed questions.

When it's my husband's turn to share Investment Banker Graham's interests and goings-on, Graham makes his first move.

His favorite hobby is reading, he notes, which draws Lindsey's interest. What has he read lately?

Graham probably could've gotten into my college theater program on the strength of the way he levels his gaze at Lindsey, full of enthusiasm. "Have you ever heard of *Notes on Tuscany?*"

I blink. When Graham was in law school and I was pursuing stage acting, we didn't have much spending money. Sometimes we went out—the Grove Farmers' Market, the Nuart Theatre, coffee in Culver City—but especially once we moved in together, we spent lots of our companionable time going on long walks in our neighborhood. With the sun setting over the power lines of Los Angeles, we'd share the details of our days, including, naturally, what we were reading, if it was interesting.

"Interesting" would describe ungenerously my feelings on *Notes on Tuscany* and its sequels *Notes on Milan* and *Notes on Florence*. They're my favorite books, which Graham knows from how I rapturously recounted to him every single detail of each on our sunset walks.

I grin over the table. He's using our unfair advantage.

Picking up the invitation perfectly, I pretend I'm flabbergasted by this happy coincidence. He's just named Vacation Planner Eliza's *favorite book*. I get to gush, entirely genuinely, over plot points Graham remembers perfectly, because of course he does. While David switches Graham's plate—they're adorably sharing the superfood salad and the fried chicken—I move the conversation gently to TV series, then to Graham's favorite legal drama. *I see you, Husband*, I'm trying to say.

While we compare favorite seasons, Lindsey looks openly surprised, like she might've misjudged our compatibility. David seems . . . less surprised. I get the feeling he might be in the know on everything. I wouldn't mind if Graham filled him in. Honestly, I'm glad Graham has a friend to confide in, one who's willing to go along.

It's fun. Not just how excellently we're playing the perfect couple, either. I'm loving the way Graham and I have folded this pretense tonight into the opportunity to share what we love with each other like it's the first time.

Under the table, I let a different sort of conversation unfold—one that starts when I shift my knee to brush Graham's. He returns the gentle press. Then before I know it, I'm running the toe of my sneaker up his calf, sorely wishing this were the type of restaurant for the heels I rescued from Graham's room earlier, ones I could easily slip my bare feet into and out of.

When dinner is winding down, Graham and I having unquestionably impressed with our connection, there's just one more thing I want to prove to Lindsey—and to Graham. Looking him right in the eye, I ask him what he enjoys about his job.

While uncertainty flickers in Graham's expression for the direction I've taken the conversation, he follows, sincerely sharing intricacies of Investment Banker Graham's job I know relate equally to his own. Listening to him, there's no denying it. Interest is sexy. This man could be describing traffic patterns or soil composition—if he were doing it with Graham's warmth, his nuance, I'd be into it.

I speak up suddenly. "I think it's really great you have so much passion for your career."

Graham's stare, which was elsewhere while he described the complexity of coordinating specialist teams, darts to me. So does Lindsey's.

Stubbornly, I go on with the truth. "We should all be so lucky.

Even if it's not work I'm interested in myself, it's interesting to hear *you* share something you love."

In the next second, with Graham holding my gaze, I see the pretense fall completely from his face. I let mine do the same. The subtle change might be enough for David and Lindsey to intuit something's different. Maybe we're blowing our stories, our whole elaborate game, in this one naked moment. But I don't care.

Right now, I want Graham to know what I'm saying is 100 percent real.

26

Graham

DINNER WAS EXHILARATING but exhausting. Not that it was hard to flirt with Eliza. *God, no.* What was difficult was staying in character for so long in front of an audience.

It's given me new admiration for what Eliza does every day. The effort of holding myself in character, of crafting every mannerism, every phrasing, every piece of backstory for the entirely different person I'm rendering, was herculean. To be in character means fighting the deepest instinct that makes you *you*. I know from now on when I watch Eliza record samples or practice lines, I'll see her with new respect.

Fortunately, I wasn't on my own tonight. When we met, Eliza explained to me the importance of a great scene partner, and tonight, she was a *fantastic* scene partner. Whenever I felt myself flagging, she was there. Prompting me with new questions, new topics.

It felt like we were really working together, collaborating instead of competing. It was incredible.

Then there was the way she praised this pretend Graham. That part *didn't* feel pretend, not with her compliments in the bathroom echoing in my chest.

Now, finally, we've paid the bill. I'm itching to leave this restaurant, my stage for the past two hours. My own words to Eliza in the restroom fill my head with their incessant charged hum. *Let's have our date first. Then we'll see what comes next.*

I'm very ready for what comes next.

"Well, we should let this table go," David says. "Does anyone want to get a drink at the bar?"

I could hug the man. "Definitely another night," Lindsey says. "I'm getting up for a sunrise hike tomorrow."

"I'm beat," Eliza adds.

I know my window of opportunity when it comes. "Can I walk you out?"

Eliza nods, pleased, like I've just accepted the unspoken invitation she knew she was offering. We head for the front of the restaurant, leaving David with Lindsey for their own dance of post-date pleasantries.

It's dark out now, only the sparse foot lamps lighting the path. The night is quiet despite the many lights on in the hotel windows. Over the past evenings, I've gotten used to the soundtrack of nighttime out here, the rustle of brush sweetened by the quiet chitter of insects. We walk in comfortable quiet, following the gently sloping gravel path into the woods.

It's a few minutes until Eliza finally speaks up. "My room isn't this way," she says, like she regrets needing to deliver this information.

"Mine is," I say.

The insinuation fills the space between us immediately. Eliza smirks.

"I know," she replies.

Then she's picking up her pace, walking—swaying—in front of me. I follow her up to the entryway of my suite, where she stops and turns. In the ethereal glow of the foot lamps, she looks up, her eyes roving over my face. When she places her hand on my chest once more, I'm locked in place, the shock of fantasy rushing to meet me.

This time, she tugs the fabric just enough to pull my face to hers to kiss me. Caught off guard, I take a moment to react. With her lips on mine, half of me is convinced this is only my imagination running away with me. The other half of me doesn't care. Whether this is dream or fantasy or impossibly, perfectly real, I wrap my arms around her the way I wanted to in the bathroom, and I hold her close.

She feels incredible. My heart pounds so hard, I'd be embarrassed if I couldn't feel Eliza's pulse racing with mine. Like I instinctively know the full experience would overwhelm me, I focus on the details. The intoxicating taste of her lower lip, the curve of her waist under my fingers. Every second is somehow forever and slipping past too soon.

It's nothing like the kisses I'm used to with Eliza. My mind gropes for why, finally latching onto something. This kiss is *uncertain*, and the uncertainty feeds the passion in ways I couldn't have predicted. Every movement is intensely charged with daring, hesitation, and hope. Every moment is question and answer—conversations Eliza and I haven't had for so long I can hardly remember them.

But I don't need to remember them. Not when they're playing out on our tongues right now.

I raise one hand to cup her face, caressing the curve of her neck, while my other snakes lower, eager to explore elsewhere. I feel her reaction in the way she exhales faintly, like a shiver held in—like she doesn't want me to know how my grip feels.

The next moment, I swear she's playing with me, leaning into me in response. *Is this what you wanted?* she dares.

Yes. Yes, it is.

I step her up to the wall, pinning her where I want her. Fingers digging into my shirt, she clings to me so hard I feel our balance shifting. Not wanting this to end, I throw a hand out and press my palm to the cold cement behind her. I don't know how I'll ever leave her embrace. How I'll ever withdraw from her mouth, hot, insistent, desperately pressed to mine. I can't get enough.

Finally, it's Eliza who draws her head back, breaking the kiss. Even though she ended it, she's practically panting, her eyes foggy with desire. The pull is wrenching, how much I want to reach out for her, her waist, her hips, *her*.

I'm ready to open the door, to take her inside, to finish this in every one of those ways I imagined earlier. Eliza, however, manages to marshal her perfect features into coy victory—like she knows where my head is. "I told you I'd make you regret it," she says, pulling away.

I have to laugh. "How much longer are we going to draw this out, Eliza?"

She lifts her lips closer to mine, the mirror of how I leaned toward her in the bathroom stall.

"Until we can't for *one second longer*," she promises.

It's nearly impossible to hear. I'm hungry for her, dying of cold, of thirst. But I push myself, intuiting what she's doing. You can't have kisses that feel like answers without leaving a few questions.

I step back, putting more space between us.

Eliza evens out her breath with effort. "I had a good time to-night," she says, her stare fixed on me. Though featherlight, her words carry the weight of real meaning. "Good night, Graham."

I watch her walk away from me, out into the darkness.

It's a few moments before I'm able to shake off the dreamlike daze and find my keycard in my pocket. Still, Eliza's scent lingers in the entryway, the imagined reverberation of her heartbeat roaring in my ears. I click open my door and step inside.

27

Eliza

I ONLY SLEEP a couple of hours. The rest of the night I spend repositioning, studying the ceiling of my room, fidgeting the seams of my pajama shorts—replaying my kiss with Graham the entire time.

It was . . . unreal. It took every ounce of willpower I could muster to walk away from his door and out onto the path into the silent forest, instead of asking if I could come in. Every instinct in me, every wave of the heat rolling off my skin, screamed for me to stay. I didn't.

In the end, I'm glad I didn't. The exhilaration of last night wasn't just from kissing my husband for the first time in days. There's something in the buildup, the deprivation, the wondering that charges our every interaction in ways I can't get enough of.

It's not just exhilarating, either. Lying in my solitary bed, I find myself convinced that the slower we take everything, the more we draw out, the better the foundation we will have rebuilt. If we were to hurry into restarting every part of our relationship, in days we might very well return to our old lack of communication. I know we can't keep up what we're doing forever, or probably even for very long, but I know I want to keep this going for now.

The next morning, I'm pulling on my shoes and heading to the hotel's Starbucks, which opens on the hour. I checked the bedside brochure somewhere between four and five a.m. I have two, or maybe more like one and a half, objectives. Mainly, my nearly sleepless night has left me intensely needing caffeine.

If, however, I run into Graham—who I happen to know generally starts his day with coffee—well, then, great.

When I walk out of my building, the morning is deep blue. I cross the patio in the direction of the coffee shop, my nerves jumpy with excitement. I can't remember the last time I felt this frazzled. It was probably after our *real* first kiss. I can't help thinking back to that night, our second date. We'd gone to a movie, and after, Graham walked me to my car even though his was on a completely different level in the massive parking structure of the Grove mall in LA.

There was no one around—I'd had to park in the very back, farthest from the elevators. We talked for an extra twenty minutes, neither of us wanting to leave. Finally, I took his hand. He leaned toward me.

It was exciting. Meaningful. The indisputable start of something.

One thing it *wasn't* was intense. Our kiss last night was intense. While I'm not exactly certain why, I suspect it had to do with the delicious in-between in which we've found ourselves. We got to enjoy the unexpectedness of strangers with the intensity of people who've long loved each other. Instead of two dates of buildup, we had years. We knew everything about how to kiss each other without knowing when we would next get to.

I swing open the Starbucks door and stop. The place is already full. *Who are these people?* Who goes on vacation only to get up at six in the morning?

Besides me, of course. But I have a very good reason.

Getting in line, I eagerly peer around. My heart flags when I don't see Graham. But I'm here now, and I did really need a latte regardless. While I wait for the baristas to work through the morning rush, my eye catches on the sign near the door advertising live music, Spanish guitar, at the hotel's fanciest restaurant tonight. I suppose it's what Graham and I would have done tonight if we were staying here together like normal. The idea makes me a little sad.

When I step forward, a familiar head of shiny dark hair is waiting at the counter where the coffees are served.

Lindsey smiles when she spots me. She's dressed for hiking, hair up, mountain dirt caked on her shoes. The flush of exercise in her cheeks says she returned recently.

"How was your sunrise hike?" I ask.

"Fantastic." She studies me. "But you're up early. I wondered if you were going to be out late with Graham, but I guess not?"

I grin suggestively. "Not late, no," I say. "Best kiss of my life, though." It's the truth, too. I've enjoyed recent synchronies like this one, where the pretense we're keeping up collides with the reality of us.

Lindsey doesn't hide her surprise. She doesn't hide much, I've noticed. It's a quality I admire in her. "I will fully admit I was wrong about him," she says, smiling. "I'm so glad your night turned around." Craning her neck over the counter in search of her coffee, she continues. "Let me know how things work out with him. I'm rooting for you two." She smiles again, chipper.

"I will," I say sincerely.

When the barista sets Lindsey's coffee on the counter, Lindsey

177

grabs the paper cup. I find my eyes following her drink enviously. *God, I need caffeine* now. She holds her coffee up in farewell and exits the café.

I walk up to the front of the line, where I order extra shots in my latte. Sleeplessness is really catching up with me. Unlike Graham, my work schedule is my own, with rarely the necessity for late nights, and I only pulled one all-nighter in college while flailing over the research paper for one of my required Gen Ed courses. I'm not used to how I'm feeling now. Exhaustion hangs like heavy clouds over me, lightheadedness warping the corners of my vision.

With my order in, I continue to the counter where Lindsey was just waiting. While they prepare my coffee, I resume my survey of the café, looking once more for Graham.

My chest deflates when I still don't find him. Not only with disappointment, either. As fun as our games are, surprising each other and improvising, I don't like the idea that Graham has abandoned who he is or who I know him to be. Even when the detail is insubstantial, like starting his morning with coffee.

Or maybe especially when it's insubstantial. On plenty of occasions recently I've had to confront how I don't *really* know my husband beyond what's on his résumé or what could be summed up for strangers in describing our romantic history. While I might not know what he's thinking at all times, I *do* know he needs his morning coffee. It's a diamond of a detail. Small, yet somehow incomparably valuable.

Picking up my coffee, which I resist sipping, knowing it would scald me, I leave the shop, dejected.

Until I spot Graham walking onto the patio with purpose, headed straight for Starbucks.

The sight lifts me in ways no quantity of caffeine ever could. Not *everything* has changed.

I see the moment his eyes find me. His stride slows, his mouth stretching into a lazy smile. Despite my quickening heartbeat, I match his demeanor, straightening my shoulders with casual confidence. "I wondered if you weren't a six-a.m. coffee kind of guy," I say when he reaches me.

"Should I be worried I'm predictable?" he replies unhesitatingly. Honestly, it requires effort to process what he's literally saying past the intense distraction of his eyes lingering on me, reminding me of our kiss. I don't have to wonder if the effect is intentional, and I know I'm doing the same. Some conversations are conversations. Others are excuses to stare at each other.

"No," I say. "I like what I'm predicting."

He has no immediate reply to this, only a new glow to his smile. Victory and invitation and hope.

"So," he says. "Last night. You kissed me."

I raise an eyebrow. "I did."

"Is there a chance for a follow-up?"

We step to the side, out of the way of people heading into the coffee shop. While I can't fight the smile wobbling onto my face for a second, I play coy. "Is this finally it? Is it happening?"

Graham's eyes sparkle. "What?" His smile says he knows.

"Are you *finally* asking me out?"

He straightens proudly. "Yes, Eliza. It's finally happening. I'm asking you out. Do you have plans tonight?"

"Not a one."

"Then," my husband replies, "it's a date."

28

Graham

THE FALCON'S EYE scouts sharply over the group of us, its head moving in precise, measured increments. It's small, housecat-sized, with speckled brown wings it fluffs in unperturbed dignity. The bird rests, then, with a quick nod from the falconer, lifts off from her glove with one powerful, calm stroke of wings.

I'm standing with David, watching the hotel's falconry experience. He requested I come to play wingman in hopes of running into Lindsey, which, twenty minutes into the presentation, is pretty certainly not happening. Undeterred, David decided he could instead diligently take notes to share with Lindsey in the one-on-one date he's hoping to ask her on.

While I'm ostensibly here for David, I couldn't help finding myself engaged in the story the falconer told, of how she'd nursed the injured bird back to health last year. Thor the peregrine falcon now helps keep the hotel grounds free of pests.

David is watching raptly. The falcon wheels in the sky, then returns to the falconer's heavy leather glove. When the demonstration ends, the falconer announces she'll hang around if anyone has questions. David promptly abandons me, marching forth with prepared falcon questions.

I check my watch. It's midafternoon, the sun blazing over the rocky bluff. I have a couple hours before my date tonight. The prospect has me itching for the minutes to pass. Weeks ago, I'd made reservations for us for every night of our stay, and for the first time, I'm not canceling tonight.

I can't deny it feels odd using the reservation I made for me and my wife. After all, I'm not certain it's my wife who will join me. I honestly don't know what versions of ourselves we'll play tonight.

The idea wouldn't leave me feeling disjointed if not for the new worry infiltrating my heart this morning. What if this version of Graham is the only one Eliza wants to go on a date with? Who could blame her? He's more charming. He works out. Perhaps more important, she hasn't spent enough time with him to grow bored of him.

I shake the thoughts off, not liking the long shadows they cast. I don't need the answer to this question right now. It won't change what I do tonight.

Tonight, I have a date. One I'm really looking forward to.

When I look up, David is returning with his loping, purposeful stride. "Did you know," he starts right in when he reaches me, "the peregrine falcon is not only the world's fastest bird, but the world's fastest animal? Dive speeds of over three hundred miles per hour. Lindsey's going to love this."

"She will, but only if you actually ask her out," I reply.

David slouches. I smile. The entire walk over here I pressed him on his next move with Lindsey, which he resisted nervously, reminding me we just went out last night. "It's too soon, dude. Obviously, it's too soon. Or—or is it charming?" He tilts his head, considering, then answers his own question. "No, it's too soon. Tomorrow?"

We head down the trail. "I don't know," I say, choosing my footing on the gravel carefully. "I haven't asked anyone out in years."

"You literally asked your wife out *this* morning."

I level him a look. "Okay, I haven't asked anyone who *isn't* my wife out in over half a decade," I amend. "Anyway, you're the one in a dating seminar. Isn't this, like, Dating 101?"

"Shit, you're right," David says. "I'll check my notes when we get back."

I laugh. Of course, David is taking copious notes. "Does the seminar cover how to eventually tell Lindsey you're not really this environmental outdoorsman?"

David's nose wrinkles. "You make it sound like I'm lying. I'm not—I'm into the outdoors *now*." He gestures past us, where in the distance the olive-green hills of the California coast slope inland. "Out here, who wouldn't be?"

"Come on," I say skeptically. "You embellished it, though, right?"

David glances over, lightly judgmental. "Excuse me, did I or did I not endure an entire meal last night of you and your wife's *embellishments*?"

"Okay," I concede. "Fair. But it's not like Eliza doesn't know who I really am." When David only hums skeptically in reply, I frown. "What's that mean?"

"Who will you be on your date tonight? Investment Banker Graham? Lawyer Graham? Does it make a difference?" David's voice is measured. He's not being flippant or unhelpful.

I don't understand the question, though. "Of course it does. She likes Investment Banker Graham better than she likes regular me. Way better." It startles even me how instantly, how readily this new mutant strain of my old insecurity slips out of me. I guess it's just the way of issues like mine—they hunt incessantly for ways to discredit what's good. What's *working*.

Right now, everything with Eliza is working. How do I hold on, though? It feels like grasping for sunlight. I can feel the warmth but not carry it with me.

David's brow furrows. "Graham," he says, "my six-year-olds can read more subtext than you sometimes. Who do you *want* to be? This isn't only about Eliza."

I plant my foot slightly wrong on the path, sending the gravel skittering under me, then balance myself. David's comment leaves me with no reply. He's exactly right—everything I'm putting into Investment Banker Graham comes from me. *Only* me.

Which means . . . maybe pieces of the person I've drawn up don't have to end when we get home. What is a self except the choices we make of who to present, how to respond to the people in our lives? Sure, Eliza and I have decided to work certain sudden changes into those presentations, then tacked on some made-up backstories. But is the process really that different from life itself? I'd gotten used to connecting this self, this performance, to this vacation.

Maybe I should learn to start connecting it to me instead.

29

Eliza

THE PATIO LOOKS fit for a movie, ready for a montage wrapped in warm lighting. The trees hold fairy lights delicately decorating their flowering limbs, while the white flames of candles flicker on each of the burgundy-clothed tables. It's tapas night, the hand-chalked wooden sign on the hostess's podium tells me. The trio of musicians with their guitars plays on a small stage past the tables, which have been organized to leave space clearly meant for dancing. Two older couples sway under the lights.

This is one of the resort's events programmed for couples, part of why the hotel is rated one of the best romantic getaways in the country. Every table, I notice while the hostess leads me through the patio, is set up *only* for two.

Crossing the space to our table, I spot Graham already seated, watching the band to his right. He doesn't notice me, not yet. He's dressed for the patio heaters, in a white button-down with the top two buttons undone, the sleeves cuffed casually to the elbows. He looks good, understatedly confident.

Part of me doubts he labored over the outfit in front of his mirror, questioning whether to opt for his coat or polos or this. It's this harsh, rational voice in my head reminding me how infrequently we dress up for each other. How far our relationship is now from nervously preening in the mirror, hoping we impress each other.

But tonight, I refuse to listen. I shut the familiar voice down. I let the endearing idea wash over me, reveling in the thought that he nervously, excitedly prepared for our date the way I did.

Because tonight isn't for painful reminders. It's for possibilities.

I let myself savor the sight of him, his forearms resting on the tablecloth, hands clasped lightly. It's been a long time since I *met* someone for a date. These days, when dates happen—only for special occasions now—they involve getting ready in the same bedroom, reaching past each other with our shoulders bumping in the closet, having him untangle one of my necklaces he's seen fifty times, then driving over together. This change, this charged little prelude, is nice. Graham hasn't seen me yet. He doesn't know what I'm wearing.

When he turns in my direction, his gaze landing on me, I get to watch his eyes light up just for me.

Good thing, too. I *really* pinned my hopes on this dress.

It's black, with a wide V-neck, thin straps, and an asymmetrical hem on the high slit that hugs my hips. What Graham can't see is the lingerie I put on in a burst of confidence. The dress required something delicate underneath, and without wearing shapewear, only the lingerie would work.

What's more, I couldn't stand the thought it would sit unworn in my bag the whole trip. Graham doesn't even have to see it. It's for me. Wearing it makes me feel like a new person.

I walk over and sit down across from him, not fighting the flush rising on my neck from how he can't stop drinking me in.

"Hi," I say.

"Hello. You look incredible," he replies a little breathlessly.

I smile, feeling practically ready to burst with quiet pleasure. "Thank you."

Our waiter comes over immediately and pours our sparkling water, then explains the specials. I process none of it, partly because of the happy haze descending over me and partly because, right now, everything sounds delicious while the waiter's explaining it.

When the waiter finishes with the specials, Graham looks to me. "If you want, I was thinking we could do the prix fixe."

I feel my eyes widen. This is not something we do at home. "I'd love that," I reply. The waiter nods, then departs. Graham and I return to taking each other in. "It's been a while since I've done this," I say.

"What? Gone out to dinner?"

This smartass reply is one hundred percent Investment Banker Graham. I sip my water. "No. Gone on a first date. You have a high bar to meet," I inform him. "My last first date was exceptional." I give him a sly smile.

His eyes sparkle. "That so? Well, tell me what I'm up against."

I settle into my seat, letting the memories sweep over me. When I've recalled them recently, they felt like cloying reminders of what we've somehow lost. Right now, though, they're just sweet. This night has some sort of wonderful Midas touch, turning everything into its loveliest version. "It was certainly nothing like this," I say, gesturing to the fairy-tale decorations of the restaurant. "We just met for coffee, but we talked for two hours."

Graham considers me. "Two hours," he repeats slowly. "I think we could go longer, if you're up to it."

My cheeks flame. The look in his eyes says he is *not* referring to coffee.

Preempting whatever reply I could have managed, the waiter returns with our first course, shrimp ceviche in crispy cones. Truthfully, I usually wouldn't go for this sort of set menu even if Graham suggested it, not trusting myself to enjoy whatever comes next. Tonight, though, I think I'm in the mood to do exactly that. I'm in character. Besides, I want to match Graham in every way he pushes us.

I eat my ceviche cone in one bite. I don't regret it.

"I like how confident you are," I remark, remembering *I* decide how Vacation Planner Eliza responds to energetic comments from attractive men. She plays it cool.

He pauses. "To be honest, I feel like you're out of my league. I have to do something to compensate."

I drop my napkin in surprise. Before I can bend down to pick it up, the waiter is there, picking it up and placing it delicately on my lap. "You think I'm out of your league? Why?"

When Graham laughs, the bashful way he does it catches me off guard. It's entirely him, and entirely not in character. "Eliza, look at yourself. And furthermore, you're . . . comfortable, charismatic, interesting wherever you are. You fit in."

Despite a different heat racing into me, I'm quick to reply. "You do, too. Besides, have you seen yourself? I'm sure I'm not even the only woman to be interested in you in the last twenty-four hours."

"So you're interested?" he says playfully.

I let my discreet smile speak for itself. But something in the exchange has snagged on my heart in ways I can't quite put my finger on. While Graham looks satisfied in the silence, I find his eyes, figuring it out while I speak. "Did the . . . last woman you were with make you feel like you were lesser?"

I steel myself, preparing for heartbreak. Frankly, I'll be crushed if I did something to make him feel this way.

"No, it wasn't her fault," he says, his expression clouding over. "I think it's just the way I see myself."

I say nothing, struggling under the complicated weight of this response, this math problem made of lead. I don't feel relieved by his reply. I'm sad—sad that Graham, the most wonderful person in the world, doesn't see himself in the full spectrum of colors I do. "Well, I'll do a better job of showing you how wrong you are," I say, then catch myself. "Better—better than your ex, I mean. She must have been a fool not to make it clear to you."

He smiles softly. "What about you?" he asks. "Something must have happened to take that two-hour conversation to feeling like your ex no longer saw you? What could he have done better?"

I gaze out over the restaurant. The answer to his question feels heavy in ways I'm not ready to face, not on this stunning "first date." Not on this gorgeous patio, this space where our real lives seem to slip into dream or fantasy.

My eyes find the couples dancing, sharing companionable silence or murmured conversation. Straightening, I face Graham with a smile. "Well, to start, he could have danced with me more," I say.

Something in Graham's eyes dims. He knows I'm avoiding the real conversation. I feel cowardly. Still, I'm grateful when he doesn't pry. I don't want to shatter the spell of the night we're having, not when everything is going well.

Graham stands up and offers me his hand. I see the new decision in him, the swift choice to enjoy the night with me instead of pressing into misgivings. It's thrillingly sexy. His next words come out low with purpose. "Eliza," he says, "would you dance with me?"

Putting my hand in his, I let him lead us to the space in front of the musicians. They're playing something slower in a minor key, the melodic line soulfully romantic. The music floats over us like the scent of flowers on the wind, intoxicating in their sweet headiness. Under the amber lights, the rest of the world melts into the moment.

Graham holds me close. It reminds me of our wedding, of the dance classes we took together to get ready. Graham is a decent dancer, and with this new confidence he's putting on, he's genuinely good. He guides us with a firm hand, which frees my mind to focus on the way our bodies brush against each other, the feel of his fingers pressed to the small of my back.

And what I hope happens after we finish dinner.

I'm not the only one, I realize. I feel Graham pressed firmly to me when our hips move together in rhythm with the music. He smiles slightly when I lean forward a little more, following the pressure of his hand, letting my thigh meet with his erection. He doesn't hide it. He couldn't if he tried.

"I suppose I should be embarrassed," he says into my shoulder.

I move even closer, swaying with him. His eyes flutter shut.

"You really shouldn't," I whisper in reply.

We lavish in our closeness for the next few seconds. I smell Graham, my Graham, under the new citrus-pine scent of hotel shower gel. The scent captures the night perfectly, the combination of home and here, of foreign and familiar. Cheek to cheek, I feel him breathe me in. "I don't know how I'm going to get back to the table," he confesses.

I laugh softly into his neck. "I could help?" I suggest.

"While it's thoughtful of you to offer," he replies instantly, "you're the main problem here. I'm pretty sure you'd only make things worse."

"Mm," I muse, seeing his point. "Sorry."

His hand slides lower down my back. "Don't be," he murmurs into my ear. "Not for a second."

I wonder if this restaurant has WET FLOOR signs on hand, because I'm presently melting into one expanding puddle of flattered joy and, frankly, lust. Does he know what he's doing to me? He must. He must know.

"For whatever it's worth," I say, "I like it."

Graham groans, pressing his face into my neck. "Eliza. You're making this harder."

I have to laugh—I'm pretty sure the word choice was intentional. Either way, it's certainly correct.

We continue to sway, losing track of time. Of ourselves. The music is dreamlike, pining, perfect.

And for the first time, I consider breaking character, because I really, really regret not sharing a room with Graham tonight.

30

Graham

DINNER IS UNBELIEVABLE. Every dish is perfection, though we have different favorites. I find myself hanging on to every word of Eliza's description of why the paella is at the very top of her list. It's funny how infatuation turns every conversation into one you want to remember for the rest of your life, no matter how insignificant the details.

When we finish our entrées, I feel certain I don't have room for dessert. Then the waiter brings out the crema catalana. We share the decadent creamy dish in the middle of the table, leaning on our elbows to spoon mouthfuls. Eliza's dress gapes a little with the movement, and I catch a glimpse of something lacy. I have to tear my eyes away.

I feel pulled in opposite delicious directions. On the one hand, I want to make this meal last as long as possible. On the other, I'm very ready to find out where the night might lead us.

From the heated smile Eliza gives me, I get the sense she's eager for the same.

The whole dinner, I've focused on asking Eliza questions. Sometimes her answers are all fabrications. Her work-perk trips for research to Prague or Vienna, or how she enjoys living on the East Coast. Now, though, I've learned not to mind the fact that *none* of this is fact. I don't want to waste the pressure-free opportunity to rebuild my instincts for curiosity, for fascination, for intuitive follow-ups in conversation with the woman I married.

I give as well, describing my fictional life in Santa Fe. In detailing workdays I've never lived in downtowns I've never visited, I realize I'm practicing something else. I'm practicing *feeling* interesting. Going into conversations with her expecting warmth, expecting enthusiasm. Feeling the confidence she says I should.

On our last bite of crema, I decide to ask the question I've been skirting all evening. "I want to hear more about your sister. What's your relationship like?"

This topic isn't just for practice. I know Michelle well. Eliza's younger sister who works in tech. They haven't spoken since Michelle's engagement party, which Eliza was upset to have missed. Now, not only do Eliza's features shadow whenever I mention her sister—I think some of our own distance started when Eliza returned from the disastrous party. My question is real, and I'm hoping this might be the chance to discuss it with her.

Eliza straightens. "My *sisters*, you mean," she says sharply. The message is clear. On this, there will be no truth discussed.

I say nothing.

"They're great," she goes on. "We have a . . . great relationship. We're really close."

It's striking how badly she's lying about this. How forced her diction, how uncreative her response. Eliza, who intimidated me with her elegant, nuanced character construction, just said "great" twice.

It makes me sad. Something in this question is such a hot stove she can't help flinching from it. While I want to press, I remember how she shied away from the real conversation earlier before diverting with dancing. One piece at a time. I let her change the subject.

"So, Graham," she says, "we're both on vacation. When we go home, it'll be to . . . different lives. What do you want out of this?"

The veiled question is one I've wondered myself this week. When we get into our car to drive home, what will happen to the personas we've constructed this week?

Considering silently, I don't let my eyes leave Eliza. She holds my gaze, worlds forming and collapsing and re-forming in the slate swirl of her irises, the calm lines of her lips, the flush of her cheeks. While this might not be everything we need, I decide, it is a chance. I can correct some of what I've done wrong.

"I want to get to know you," I reply.

Her smile softens. I don't know how I know it's not part of her performance. "What do you want to know?"

"What makes you happiest right now?"

Eliza sets her spoon down carefully. I know we both know it's time to be real. Still, I'm grateful for this charade. Back home, I felt like I should know what makes her happy. Shouldn't her husband never have to ask that question? But on a first date, it's easy. Expected.

"Adventures like this, and long conversations," she says. "What about you?"

I file this information away with care. I can do this. I can give her what she wants. It's only as hard as asking.

Asking and answering, I suppose. With Eliza's eyes on me, I decide I won't overthink the first response my heart supplies.

"I want a family."

I don't hide my honesty in my character's bravado. While it feels huge, I'm instantly glad I said it. Having children is something Eliza and I have discussed, something we want in general. When we got married, we were twenty-four and in no hurry. Over the past year, though, I guess something shifted in me, and not knowing how to raise the subject, I let the idea hide in my mind. This is the first time it feels easy to say.

Obviously, I watch Eliza's reaction with intense focus. She blinks, but even while I prepare myself for disappointment, for re-direction, I don't find reluctance in her expression. Nevertheless, I remind myself, it could just be her character's reaction. Not my wife's. I'm not certain she knows what I'm saying is the truth, either, instead of part of our collective charade.

Her measured voice offers no indication when she replies. "It would require meeting the right person, of course."

"Of course," I say. My heart races, but not unpleasantly. In these things it's sort of impossible to know where nerves end and excite-ment begins. "And making sure the time was right for her," I go on.

"Naturally." Eliza's eyes dance with unspoken conversations and quiet joys.

I feel emotions too enormous to name swell in me. Chasing my instincts, I channel them into the bravado I've felt since Eliza sat down with me, wrapped in the confidence of this character and this clean slate. "So the guy you met for coffee," I say. "Did you go home with him after the first date?"

When she smiles, I'm pretty sure I see the same raging hope lighting up her expression. "Not the first date, no."

It's the response I was expecting. I remember our coffee date perfectly—including how I'd *wished* I was going home with her. Removing my napkin from my lap, I toss it gently onto the table in front of me. "I think we've outdone him, though, wouldn't you say?"

Eliza eyes me. "What exactly are you asking?" She smiles again, lips pressed together seductively. It takes everything in me to keep from reaching forward, caressing the lithe neck I murmured into while we danced, and crushing my mouth to her red-velvet lipstick.

Instead, I only match her expression.

"I'm asking if you'll spend the night with me," I say.

31

Eliza

I SAY YES.

Graham glows while he hurries to pay the bill. I would find his obvious eagerness cute or sweet, except right now, much hungrier descriptions fill my mind.

We walk the path from the restaurant to the forested grounds of the hotel, not speaking while slate changes to gravel under our feet. I get the unexpected feeling everything is *new*, the first time I've walked this way, though of course it's not. There's expectation lighting up every color, singing in every quiet sound, humming in the gentle wind on my cheeks. Excitement prickles me like prodding fingertips.

Context, I guess, is everything. We know *exactly* what we'll do when we reach our destination.

In the dark, I feel intensely the feet separating us, until suddenly, Graham's arm encircles my waist. It is its own impossibly enticing promise. The casual pressure of his hand on my hip invites me to imagine everywhere else I'd like to feel it. I don't fight my imagination, instead letting fantasy preoccupy me the rest of the walk.

Graham holds the door open for me when we reach his room, which is technically *our* room. I walk in, my eyes sweeping over the details. The soaking tub in the lavish bathroom. The wide living room. The balcony with the Jacuzzi. While I would guess the view is incredible, right now there's only black night sky.

In front of the bed, I stop. I could be reflecting on everything I've deprived myself of, everything I felt I needed to deprive myself of for this unlikely, unconventional, improbably wonderful game we're playing, but—I'm not. Instead, I'm just grateful for everything I get to experience *now*, in exactly this way. I'm grateful for how this moment will be made sweeter by everything I'll get to explore.

Grateful for the reason I'm here, too.

I turn, finding Graham standing behind me, silently watching. He pushes off the doorframe, walking into the room with mesmerizing, slow strides. *Is this . . . swagger?* Whatever it is, I'm fixated.

"Do you want to use the Jacuzzi?" He nods toward the glass doors leading out to the balcony. His voice drips with invitation. He's projecting the confidence he had during dinner but—finally, for once—I catch the hint of unsteadiness in his delivery.

It is somehow endearing in ways no swagger ever could be. This man who's been with me countless times is . . . nervous with expectation. He's jittery.

In the next moment, I realize I feel the same way. What's more . . . I love it. I love the shallow hitch in my chest, the pounding of my heart, the charged focus of my mind searching every moment for clues to what'll happen next.

"No," I say. I decide to race headlong into the feeling. "I'd like to put my hands on you. Kiss you. I'd like to do everything with you."

I'm honestly impressed when Graham's eyebrows rise only slightly. Even to me, the question felt like plunging down a roller-coaster drop while forcing myself not to scream.

Which makes me want to push us further. I cock my head, playing curious. "Unless you invited me to your room for something else?"

"No. I didn't." Graham *swaggers* in my direction, recovering his stability. *He's good. He's very good.* He plants his feet in front of me, some inches separating us, like he's showing off his self-control. "I just didn't expect you to be so . . . direct," he says.

Fuck your self-control. I want his heart galloping like mine. I want him stiff in the front of his pants, like when we were dancing. I want him driving his fingernails into his palm to keep himself from ripping the clothes from my body. *I want him to feel like I feel.*

"What?" I whisper. I step up to him, making my limbs soft and seductive. "Was your wife not *direct*?"

He swallows. "She made what she wanted clear," he replies. "Just not quite this frankly."

"Do you like it?" I rasp.

His expression flashes desperately. He nods, his throat bobbing.

I don't even know myself right now. The guttural Eliza cooing to the man in front her while pressure pounds between her legs isn't just in control of Graham—which she is, I know from the ship-wrecked look in his eyes—she's in control of *me*.

I love her. I unleash her.

"Then undress me," I say.

The invitation consumes him. I watch the moment it does. Usually, I undress myself—often quickly, only logistics. We've had sex so many times, removing my shirt or my underwear feels like nothing.

Tonight, it does not feel like nothing. Concert violinists have bowed their instruments with grace outdone by the way Graham's fingers slide under the straps of my dress, removing them delicately from my shoulders, his touch sending shivers down me. Nerves explode in my stomach when, in one impossibly smooth motion, he unzips the zipper, dropping the black pool of my dress to my feet.

I feel Graham go still, lost in the sight of my lingerie.

The moments when I fretted over Nikki's gift, the way every sculpted, lacy hem seemed to laugh in my face, feel like some other life. No one or nothing is laughing now. Graham is silent, his whole existence fixed on the fabric curving perfectly over my hips and chest.

Moving like he's possessed, Graham's hands slide up my sides to my breasts. Then, though, it's *my* Graham who takes over. I know because his gentle fingers find the chain where I've kept my wedding band. He thumbs the rings, noting their presence, the fact I never took them off.

We don't speak, though. We don't have to.

I sit down on the bed, where I work on Graham's belt buckle while he stays standing, his breathing heavy. When my hand brushes the hardness in his pants, which is no surprise but no less exhilarating, he exhales deeply, his eyes fluttering closed.

The excitement we felt on the walk here prodded us with prickling fingers. Now, it's got us firmly in its grip.

His pants fall. Hurriedly, forcing myself not to fumble, I continue to his shirt, unbuttoning with near-frantic eagerness. Exposing the flat stomach I saw poolside, when I didn't want to tear my eyes from him. Now, I'd rather do other things. I kiss him there while I work, finding his hand cupping the curve of my neck in return, his lips finding the top of my head, unimaginably delicate.

Once I've pushed his shirt from his shoulders, I slide back on the bed until I reach the pillows. The lace of the lingerie is impossibly smooth on the sheets. Graham's eyes trace every delicate frill, every stretch where skin peeks through. My chest heaves under the crimson bra. Sometimes, good lingerie makes you feel like you're not wearing anything at all.

I nestle into the pillows, heart pounding. The hushed hotel room, this extravagant underwear—everything contributes to the feeling of *newness*. Like we're really strangers. Like this really is our first time.

I hold on to the feeling hungrily, wrapping myself in our pretense while Graham slides one finger up the outside of my thigh, then drags the underwear down my legs. Somewhere between devotion and desperation, he presses his face into what he's exposed.

When he kisses me deeply—*not* on the mouth—heat explodes in me.

I could lose myself right here. Instead, I fight through the feeling, restraining myself while I grope for inspiration. I want to do something *new*. Something to keep surprising ourselves, to keep this mystique between us.

I grasp on to an idea, and shudder out my order. "I want you to lie down," I say.

Graham looks up, his eyes glazed with desire. He knows exactly what I'm doing. This Eliza is taking charge.

"Tell me what you want. Tell me everything you want." His stare sears into me. "This is our first time—it's important we get it right."

I wonder if he knows how perfectly his words strike on exactly what I'm feeling, like a match swiped on a rough surface hissing into flame. I'm pretty sure he does. He's smirking when he crawls onto the comforter next to me and permits me to gently push him over, until he's lying flat.

Savoring the stretch of him under me, the symmetry of his freckle-scattered chest, the shoulders I'm going to run my hands over, I place my knees on either side of his body. Mesmerized, he moves his hands to the elusive soft skin of my pelvis. It makes me slicker, which he'll know soon enough. Slowly, I move up his body until I'm closer to his face, over him so he can kiss me there again.

His eyes flit to mine momentarily with the spark of comprehension. He knows what I want.

He falls into rhythm immediately, knocking my head backward with one stroke of his tongue. Then abruptly he's gripping me from behind, holding me in place. It is everything. His hands keep me firmly in position exactly where he wants me while waves of pleasure roll over me, dashing every coherent thought in my head into chaotic ecstasy.

The feeling is overwhelming, and my orgasm catches me quickly. His hands hold me, gripping my thighs with the same hunger I feel in me. I shudder into his face, exhaling hard while heat lightning shoots through me.

When finally I still, panting, I look down to find Graham smiling up. Or grinning. No, I decide—some of each. He looks like a man who's just had his mouth where it was. But he looks like a man in love, too.

His hands stay where they were, but softly. He traces one thumb gently up my leg.

"Now what?" His question comes out low, like he's eager for dozens of possible responses.

There's only one I want to give him, though. Still over him, I place my hands on his shoulders, lavishing in the cat-in-the-sun pleasure filling me.

"You tell me," I say.

He doesn't hesitate. He sits up, letting me watch those stomach muscles do swift, seamless work while he pulls me firmly down onto his lap, onto him. I gasp softly even though I know how he'll feel—partly because I'm lost in the pretense that this is really our first time, partly because the contact sends more delicious static into where I'm still sensitive.

Then we're moving together, rocking together. Graham is everywhere, kissing my neck, the tops of my breasts, the curve of my collarbone while our chests come together. It's mind-scattering, dizzying, consuming.

It's the first time we dispense with one piece of our pretense, I recognize distantly. There's no need to confirm birth control when he knows I've been on the pill for years. In every other way, though, it's different. We're running on the edge of this newness together, hand in hand, chasing this electricity we've learned how to create.

Graham tells me what he wants, and tells me again, and again. Wordlessly, he moves us onto our sides. I race to follow, improvising with him, stretching out in mindless pleasure with him behind me while he snakes one hand up my stomach to cup my breast. He's feverish, kissing my back, pressing his face into my neck while he pushes into me. It's a side of him I've never seen, and I don't know how much is character and how much is real.

Either way, I like it. Graham's unleashing something, too. Something I very much desire.

With our rhythm growing fiercer, we lose ourselves entirely in each other.

32

Graham

ONCE I'VE FINISHED—or *we've* finished, her for the second time—I pull her close to me. I pushed myself to last as long as I possibly could, fighting with every movement not to give in. Finally, I couldn't.

Now, lying with her, both our bodies sweat-slicked, I just want to drink Eliza in. The scent of her, the way her disheveled hair spills over her shoulders, the supple flexes every one of her curves makes while she breathes deeply. It's *never* been the way it just was between us. I felt unbelievably *free* to give and take, to chase and lead. The results were . . . well, beyond rewarding.

I send my silent thanks to Investment Banker Graham. He deserves it.

Quickly my thoughts shift from reliving every glorious second of what just happened to figuring out how I can make it happen *again*.

Beside me, Eliza lets out a sated laugh. I roll onto my side to face her. "How do I measure up?" I ask. Pure happiness is making me cocky. I hold the feeling, not wanting the energy between us to flicker even for one relaxed moment.

Eliza chews her lip, her eyes round behind her lashes. "With my ex I never had any complaints," she says, tracing one fingernail up my chest. "But I've also never had sex like that before. You?"

"Me either," I say. I hold her gaze. "Not like that."

Exhilarated, I leap up from the bed. Ordinarily, I'd probably be self-conscious standing in the middle of the room completely naked, but right now, I continue to channel the confidence of my investment banker persona. *He* works out. He regularly has mind-blowing sex. He's like my superhero suit, if the suit came with the superpowers. Shoulders held high, I walk to the balcony doors and push them open.

Conscious of Eliza watching me, I stride to the Jacuzzi, where I flip open the cover.

Behind me, Eliza is giggling. "What are you *doing*?"

I turn to her, feeling the night breeze on my butt. "No one can see us," I reply, gesturing to what is only cliffs and forests all the way to the ocean. Each suite like mine is its own bungalow, out of view of the others.

Eliza says nothing, eyeing the steam rising off the water.

I step in, enjoying the prickling heat enveloping me, then place my folded arms on the rim of the Jacuzzi to face her. "Care to join me?" I ask. I raise an eyebrow in a dare.

Eliza laughs again. Her eyes dart from me out into the night. Watching her, I feel my heart pounding with the same near-painful wild hope coursing in me when we reached my room. After a moment, she stands up with the sheets held around herself, her expression naked with wavering excitement.

With a delighted shriek, she lets the sheets fall behind her. She springs for the door.

She's shivering when she reaches the Jacuzzi, and she quickly lowers herself into the water. Hearts still pounding, we look at each other across the steam. It's perfect—only us, the gentle hum of the Jacuzzi, and the incomprehensible vastness of the night. We're alone together.

Eliza smiles, her cheeks flush with heat.

I lean forward to kiss her. The kiss is slow but not chaste, my lips sticking to hers like honey. Feeling her nakedness under the water, my body responds immediately. I know we'll be getting that second round before too long.

While I return to my bench, my eyes never leave her.

"You're incredible, you know that?" she asks.

Though I return her smile, the compliment feels precarious, like holding sand in cupped palms. I wonder if her words are for *me*, the man she married in the Huntington Gardens two days shy of five years ago, or the character I'm playing. David's point from earlier echoes in my head. What's the difference, in the end? Does it even matter which me she means?

It doesn't, I decide. *If this is who she wants, this is who I'll be.* Doing it might not be easy, but my new resolve suddenly feels like the simplest thing in the world. Because this is Eliza. This is our marriage. I'll do anything to make her happy.

Finding her hand under the water, I pull her to me, the way the new Graham would.

33

Eliza

I WAKE UP before Graham. The sun glows past the crack we left in the curtains, warming the room just enough for coziness. Staring up at him, I remember last night. He held me close while we slept, closer than he has in months. I can't help grinning, realizing what this means.

This is *working*.

The improbability of it only makes me more grateful. In our familiar house, I was shadowed by conversations I couldn't imagine having—interrogations of *what's wrong* and *whose fault* and *now what*. Now, instead, circumstance has delivered us this unique way forward, and we're finally making progress. We're closing the distance between us, reforming connections.

It's thrilling, but for the same reasons, it's terrifying, because we can't keep up this charade forever. Nor would I want to. I don't want to lose this connection, but I don't want to forsake the real Graham either, the one who's never been to Santa Fe. If I focus on this riddle too much, it daunts me—until I remember this pretense was itself the very unforeseen solution to other problems that felt like they couldn't be fixed. We just needed to not give up.

I nestle into Graham, content to relax into this moment before we have to figure out what's next.

My phone vibrates suddenly on the nightstand, jarring me out of my rest. Reaching over to check the screen, I find it's my mom. I dart a glance at the still-sleeping Graham—he looks soundly out, which doesn't surprise me given the night we had. I slip out of bed and quietly shut the bathroom door before picking up the call.

"Mom," I whisper, "if you're calling about Michelle's wedding, I need to remind you I wasn't invited." Unlike the bedroom, the bathroom is chilly, especially because I'm only wearing one of Graham's T-shirts. With the phone held to my ear, I cross my free arm over my chest and sit down on the lip of the massive tub.

"Why are you whispering?" Mom asks.

"Graham is still asleep," I tell her. For the first time, I don't have to lie to my parents about where Graham is. It's a relief.

"Well." I feel my mom change conversational course effortlessly. "Your father invited you," she says.

I exhale quietly. Of course it's one more protracted negotiation on the subject of the goddamn wedding. "You do know that's not good enough," I reply, practically feeling my thumb itch to end the call. "Don't you think Michelle might get a little pissed at you if you invite someone she expressly *doesn't* want at her wedding? We don't have to turn her day into family drama."

"Oh, it's already family drama," my mom announces. I wince. If my dad imagines himself Phil Dunphy on *Modern Family*, my mom drapes herself in the robes of Judge Judy. She loves to play the fearless, fearsome adjudicator, arbiter of the Right Way. It's not necessarily the friendliest quality, even when she eventually apologizes for, oh, declaring *no one these days* gets engaged when they're twenty-three or makes a career in acting. I've never welcomed her relish for picking fights in the guise of "discussion."

"I just wish you both would grow up and have a conversation," she says.

Feeling my chest constrict, I reply coolly. "She can call me anytime she wants, but she won't."

"You're the one who missed her party," my mom returns.

I taste something sour, practically hearing her enjoyment of this *gotcha* moment. Fighting to keep my composure, I focus on the cold bathroom floor under my bare feet. "It's not like I wanted to," I reply patiently, ignoring the fact I've reminded every individual member of my immediate family of this multiple times.

"Does Michelle know that?"

I sigh, pinching my brow. Outside the bathroom, I hear bedsheets rustling. Clenching the phone, I decide I've had enough. "Mom, we have to talk about this another time. Maybe when I'm not on vacation for my *anniversary*."

"Oh, right." Mom suddenly sounds interested, performing magnanimity. Like we're catching up in the produce aisle. "What is it, three years?"

My heart hammers. "*Five*."

She pauses. Enough for respectfulness. "Well, you really need to call your sister. I'm trying here, but I don't understand why you couldn't spare five minutes for her." In my silence—which is sprung of stunned incomprehension, not to mention hurt, of how she just outright ignored me—she goes on. "We have to—"

I find my voice enough to cut in. "Mom—"

"We have to tell the caterer the final head count next week—"

"Mom," I repeat, fraying. *"We'll talk some other time."*

My sharp tone quiets her, but it's a petulant quiet. "Okay. Talk to your sister," she says in parting.

I hang up, clenching my lips together. Part of me feels guilty for snapping, honestly. I can't do this with her. Can't *keep* doing this. Every conversation escalates into a nuclear-weapons stockpile of snide remarks, priorities questioned, misspoken phrases interrogated. So I panic. I shut down. I do what I just did.

Quietly, I set my phone on the marble counter. I'm pretty sure my mom knows Graham and I are on our anniversary trip and chose to disregard this inconvenient fact. Or, I don't know, it's possible she didn't. Either way sucks.

I just want to have my one week of vacation.

Walking out of the bathroom, I find Graham sitting up in bed, scrolling on his phone. His eyes dip to my bare legs for the briefest moment before finding my face. "Everything all right?" he asks. He searches my expression, his voice somewhere in the middle of concerned and casual, like he can tell I'm a little off.

I consider confiding in him, I really do. I feel close to him in ways I haven't in months. It's just . . . I would rather not dwell on this family drama right now. I don't want this feud to distract us. Even more, I don't want our real lives, our real selves, encroaching on this new, still-fragile thing between us. This is working. Why burst our bubble early when we have two days of vacation left? It can wait.

So I school my features into pretense. I put on overworked agitation, the face of someone who's had to get on a call with her office while on vacation. "Just a double-booking client hotel crisis. All fine now," I joke, walking over to him.

Graham's expression flickers, but he doesn't push me to drop my performance. Instead, he reaches for my hand, pulling me into his lap to kiss me. He lays me down, letting the kiss drag on, his fingers lightly stroking my hair spread out on the pillowcase.

"What do you want to do today?" he murmurs into the side of my face.

I want to stay in this moment forever. Right here, in this gorgeous hotel room, with the man I love whispering sweet questions into my ear. At the same time, though, I'm sort of scared to. In every perfect second, I feel the pull of normalcy, the instinct to return to our regular married life. To lapse into familiar patterns, which might just return us to familiar doldrums.

Jumping out of bed, I spring lightly into the hallway, where today's schedule has been slid under the door. What I need to do is keep the day moving. I scan the cream-white paper, looking over the itemized list of the hotel's offerings. It's exactly what I'd hoped. The day is packed with a mix of dating workshop programming and dedicated couples' activities. Nearly every hour is accounted for.

Graham crawls to the edge of the bed, peering around the corner. "Anything you like the look of?" he asks.

I face him, feeling myself glow.

"Everything," I say. "Let's do everything."

34

Graham

WHILE ELIZA GETS dressed, the morning takes on the kind of excited haze I remember from times like this early in our relationship, minus the sculpted modernity of our hotel room. Zipping her up with quick, wordless smiles, bright glances whenever we catch each other's eyes, the breathlessness under our goodbyes in the doorway.

We part for thirty minutes to change before beginning the day's hotel marathon. Eliza didn't offer to bring her luggage over to the suite, nor did I inquire. I think both of us want to draw out this feeling that we're *dating* again.

I head out to wait for Eliza where we agreed, the outdoor couches on the patio overlooking the gorgeous scenery. I don't know if I'm still high from the previous night or if the morning is exceptionally beautiful, the hills drenched in dazzling emerald like some divine Photoshopper cranked up the saturation. I'm excited for the day—first jam making, then couples' yoga, wine tasting, and finally stargazing.

But I'm trying not to be nervous, too.

What we're building is both real and not real, I remind myself. I shared real pieces of myself last night. I'm pretty sure Eliza did, too. Though I'm not certain how I'll continue to meld myself and this other me. When we got here, I couldn't imagine having even one night like the one we just did. I'll figure this out, too.

Because I have to.

I'm working the question over when my phone buzzes in my pocket. Pulling it out, I expect to find Eliza saying she's running late. Instead, I see my mother-in-law's name. My brow furrows. I have a cordial, if distant, relationship with Laura consisting mostly of coordinating dinner plans when Eliza's unreachable in the studio.

> Hey Graham! I hope you're having a
> nice trip. Just texting to get your meal
> preference for Michelle's wedding. Fish
> or chicken?

I blink. This message is incomprehensible to me. Not literally, of course, but in its very presence. As far as I know, we never received an invitation to Michelle's wedding. With her and Eliza on the outs, I figured we weren't going. If Laura's hitting me up while I'm celebrating my anniversary with her daughter, wondering if I want the fish or chicken, then I'm missing some key details.

Furthermore, if she's asking me instead of Eliza, it's probably because, for whatever reason, Eliza's not responding. Laura has turned to me just like we're planning dinner while Eliza is in the studio.

Or Eliza *is* responding, but not the way Laura wants.

Of course.

This, I realize, was the whispered phone call Eliza took in the bathroom this morning. The reason for her strained demeanor when she came back out. Eliza struggles with her relationship with her mom, I know from having listened supportively to impassioned accounts of my wife's insecurities and resentments on plenty of car rides home from evenings with her family. I remember now the times I've seen the rattled, drawn, deer-in-the-headlights look she had this morning.

The implications of this suck some of the spirit out of me. Eliza is evidently going through something, something she doesn't yet have the heart, or the strength, or something, to share with me.

I type out my reply, telling Laura I'll check with Eliza, then stare out over the hills. This means we have more work to do, I realize with the inching illumination of the sun climbing up the hills. *I* have more work to do, becoming not just someone who can charm her into my Jacuzzi, but someone who Eliza feels she can confide in. Helping her recognize we can be completely real with each other, even while playing these parts. It won't be easy, but I'm not giving up.

In fact, after last night, I'm more determined than ever.

"Hey, ready?"

I look over, finding Eliza walking up to me, dressed in athleisure and heartbreakingly pretty. Everything about her is relaxed, content.

"Ready," I say, and I am.

35

Eliza

MY STOMACH FEELS uneasy when we walk into couples' yoga. It's not just from the quantity of preserves I tasted on little toasts, either. The preserves, for the record, were delicious.

What's upsetting me is the lingering echo in my head of the call this morning with my mom. Right now, I feel like the wonderful synchrony I've found with Graham these past few days is sculpted out of sand, not stone. One gentle push could send it collapsing into nothing.

One push like the prying reminders of one relationship I can't seem to fix.

Graham, fortunately, has been wonderful—if he understands something is up with me, which the shadow flitting over his expression when I left the bathroom in his suite said he maybe does—he's been nothing but boyish bravado and eager reassurance this morning.

Still, I'm nervous. I want to just stay with Graham in the private climate of this getaway. The problem of my sister's wedding is threatening to pull me out. No delectable boysenberry spreads could distract me from what's waiting for me outside this hotel.

I hate how much it scares me.

The yoga class is being held outside, on one of the grassy slopes. Impulsively, I reach for Graham's hand.

He entwines his fingers with mine. It's impossibly reassuring, like he's somehow literally wrung the toxic tension out of me.

"You good?" he murmurs, leaning toward my ear.

"Yeah," I reply, feeling it for the first time since the call.

Right then, a woman in a Treeline Resort yoga top approaches us. "Please take a mat and find a seat wherever is comfortable," she says, smiling. "I'm Trish."

"I'm Eliza. This is my—this is Graham." I catch myself.

Graham notices. I'm undoubtedly the only one who can read the meaning in the slight movement of his head. His smile catches the hint of knowing humor, like he wishes I'd blurted out *This is my Graham* instead. I nearly laugh myself.

"How long have you two been together?" she asks.

I grab on to the chance to restore some of the spontaneity between me and Graham, to take the pressure off. To return myself to the private world where I feel comfortable, not the one pervaded by the pressure of my family.

"We just met here on vacation, actually," I reply.

Trish brightens. "Oh, how romantic. Most of our participants have been together for years. I love that you two are only just finding your connection."

Graham squeezes my hand. It's one of those moments where the simple, quick gesture says something words can't. He reaches for two mats, then walks a few feet away to unroll them while Trish glides past us to greet the next group.

I join Graham right in the middle of the class. He's stretching, clearly taking this yoga thing seriously. Part of me wonders if he's trying to invite me to do the same—saying, *whatever's on your mind, let's get distracted together.*

"Partner yoga not only can help with stretching and strengthening," Trish explains, coming to the front of the group. "When done with a romantic partner, yoga can help deepen a couple's connection in communication, trust, grounding—even sexual desire. Exercise and arousal are similar physiological experiences, after all."

I watch the effect this has on my fellow participants. Part of me is just curious to people-watch the group, who do not disappoint—the older woman who harrumphs good-naturedly, the good-looking men younger than us who exchange smiles glowing with insinuation, the wife in expensive yoga wear who grimaces when her husband in his golf clothes plants his hands in his pockets. But part of me is wondering whether I'll find my fragile hopefulness mirrored in other guests.

I don't. Plucking up my confidence once more, I face forward.

"Sit back-to-back in sukhasana," Trish instructs us from the front of the group.

Never having done yoga before, I don't recognize the terminology. I wait for Trish to demonstrate the pose with her partner, the young woman who's joined her on their mats. They sit cross-legged, facing opposite directions, spine to spine, postures perfectly aligned.

Graham has lined the mats up end to end. Following the group, I position my back against his.

The feeling of him jumbles me up. The contours of his muscles make me remember when I stared, watching him walk cavalierly from our—from *his* bed to the Jacuzzi, not to mention remembering everywhere my hands roamed last night and everywhere I want them to in nights to come.

I want to match the ease I feel in his posture. The depth of his breathing, the low slope of his shoulders.

Despite how kind he's been, despite the perfect conditions of the sage-scented Big Sur breeze rolling over us, I can't. I'm certain Graham feels the sharp stiffness of my posture. I'm guessing he knows it's not entirely the product of good yoga form.

"Breathe together," Trish tells us. "Focus on your grounding."

I close my eyes, concentrating on the movement of Graham's back behind me. I work on timing my breaths with his, letting our rib cages expand together. But we're out of rhythm. *I'm* out of rhythm. Whenever I start focusing on finding our flow, questions of my mom, Michelle, the wedding, nudge me in delicate places, distracting me from the calm I'm chasing.

I try not to let the desynchrony frustrate me. Not being frustrated is kind of the point of yoga, I think. Within a couple minutes, we start to find our harmony.

Right then, of course, Trish introduces the next pose, moving on to some seated swaying movements designed to stretch our spines. I reach outward like she's doing, letting Graham clasp my forearms.

He helps me move, bending over from side to side like we're supposed to. But somehow, the movements don't feel natural like they did when we danced. I feel myself resisting his pressure. When it's my turn to stretch him, I'm relieved the pressure isn't on me to perform relaxation.

"Now stand," Trish instructs. "In these next poses, you're going to work on balancing with each other."

Do they want this stuff to be some sort of metaphor? Renewing my resolve, I stand with Graham, who silently imitates Trish's movements with her partner.

Unlike in the previous exercises, we're now facing each other. I can feel Graham trying to meet my gaze, his eyes like flashlights searching for survivors under rubble.

It's just . . . too much. I skirt his stare, embarrassed by my own evasiveness. I can't help it—I'm proud of how I've worked this week to open up, but right now, I feel myself putting up distance.

Frustrating, familiar distance.

We end up pulling the poses off well enough, but honestly, it's discouraging how disconnected—how frankly unsexy—everything is. Our inelegantly synchronized movements must look more like airport security than yoga. Wobbling on our mats, I feel distinctly uncoordinated and out of touch.

In fact, with the way we're struggling to connect, it's like we really did only just get together, unlike the other couples surrounding us, most of whom seem comfortably in tune with each other. We've spent the week pretending we don't know each other, but right now we don't have to pretend. Regret courses through me. If I'd only not answered my phone this morning, I could be in the moment with him.

The instructor calls for one partner to go into balasana, or child's pose, while the other stands behind them to lean on their back. Graham and I pause, indecisive for a moment before he folds himself over into the restful pose. I stand over him, preparing to bend forward the way Trish showed us, my cheeks starting to flush. Not the good kind of flush, either. How is this so uncomfortable? So dysfunctional? Nevertheless, I gamely reach forward, leaning the way we're supposed to.

Unfortunately, I end up startling Graham, who jerks a little, causing my hand to slip. I very nearly bust my chin on his shoulder. Instead, we lurch together, my stomach pressed precariously to his back.

Of course, right then Trish walks by, smiling magnanimously. "If you two aren't up for the more intimate poses, don't worry," she says. "You're still early in your relationship, still finding your connection. Don't overextend. Why don't you sit in sukhasana and focus on your connection? Feel each other and really breathe together."

While she couldn't have spoken more gently, the suggestion makes embarrassment flame hotter in me. I have searing flashbacks to my freshman seminar professor, who in front of my entire cohort informed me the Juliet I was proud of was "devoid of romance." Noticing the other couples balancing smoothly, I muster up my effort to keep frustration from seizing hold of me.

I'm grateful when Graham replies from where he's kneeling with more patience than I could have managed. "We'll stay with the class, thanks. Eliza," he continues, "why don't we switch positions?"

I withdraw, letting him stand up. I'm honestly a little surprised he wants to continue, with what a nervous mess I obviously am. Kneeling in front of him, I press my forehead to the mat. When Graham's hands press into my back, I congratulate myself for not flinching in surprise. He shifts his weight forward gently, stretching my spine. It feels good, if strenuous.

Suddenly, his face is near mine. His scent is everywhere. He exhales—like he did last night, when he was close enough to press his lips to my neck, close enough for his breathing to play with my hair. *This* close. While he doesn't do those things now, the moment is surprisingly intimate, the signals in my body chaotically confusing.

"You have to listen to each other," Trish says. "Hear each other's limits and work within them."

Graham's hands walk down my back, elongating my tendons pleasantly. "More," I tell him.

"My pleasure," Graham exhales, which leads me to consider my word choice.

"Oh, very mature," I reply, nevertheless warming with my unintentional insinuation. It is not the heat of embarrassment. Who knows—maybe what I said was a subconscious slip instead of poor phrasing. "I meant, you can press harder," I clarify.

He does. The sweet burn of pleasure fills me—momentarily. The next second, my mind snags once more on what's waiting for me. Michelle. The wedding. How I'll probably forever be the maid of dishonor in my family. My muscles clench, turning Graham's massaging presses into pounding strain.

Graham obviously notices. I feel his hands leave my back, ending the pleasant pull of the stretch. He sits down on the mat behind me.

Unfurling, I look over my shoulder, my heart racing with uncertainty. I wish I didn't feel this way. But part of me is glad he withdrew. If we try to be flirty, to have fun, and I *still* can't pull myself from what's distracting me, it might hurt worse than not trying in the first place.

Graham, I'm relieved to see, is eyeing me with playful patience. "You know, we *did* just meet," he says. "Maybe the instructor's right. We can feel out our connection first before jumping into the other stuff."

Ignoring how every other couple here is finding their balance in the new pose under the gorgeous, cloudless sky on this hillside—ignoring my disappointment in myself—I sit, crossing my legs, facing him.

The other instructor, the woman who is not Trish, comes over to us. She places our hands on each other's legs. "Eye contact," she says encouragingly.

We follow her instruction. Finally, I stare into Graham's eyes. It's impossible not to see the feelings coursing in his emerald irises— so profound, so loving. My instinct is once more to divert, to withdraw, even when forced into this ironically tranquil standoff.

But when we refuse to break each other's gaze, something . . . starts to happen. Our breathing evens. Our movements start to synchronize, chests rising and falling in unison. Like parts of one whole.

I don't notice when the instructor guides us gently into clasping hands for side-to-side twisting motions. In fact, *everything* starts to disappear—the clear sky, the mats, the grass, the whole world shrinking down into my rhythm with Graham. We never drop our eye contact. Sweat springs to my skin, not just from the movements.

With my gaze locked with Graham's, I feel our charade crumbling, feel myself looking into the eyes of my husband once more. We move together, sweat-slicked arms sliding in unison, chests heaving, and I'm not prepared for the vulnerability. With each stretch, each exchange of straining muscles and skin on skin, I feel like I'm physically pulling inner parts of myself forward, exposing my soul to the sunlight. Like the stretching, it's strenuous, even sometimes searing.

I register my own instinctive reaction to what's happening—I want to hide. I want to let those pieces retreat into their interior walls.

But I don't. I make myself stand naked in the day, because Graham is with me. We exhale in unison, our movements fluid. I have to fight tears from springing to my eyes while Graham holds my gaze, his grip on me tightening. For months, I found him unreadable, impossible to decipher. Now, it's easy, even innate. I can feel his feelings, how he's urging me to stay with him, to be bare. To keep my emotions exposed instead of masking them in performance. Not just of Vacation Planner Eliza, either. Longer performances, deeper ones. Someone who's fine when her marriage, her relationship with her sister, start to suffer.

I'd normally be uncomfortable with this openness. Instead, it's tiring, but—wonderful.

I lose track of how long we hold these poses with each other. Eventually, the class ends. I'd only envisioned this morning yoga session would be something invigorating in our day together, but it's become something more. I feel genuinely peaceful.

We start to walk up from the grass, hand loosely in hand. Instead of stopping myself, I speak up.

"Hey," I say to Graham, who looks over. He's calm. I feel the same way, I realize, not because what I'm going to say is effortless, but because, right now, I'm suspended in the unfamiliar conviction that it'll be okay. "It—wasn't a work thing this morning. It was my mom calling. She wanted to know if I'm coming to my sister's wedding."

I pause. Graham stops with me, his hand not leaving mine. He nods. My heart is pounding, but my breathing comes evenly, my face cool in the morning breeze. Sometimes, I think to myself, spontaneity doesn't look like prix fixe menus or feigned boxing experience. Sometimes it looks like this, true honesty toward the person you trust most in the world.

Graham is waiting for me to go on, letting me decide what to say. So I do. "I don't want to discuss it right now, not while I'm on vacation, but . . . I wanted you to know that it's on my mind," I say.

There's nothing prying or uncertain in Graham's expression.

"Thank you for telling me," he says. "We don't have to talk about it until you want to."

I nod, feeling inexpressibly light. I say nothing more, not because I'm hiding or because I don't know how, but simply because there's nothing more I *need* to say. With Graham's response, I'm starting to feel like there's a way to let him into my problems without letting them consume everything—proof I didn't know I desperately needed.

Together, we walk up the hill into the sunlight.

36

Graham

I STAND UNDER the spa's unfairly good shower, letting the water soothe me. Yoga was intense. It's hard for me to describe or entirely understand what happened, but something did. I felt something shift while we looked into each other's eyes. I felt her realize I was there for her, both in and outside this game.

It was real, not just the pretense we've performed for the last few days. It was only me and Eliza.

She'll tell me more when she's ready. If she doesn't, I have to do my part, too—I have to ask. I just have to show her I'm there for her, for everything she's going through. It's what I hope I communicated today. It was a step in the right direction. A step back to us.

We both brought fresh clothes to change into, knowing there wouldn't be much time between showering and wine tasting. In the elegant, wood-paneled bathroom, I shave and permit myself to enjoy the range of bougie skincare products. I throw on my jacket—the charcoal topcoat Eliza got me—over my turtleneck.

When I exit into the lounge, I find Eliza waiting. She's tucked her black sweater into a high-waisted dusty pink skirt over black tights. Small gold earrings dangle on her ears. With her hair up in a sleek ponytail, she looks fantastic.

Fantastic, and impatient.

"Did you try *every* product in there?" she jokes. "How could I have possibly gotten ready before you?"

I smile. "Hi. You look beautiful." She rolls her eyes, looking pleased. "And yes," I go on. "I did. You'll be thanking me later when you feel how smooth my face is."

Eliza folds her lips to hide her grin. "Oh yeah? Why is that, exactly?"

I sweep in, kissing her smoothly on the lips. "You know why," I say close to her ear. I feel her shiver, no doubt remembering where my face was last night.

Playing it cool, I withdraw my hand, then walk without hesitation out of the spa and head toward the wine tasting. I'm not a huge wine guy, but Eliza was adamant we do everything on the hotel's agenda. I don't mind, of course. Still, what I'm really looking forward to is the stargazing later tonight.

In the crisp early evening, I'm glad for my coat. The sun is starting to set, the daylight fading into the purple-orange umber of dusk. We cross the patio to the main hotel, where we ride the elevator up to the rooftop. The space is normally closed for private events, but Eliza explained the wine tasting was being put on by the dating workshop as a celebration for its final night.

In the cramped elevator, my hand finds the small of Eliza's back with possessiveness I don't restrain. Saying nothing, Eliza leans into my touch nearly imperceptibly. Just enough for me to know she likes the gesture.

The doors open. The view is stunning, momentarily stopping me in the elevator. The sprawl of the hills looks like it's pulled from landscape paintings, everything colored in warm olive or swathed in deep forest green. In the dusk, every contour of the cascading mountains and slope of the countryside is in focus. High walls of glass enclose the terrace itself, where small decorative trees stand, decked with lights like the restaurant downstairs.

Only Eliza walking forward—out of my grip—helps me remember to follow her.

We walk to the hostess's podium, where we join the line of people waiting, then charge the wine tasting to our rooms. While I'm signing the bill, the hostess hands us name tags and pens to write our names, no doubt some formality of the workshop.

Glancing over, I'm caught short for a moment. I notice Eliza's drawn a small circle instead of the dot on the *i* in her name. From years of grocery lists and birthday cards, I know my wife's steep, professorial handwriting well enough to be certain Eliza does *not* colorfully dot her i's.

The next moment, I realize what she's doing. I remember how jarring her modulated Vacation Planner Eliza voice was. She's matching the effect in handwriting.

Smiling, I make sure to add a sharp right angle to the usual curl of my capital G.

I stick on my name tag and follow Eliza toward the tasting. Reaching the terrace, though, I falter. This does not resemble the other wine tastings in my limited experience. Two-person tables run in one perfectly straight row down the length of the terrace. No one is seated yet. In confusion, I glance to Eliza.

"Hey, what are you two doing here?"

I recognize David's voice immediately. Turning, I find our friend, looking jubilant like usual.

"We're here for the wine tasting," I reply.

David's brow furrows. "You know it's not just wine tasting, right?" His eyes flit briefly to Eliza, then back to me. "It's wine tasting," he says, "while speed dating."

I round on Eliza. She must have known. She had the schedule.

Unbothered, she shrugs. "It's not like we have to participate. We're just here for the wine tasting."

I hide my satisfaction, knowing the prospect of speed dating wouldn't ruffle Investment Banker Graham in the least. Inquisitive, I face David. "Wait, what are you doing here? Where's your soul mate?"

David claps one reassuring hand on my shoulder. "This isn't supposed to be *real* setups," he says encouragingly, like he's explaining you get green when you mix blue and yellow paint together. "It's one of the workshop's exercises. Everyone here is returning home to different cities in the next couple days. It's just for practice, and I need all the practice I can get before my first solo date with Lindsey tomorrow."

I straighten, genuinely excited for him. "You asked her out?"

Impossibly, David's grin widens. "I did. Dinner tomorrow, my last night here."

Our conversation is halted when an older woman walks into the center of the terrace, ringing a handheld bell. "We're going to begin now," she says. "Half of you, please sit on the left side of these tables. The rest of you will float from table to table when I ring this bell."

"I'll go tell her we're just here for the wine tasting," I say to Eliza under my breath.

When she looks up, the glow in her gray eyes is intoxicating. I could lose myself in their fog, drifting on their oceans forever. "Or . . ." she begins, the syllable heavy with suggestion.

"Or what, Eliza?" I prompt skeptically.

"Or you could trust me."

I know I'm done for. I prod her playfully, nevertheless. "We made very clear rules on the subject of dating other people."

She squeezes my hand. "I know. It'll be fun," she promises. "We won't talk to anyone else."

I eye her, pretty sure this is the exact opposite of the premise of speed dating. "How, exactly?" I ask.

But I get no clarification. The woman rings her bell, sending the crowd into motion. David steps right past us with more smiles.

With Eliza's hand still clutched in mine, I don't move. I'm fighting the doubts I couldn't help but indulge for most of the day. Vague reassurances notwithstanding, it's hard not to imagine this is Eliza once more skittering to distance, to performance, to the pretend comfort of casual, no-strings-attached acquaintance.

But when I look in her eyes, I see she's not. I hold her gaze, seeing in her imploring expression the same thing I did during yoga. She's not hiding—she's asking me a question.

"Okay," I say.

Her shoulders relax in relief. The corners of her mouth start to lift.

"But if this gets weird," I go on, "we're leaving. I have no interest in dating anyone else. Nor does Investment Banker Graham."

Eliza smiles. "I'm glad to hear it."

Releasing her hand, I walk toward the tables. I feel like I'm entering some sort of gladiatorial scenario, though I doubt Rome's fighters had the pleasures of rooftop views or twinkle-lighted trees.

Joining my compatriots, men and women, on the left side of the tables, I hover over the open chairs. The choice of table feels simultaneously critical and completely unimportant. While I hesitate, Eliza's words replay on a loop in my head. *Trust me.*

Done hesitating, I sit, watching her from across the room.

37

Eliza

WHEN THE MODERATOR rings the bell, I sit down opposite Graham, obviously.

"Nice to meet you," I say. "I'm Heather."

His eyebrow rises. It is delightful. Honestly, the entire thing is delightful, this spectacular view, the perfect chill of the evening, how *good* he looks in this unlikely turtleneck-topcoat situation. The waiter comes over, serving us the first wine. It's white, deliciously sharp on my tongue when I take my first sip.

"What are you doing?" Graham asks.

Knowing I owe him an explanation, I swallow. I remember everything in our real lives waiting for us in just a couple precious days. "I just . . . don't want to put pressure on ourselves yet," I reply, dropping "Heather's" voice.

Graham's eyes cloud. Not with resistance, though. He's trying to work with me. "You know we can't do this forever," he says.

"I don't want to do it forever," I reply immediately, starting to hear the strain in my voice. I'm not pleading, not exactly—not yet. "Just a little longer."

Graham pauses, pensive. I wait, wildly hopeful, wondering if he's hearing in his head what I told him earlier. *Trust me.*

He tastes his wine, then looks up, his eyes sparkling. "Hi, Heather. I'm Liam. What do you do for a living?"

"Really?" I sip from my glass. "That's your opening line?"

Meeting my gaze, Graham smirks. I sort of knew he would. You don't get to be a litigator without a competitive streak. "You have a better one?" he asks.

I consider for a moment. "How important is love to you?" I counter.

"More important than anything," he replies unhesitatingly.

I narrow my eyes, putting on skepticism. "Anything?" I press him.

"More important than a job, or where I live," he says.

I have to smile, recognizing he's referencing our game, our first pieces of character construction. What's more, there's tenderness in what he's saying, romance in his references. Santa Fe Graham loves me. San Diego Graham loves me.

I'm opening my mouth to say the same when the bell rings.

"People on my right, take your wine glasses and move to the next table," the leader instructs.

I stand swiftly. Perusing my eyes over the tables, I make like I'm going to walk away. To my left, someone veers in Graham's direction. Abruptly, I turn back and drop into my old seat before the other person can.

I change my voice once more—perkier, the voice I use for characters in their early twenties. "Hi. I'm Alex," I say. "What do you want your life to look like in five years?"

Slowly, Graham grins, catching on to my ploy. He enthusiastically plays along, answering my questions while fabricating an entirely new persona. He's a screenwriter—then a surgeon. He inquires what my dream date is (drive-in movie), whether I prefer brunch or dinner (brunch), where my favorite place to travel would be (Venice). Not only is it fun and easy, I'm moved by the genuine care Graham puts into each question.

Every time the bell rings, I stand up, do my best impression of someone leaving the table for other dating pastures—then promptly return, making sure no one else claims my spot. I pay no mind to the confused glares I elicit.

We do this for four rounds. Four glasses of wine. The constant character reinvention is a new level of our game, and while exhausting, it's a hell of a lot of fun. Like memorizing lines all night with your best friend, lapsing into sleep-deprived laughter over your scripts.

When I sit down for round five, I start in like usual. "Hi, I'm . . ."

I stop. For the first time, no new name comes. I've forgotten my lines. I'm blank. Except, with Graham watching me, smiling half-expectantly, what I'm feeling isn't the onstage terror of having misplaced the beginning of my soliloquy—heart racing, palms coated in sweat. It's something deeper, more fragile, more fundamental. I push myself, working with desperate hope to find my next personality.

Preempting me, Graham sticks out his hand.

"Hi," he says. "I'm Graham. I live in San Diego and I'm a lawyer. It's wonderful to meet you."

My eyes widen a little. Then I feel my expression soften. It's unexpected—which is itself something I'm starting to expect. Graham is being spontaneous, even courageous. He's putting himself out there, his real self. It's not how I envisioned this evening, but it's incredibly endearing. "Hi, Graham," I say, taking his hand. "I—" I hesitate, hitching for a second on this new direction. But I press on. "I also live in San Diego. I'm a voice actress. It's nice to meet you, too." My voice is my own, the one I said I would marry him with, the voice I read my vows with. It feels like breathing.

His eyes never leave mine. "Are you having a nice time?" he asks.

"I am." I smile, my fingers rolling the stem of my wineglass. "My date has been wonderful company. He's really incredible." I feel my gaze warm, the pull in my heart of how deeply I mean my words—what I wished I'd helped him to believe before.

He hears me. He understands me, I know he does. He's glowing like the lights strung on the rooftop. "I'm glad to hear it," Graham replies. "Do you like voice acting?"

"I love it," I say, gathering momentum. Relaxing into myself. "I just landed the job for this new book by Katrina Freeling and Nathan Van Huysen. I can't wait to record."

Graham drains his glass. His eyes sparkle.

"Tell me about it," he says. "Tell me everything."

I do. The current of conversation sweeps me forward effortlessly, into the parts of my job I love, the details of my days, the things I'm looking forward to. Graham leans forward, listening carefully, asking more questions. While I speak, I gradually figure out why exactly this feels right. It's personal, this return to my real self. And it's partnership, this give-and-take with Graham, with my husband. I'm me, and we're us.

Of course, the bell rings. When I start to get up, Graham reaches out and takes my hand.

"Let's get out of here," he says.

I still. With a gentle smile on my lips, I nod. My fingers tighten on his, and when I stand, I pull him with me.

38

Graham

IN THE ELEVATOR down, Eliza's fingers find mine. We don't speak, though not for lack of something to say. In fact, I feel more conversation, more questions, ready and waiting on my tongue.

What's stopping me is only giddy expectation. Not wanting to disturb the perfect momentum of now. It has its own sweetness, this conversational pause—something, frankly, not unlike the walk down to my room last night. We know the silence is only prelude, not some endless expanse past the coda.

We grab premade sandwiches from the hotel café, our interactions still passing only in quick smiles exchanged and gentle touches. Once we've finished this short, practical dinner, we get onto one of the hotel golf carts circulating for the night's event. When Eliza puts her hand in my lap, the patio beginning to recede behind us, the gesture feels quietly meaningful. I place my hand over hers.

We're driven up one of the ridges, leaving the lights of the hotel far behind us. In the dark, the grasses on the hillside sway, hard to make out except for the sense of motion and the cast of the moonlight on them. It's quiet out here like the hotel isn't, the hum of the golf cart practically disappearing into the vacuum of rustling plants and the night wind. Our cart climbs higher, winding up the path.

When Eliza shivers, I put my arm around her. In my head, I keep seeing the way her face lit up the more I asked what she loved about her job. It was—magical. Like spinning thread from the fabric of our lives into gold. I should have asked her those questions every day just to see her react the way she did, the gleam in her eyes.

Deep down, I'm ashamed for having ever stopped. I know why I did. I felt like I knew what she would say, like there was nothing new to discover. But what does that matter? Absolutely nothing, I've realized. I'm not marshaling evidence for one of my cases, not hunting for clues like some dauntless private investigator. I'm doing it because her answers are a joy to hear over and over.

After fifteen minutes of following the mountain road with only the small headlights guiding us, the cart parks next to several others from the hotel. Eliza and I get off. My arm doesn't leave her waist for even a moment. Near the edge of the cliff, one of the hotel guides stands, gesturing to the sky. Eliza and I join the group.

Immediately, we look up. The expanse stretching over us is . . . stunning. Dizzying, even. The night is perfectly clear, stars splayed out in every direction. The darkness itself is rippled with color in ways you don't see in the city, streaked with deep purples and blues like running watercolors.

But it's the band of light directly overhead to which the guide points us. This, the guide explains, isn't just the endless scattershot of stars. It's the Milky Way. Our own galaxy, our cosmic neighborhood. It is otherworldly—one dark slash down the starlit sky, spitting out stars in its wake in an opal kaleidoscope of color.

Holding Eliza, we stare up together. The feeling is profound, of seeing our galaxy from one of the vast spreads of planets in its swirl. It's the rarest of gifts—the opportunity to view something from within it. This kind of perspective isn't something you see every day, but sometimes, you find yourself on a hilltop, immeasurably grateful for the chance.

While the guide points out constellations, Eliza and I don't speak. We don't have to. Holding my wife close, our connection feels undeniable, invisible yet present, like gravity.

Underneath the constellations, I feel the hugeness of the universe. Hundreds of billions of stars form the Milky Way, and while I can't make them out individually, what they create together lights up the sky. It's wondrous. I could look into this sky every single night and still find new views, new unexplored worlds overhead. Eliza's vibrant expression dances through my head, her eyes illuminated like the reach of the galaxy—how much more of *her* is there left to uncover?

I want to know. I want to spend the rest of my life finding out. I want to see her in every light, to study her under clear skies like this one, to see the sunshine of her joys, to wipe her tears in thunderstorms.

Eliza turns to face me like she's thinking the same thing—or maybe she isn't, I don't know. Not yet. In the quiet of the starry night, I kiss her like we're starting over.

39

Eliza

WE RETURN TO Graham's room. Except now, while he holds the door for me, I notice it's begun to feel more like *our* room. Like I'm meant to be here instead of just choosing to be. I like both feelings, but in the moment, I nurture this one.

When the door closes behind us, we don't turn on the lights, leaving the room shadowed in starlight from the wide windows. We didn't discuss coming back here when stargazing ended. The conclusion was foregone. But for whatever reason, I'm nervous in ways I wasn't expecting, my pulse beginning to pick up while I follow Graham down the entry hallway. I don't know why—we had sex here *last night*, wild, fantastic sex. Not to mention what went on in the hot tub. Today was perfect in different ways, counter to the game we've been playing but, unpredictably, exactly what I needed.

Still, reaching the darkened living room, I shiver. Graham slings his jacket onto the nearby chair, then slowly walks up to me.

He stops close enough to kiss me, to put his hands on my body.

But he does neither. He only looks—no, stares—holding my gaze. He's half in shadow, the lines of the windows cutting his features into pieces of him.

I feel my heart pounding. It's intoxicating, so I let myself lean into the rush, lifting one hand to his chest. On the cliffside, the guide noted we were just one system on one spindle of the Milky Way. Right now, I feel like the center of the galaxy.

Graham's eyes follow my movement, then return to my face. It's impossible to miss the quiet explosion of heat in his gaze, like my first touch, even over the fabric of his sweater, suddenly ignited unconcealable hunger for more. It makes my breathing go uneven, goose bumps rising on my skin.

With the same fusion of boldness and restraint, he reaches forward to run his fingers up my arm.

I can hold myself on this precipice no longer. My question comes out whispered. "What do you want?"

Graham looks right into my eyes. Then he steps forward, his hand moving with featherlight fingers to my neck, my cheeks. I lean forward, unable to stop myself, feeling like my skin is searing from the molten core underneath. Graham's hand moves to cup my chin, his thumb gentle on my jaw.

"I want to be with my wife," he says.

There isn't only desire in his voice, though there *is* desire, unhidden. It mingles with yearning so deep it pulls my heart to him. In the moment, I realize he's exactly right. It was the perfect thing to say. It *is* the perfect thing to be. While he watches me intently, intimately, I nod, letting myself slip into the real us. There's no more pretense now. Lifting myself onto my toes, I kiss him.

His mouth moves with mine in the way it has hundreds of times. It's familiar, like a well-learned dance. The continuation of a kiss we've been having for years. But right now, I'm the furthest thing from tired of the motions—I enjoy every step of this dance, leading, following, joining with him. Moving from my face, his hand slides into my hair, drawing me nearer, our bodies fitting together.

Then he's moving his lips to my neck, his hands to my waist, where they slip under my skirt to pull the garment and tights down, past the hem of my tucked-in sweater. When skin meets skin, I hear myself exhale sharply from the quiet rush.

His hands rise, gently clutching the sweater's hem to pull it seamlessly up and over my head. The exposure is exhilarating— while he's fully clothed, I'm standing in front of him in only my underwear, painted in moonlight.

This contrast clearly works the same effect on my husband. With new intensity, he stares. I don't shy away, watching him take in the curves of my bare skin. Then suddenly he's bending down, hands underneath my thighs, lifting me off the ground. I embrace his neck, clinging to him while he walks us both to the bed in the dark.

He lowers me, laying me on the cloudlike comforter so tenderly I feel tears prick my eyes. Now he unzips his pants and pulls off his shirt, moving with sharp efficiency, like he refuses to languish one unnecessary moment before getting closer to me. Moving gently, he joins me on the sheets, his eyes like worlds of expectation.

I meet his gaze in the moonlight, knowing which Graham I'm seeing. This is the man I shared coffee with on our first date, whose law school graduation I captured with eager iPhone photos, who listened to my recordings with wonder written on his expression. It's the Graham I know, my husband, looking desperate for me like he's been on so many nights.

What's more, it is exactly who I want. Not the handsome stranger I met on vacation, who's been wonderful to me over the past few days. I don't need the character—I need *him*.

I strip off my underwear, laying myself bare for him. His eyes follow my every movement like he's memorizing them. He probably is—I know I'm inscribing on my pounding heart every flicker of lust in his features.

When I'm entirely naked, my body stretched out wanting on the bed, Graham wastes no time. He's over me in one swift, seamless motion, one controlled swing of coordinated shoulders and flexed stomach, pinning me with his kiss into the comforter. He starts with my mouth, drinking me in, then moves with impossible gentleness to my cheek, my jaw, my neck.

My breathing begins to heave, the tops of my breasts brushing against his chest while he continues to decorate my skin with kisses. In the starlight, we're rhythm in motion, hunger made human. I reach down, half instinct, half daring, to grasp him. It earns me the softest of disarmed sounds from him while he pauses in kissing me, smothering his face in my hair.

His whole body ripples with expectation while I guide him where I want. Where we want.

When he fills me, we gasp together. I close my eyes, tipping my head back, letting Graham hold my wrists up over my head. I'm ready to surrender to the swirl of nameless feelings, of sound without words, to vanish into the collective current where there's no him or me—only us.

But when my eyelids flutter open, I find Graham's gaze fixed on mine. I understand immediately, implicitly, the tender need in his eyes, past the craving for my body. He doesn't want only us. He wants *me*—the way I wanted my husband instead of his character. He wants to be with his wife.

So I give her to him. I don't shy. I don't put up walls. Holding his stare, I stay here with him, myself, even though it's nearly *too* intimate. I take with every movement he gives, give for everything he needs. We move together deliciously slowly, with more than hunger now—with love. In my eyes, tears of joy glisten.

Graham rocks inside me while I roll my hips with his, his forehead pressed to mine. When he releases one of my wrists to caress the underside of my leg, I reach up to hold his neck. Saying, *I'm here with you. You, Graham.*

It's different from last night, but perfect in its own way. Instead of losing ourselves in the heat, the pounding rush of feeling, we're deeply, profoundly present. I'm caught up in the sensation of nothing left between us. No games, no distance.

It's only us.

40

Graham

ON THE MORNING of our anniversary, I wake up with the rising sun. Instinctively, I reach for my wife next to me.

For the first time on this trip, my hand doesn't find only the cool sheets of my otherwise empty bed. Eliza is there. I shift onto my side, finding her breathing slowly, the morning light setting her soft skin to glowing. With my chest full of raw happiness, I pull her close.

She wakes just enough to settle herself more comfortably onto me before promptly dozing off. She smells like her—my favorite version of her scent, no shampoo, nothing of the day. The moment is everything.

I stroke her hair, remembering waking up on this day five years ago. We broke the rules and spent the night before our wedding together, neither of us wanting to be without the other. But when we woke up, Eliza made me promise not to open my eyes.

She kissed me with my eyes closed. She did *more* with my eyes closed. While she took her time, I pictured the woman who would, in only hours, become my wife—pictured and pictured.

I wasn't nervous on the morning of our wedding. Despite our youth, I went into our marriage with nothing but confidence in our decision. While I never imagined we would reach a point where I wouldn't even know how to talk to Eliza, the problems we've been facing don't represent the crumbling of unsound foundations. Now, with Eliza curled on my chest, I know I was right not to be nervous.

Eliza sucks in a breath, the sound I've learned over five years means she's awake. Her eyes open, focusing on me slowly.

"Happy anniversary," I say.

She starts to smile. "Happy anniversary," she replies, her voice adorably groggy.

When her eyelids flutter closed, I feel her drifting off once more. I stroke her hair, the way I know relaxes her. *What if we just didn't get up?* one very inviting voice in my head whispers. *What if we simply spent the entire day here, under the covers, wrapped in each other?*

Snapping me out of this delicious speculation, Eliza's phone vibrates on the nightstand. With a groan, she rolls over and checks the screen. I watch her read, then frown. "You've got to be kidding me," she mutters, before returning the phone facedown to the nightstand.

I sit up, propping the pillows behind me. I could give her space like I did yesterday. Instead, I decide I'll let her know there's an open door.

"Who was that?" I ask.

She meets my eyes, looking nervous, until resolve enters her expression. "It's my mom calling," she says, like she's out on a ledge, uncertain if it'll hold her. "On our literal anniversary, she's pressuring me into RSVPing to Michelle's wedding, which we weren't even invited to. *Ugh*," she sighs harshly, her nerves overcome by frustration. "I just want out of this mess." She draws her knees up to her chest under the covers. The posture is defensive, hiding her vulnerability.

While her discomfort pains me, I'm relieved she told me. Incredibly relieved, in fact. Though nothing she explained was new information, what's important is she was willing to share. Recognizing this progress, I keep going. "Do you want to go to the wedding?" I ask gently.

Eliza speaks to her knees, her voice small. "Of course I do, but Michelle doesn't want me there. I think just showing up would ruin her day."

I consider what she's saying. I have to navigate this conversation carefully, the way I would in court. It's obviously difficult for her to open up on the subject the way she is. I'm sympathetic—I want to help her figure out the question of Michelle's wedding while simultaneously showing Eliza it's okay to be candid with me. I keep my question even, directionless, nonconfrontational. "Have you asked her, though?"

Eliza doesn't move. "She doesn't want to talk to me. She made that clear. In her eyes, I'm just the full-of-myself actress who flaked when she needed me."

"I'm sorry you feel that way," I say. "Anyone who knows you should know how caring and generous you are. I wish she saw that, too."

Finally, Eliza looks at me. When I find gratitude in her eyes, my heart races with joy.

I go on, feeling like I can. Feeling like we're really doing this. "Even so, maybe you should just tell her she has it wrong and ask her if you can go to her wedding."

"I don't have to ask her," Eliza insists. She sounds frustrated, but not with me. "I never got an invite."

"I know," I say patiently. "But . . . maybe she doesn't know you want to come. People . . ." I pause. Giving honesty might be the way to receive honesty, I decide. "People get insecure sometimes. They close off, even if inside, they feel differently."

Eliza stares into my eyes. There's nothing hidden in hers. "We're not only talking about Michelle, are we?"

I smile softly. "I'm just suggesting you do with her what you've done with me this week. Show her she's worth fighting for."

"The situation with Michelle is nothing like ours," she says hastily. Her gaze drifts from me. She stares into space. The pause stretches, the silence filling the room. My pulse pounds, no longer with joy—right now, I'm out on her ledge with her.

Even so, I see the moment it happens. The wall goes up. The gray in her eyes changes from fog into slate. From navigable to impassable. "Could I think about this later? I just want to . . . have fun right now," she says.

Quietly, I'm a little crestfallen. *Fun.* I understand what's really happening here. Eliza is reaching the limit of how open she's willing to be with me, or how open she's capable of being. Out onto the ledge is the farthest she'll go. What she's saying right now is—she refuses to leap over the chasm to the other side.

Which . . . maybe isn't her fault. It occurs to me with the suffocating weight of obviousness—maybe it's me. Were I more confident, more fun, more insightful, more everything all the time, I would be worth investing her worries in. Worth coming to for support.

But I'm not.

If my wife can't confide in me, I might as well be a guy she's met on vacation.

I pull on the persona I've worn for the past week, despite it not fitting quite right. It's difficult, after the night we had last night. I feel like I'm smiling with sore muscles, putting on cockiness with pained posture. If it's the *fun* Graham she wants, I'll give her the version who offers plenty.

"Of course," I drawl. "I was thinking of meeting up with David for a run, but maybe we can get together later?"

Everything in me wishes she would push back, would even question what I'm doing. Would offer me the faintest sign lighting up the fog that it's not just this Graham she wants.

She doesn't.

"Sounds good," she says in her character's voice. "I'll text you later."

41

Eliza

I RETURN TO my room, walking with fast, frustrated steps. I wish I hadn't opened the Michelle issue today. *Of course* I'll have to talk to her eventually—but Graham was wrong when he said it was no different from my relationship with him. I didn't want to fight with him, though. I just wanted to spend today with him.

Except now I'm not with him.

I don't really understand why. Why I'm here, in my generic hallway, keying open the door to my solitary room. I can't help grumbling in my doorway, comparing my space with Graham's lavish suite. Of course, what I'm missing most isn't the Jacuzzi, the gorgeous living room, or the bed I wish I could have spent hours in this morning. It's the occupant.

The riddle frays the edges of my mind. Why did Graham retreat immediately into role-play? Caught off guard, I'd followed his lead. Vacation Planner Eliza put on last night's clothes, then left with a forced smile. It leaves me wondering how much of today we're even going to celebrate. Clearly, we need to discuss this pretense, but we can't right now. Because my husband has plans with *David* on our *five-year wedding anniversary.*

I drop into the chair near my bed, grabbing the book I'm reading for work from the narrow desk. Unenthusiastically, I crack the pages to practice voices and delivery. It's not particularly easy work—I'm trying to use pitch changes to signal the book's flashbacks. But I only get two pages in before I find myself losing the line I'm reading.

My voice catches. I flip the cover closed, groaning in frustration like one only does when no one else can hear.

Nothing is working. I haven't sunk into the role yet, haven't even found the character. My head is overstuffed with other performances. Performances with Graham, with my family. Sometimes even performances for myself. How often have I gotten through the day pretending *siblings fight, it's normal, it'll blow over* or *oh, what do I care, it's not like Michelle and I were* that *close?* Easy resolutions to problems I didn't want to face.

Of *course* I want to be at Michelle's wedding. I just knew confronting the problem would make me miserable.

But here, in my hotel room, I'll be miserable regardless. I'm not celebrating my anniversary right now. I can't even focus on work. Instead of just moping, the least I can do is get an answer to one part of the Michelle question.

I reach for my phone and quickly find Michelle's contact information, not letting myself overthink my way out of it like I've done countless times before. I'll just ask if I'm invited to the wedding. If I am, great. If I'm not, then I can tell my family the decision isn't up to me. Either way, I'll be okay.

With the energy of my new decisiveness, my fingernail clicks sharply when I hit the phone icon. I listen while it rings. The tone is weirdly peaceful, anticlimactically slow. I start preparing my message, expecting to be sent to voice mail. The waiting starts to stress me out, each new ring sounding like years onto this sentence of sisterly discontent I'm serving.

On what must be the final ring, though, Michelle picks up.

"Are you dying?" she asks humorlessly.

I reach for words, still shaking off my surprise. "No, I'm not dying," I finally manage, throwing out the voice mail I was preparing in my head.

"Then why are you calling after—how many months has it been?"

Defensive instincts rear up in me, probably one of those inescapable legacies of sisterhood. "You could have called, too, you know," I reply.

"Yeah. I chose not to." She's relinquished some of her sarcasm. Yet her quiet finality cuts deeper.

My cheeks flush. I remember the stupid fights we had when we were kids. Copied hairstyles, sharing the family computer, who finished the last piece of birthday cake in the fridge. Nothing that mattered like this.

"Right. Well," I say, performing once more. Pretending I'm not stung. "Mom and Dad keep calling, wanting to know if I'm RSVP-ing to your wedding."

There's only silence on the line.

I clench my jaw. *This* is the type of improv I don't enjoy. I desperately wish there was some sort of script for conversations like this one. Even if it was clumsily written, or I could only remember half of my lines, I just wish there was *something*. Instead, Michelle is determined to not make this easy.

"I've tried to explain to them I'm not invited," I say, with the most patience I can muster. Which is not very much. "But I figured I'd call and just make completely sure my invitation wasn't lost in the mail."

I examine my fingernails while I wait. Honestly, Michelle's response feels somewhat unnecessary, with the way this conversation is going. Closer to a formality. Glancing up past the sunlit curtains of my room, I wait for her to confirm. To tell me no, my invitation was definitely *not* a casualty of the postal service. No, my sister wants me nowhere near her big day. No, I'm too *selfish* to let into her life.

Michelle's voice returns, grudging cold in every syllable. "If you *were* invited, would you show up?"

I bite back the retorts immediately springing to my mind. Staring out the window, I focus on the green hills, the crystal sky. I don't need to give Michelle the satisfaction of the low blow she's struck, don't need to let bitterness betray my wounds. There's no point making this worse. I just have to get through it.

I can't believe I let today weaken me into this impulsive, useless phone call. I knew this would happen. It's exactly why I hate prying open conversations like these. My family, no matter how much they say they love me, can't resist hitting every sore spot, drawing everything out into tortured interrogations full of performative indignation and petty cruelty. These discussions go nowhere except down.

"Of course I would," I say hollowly. It's the truth, obviously. I'm just waiting for the next stinger it will earn me.

"Fine. I guess you're invited, then," Michelle replies. "January twelfth in Boulder."

My mouth literally falls open. Michelle, however, doesn't give me time to be stunned.

"Fish or chicken for you and Graham?" she goes on.

"Um." I need a second for my mind to unlock. "Chicken for Graham. Fish for me. Michelle—" I start.

My sister cuts me off. "Great. I have to go. Oh, happy anniversary, by the way."

I pretend I don't hear the venom in her parting words, the spite I expected. "Thanks," I say, but she's already hung up before the word is out.

I calmly put my phone facedown on the desk. Impossibly, I feel . . . worse. Not pulling my eyes from the hills outside, where I hold on to the view like some sort of refuge, I find myself biting the inside of my cheek. This hurts. Like I've swallowed ice, but it's gotten stuck on its way down in the middle of my chest.

While I expected steely refusal and simmering resentment, what I got was . . . the path of least resistance. Dismissal in the form of cooperation. I thought it was the worst thing to be not worth inviting. Now I know it's worse to be not worth *uninviting*.

We didn't talk anything out. Michelle didn't ask me to explain what happened with her engagement party. Her invitation might as well have been a closed door. On the day of her wedding, she won't even glance in my direction. It'll be the furthest thing possible from the sisterly wedding experience we've envisioned since we were kids—me her maid of honor, the cozy photos, the tearful toasts.

I almost wish she'd told me not to come.

42

Graham

I LACE UP my running shoes with quick, deliberate strokes. It's funny—somehow, my hotel room now feels empty without Eliza. Like, overnight, some marital magic turned this place once more into hers, too. Underneath my frustration with how quickly she reached for *have fun* this morning, I miss her. I hate how empty the sterile white hallway feels, how vacant the half-made bed looks.

The run, of course, was David's idea. Regardless of my disinclination for trail running right now, I'm eager to fill him in on everything going on with Eliza. Honestly, I'm hoping for some words of wisdom before David checks out tomorrow. I'll need help if I'm going to pull off the tightrope walk of tonight. I know I have to play the parts of my persona Eliza likes, but I want to celebrate my anniversary, too, which means getting her to fall in love with the *real* Graham.

As I'm finishing my laces, the doorbell rings. I stand, grimacing from how unprepared I feel. I ran in college, but in the years since, my legs have grown unaccustomed to the prospect. What's more, if I know David, he's some kind of serious marathoner. I reach for the door, expecting I'll find him in an armband, headband, the whole nine.

When I open the door, though, it's not David.

"Surprise!" my mother says. "Happy anniversary!"

On my doorstep, my parents look incredibly pleased with themselves. My dad is dressed for golfing, my mom for tea. She's holding flowers, the bouquet so big she can barely see me past the daffodils.

Stunned, I can't react. I just stare, struggling to comprehend. "What are you *doing* here?" I finally manage. "How did you even know this was my room?" Possibilities start to swirl in my head. Dark, unsettling possibilities. Have they been staying here this entire week? Did we just not notice them on the beach hike because we weren't looking—or, god, during *couples' yoga*?

It wouldn't be unlike them. While entirely well-intentioned, my parents have been known to cross boundaries. I've patiently explained to Eliza they only want to be friendly, sometimes without considering the way their presence changes situations—like the memorable night I finished finals for the first semester of my final year of law school. When Eliza posted on her Instagram story the West Hollywood restaurant where she took me to celebrate, guess who decided they'd "just drop by" to join us for drinks?

I reassure myself I would have noticed Helen and Conrad Cutler on the nature hike or during yoga. With the full foot of height difference between my swaggering Germanic father and prim, petite mom, not to mention the former's lively tendency to speak two ticks on the volume knob louder than normal, they're not easy to miss.

Dad throws his arm around my mom. "We booked the room for

you, didn't we?" he exclaims. "Your mom and I have stayed in this specific suite on several occasions."

"Isn't it wonderful?" my mom chimes in. She shares the same inability to stay silent as my dad. "We just had to get it for you. Where's Eliza?" She peers around me into the messy room. I fight the instinct to step in front of her gaze, knowing if I did, she would realize something was up.

I plaster on the fake confidence I've gotten so good at. "She's on a hike. Are you staying here?" The question flies out of me with the speed of dreading one particular answer. Running into them while I'm desperately working to figure everything out with Eliza is an unpleasant prospect.

"Oh, goodness, no," my mom replies. "We don't want to crowd you. We're on a little trip to Carmel, but we had to come by for your big day. We were thinking celebratory brunch?"

My relief over them not staying here is short-lived. Instead, I have to hide my displeasure. *Brunch?* I know my case for frustration isn't very strong—this trip is very generous, and in general, my parents are supportive. But they do things like this, too. They're pushy, overly present, insistent on shaping everything into their view of what's ideal. It registers with me now how unsurprising it is that the room they booked us is one they've enjoyed before. Brunch is just one more step toward designing our day for us.

"We already have brunch plans," I say. "I really wish you would've called, then we could have scheduled something."

My mom's expression doesn't change. Only her son would recognize the subtle shifts, the way her stare fixes, the sharpening of her features, like fire lit inside a ceramic vase. "Graham, we paid for this entire vacation of yours," she reminds me with cutesy incredulity that poorly conceals sternness. "Can't you reschedule whatever your plans are? When does Eliza get back from this . . . hike?"

I hear the suspicion hiding in her words. She makes like she's going to walk into my room, which I can't let her do. If I did, she'd see none of my wife's clothes or luggage, not even her phone charger on one of the nightstands.

I move quickly. Like I think she only means to bring the flowers inside, I take them out of her hands, deflecting her entry. It's weaponized politeness. I wonder if my mom recognizes the instinct—she should.

Still, it was close. I remember what I've been taught on hostile witnesses, on regaining control of the conversation. I need to deescalate. "Of course, Mom," I say. "We can reschedule. Brunch would be . . ." With the beginnings of panic, I realize, to pull this off, I'm going to have to figure out where Eliza *really* is instead of on her nonexistent hike. "Brunch would be great," I finish.

My dad grins. "Perfect! Well, you look like you're heading to the gym," he says, removing his arm from my mom to clap me on the shoulder. "We don't want to *completely* derail your day. How about you do your workout, and Eliza doesn't have to cut her hike short? Your mother and I will book treatments at the spa. It's a fantastic facility. Then we can convene for brunch at, say, one?"

I nod, recognizing my dad is providing me with the smallest window of flexibility. It's how he is—while he's enthusiastic enough to indulge my mom's every suggestion, even the overly involved ones, his good nature makes him diplomatic and solution-minded in ways my mother is not.

Still, his cheerful suggestion ultimately does nothing for my problem. My wife is—*still*—not on the hike I'm pretending she is.

Faced with my mom's mandate, I have a little over an hour to find Eliza and convince her into surprise brunch with her in-laws.

"We'll see you then," I say stiffly.

My mom's smile practically glows. "Wonderful," she says. "I can't wait to hear everything about your stay."

43

Eliza

I COULDN'T KEEP waiting in my room, the pale imitation of where I woke up this morning with Graham. I just couldn't. Instead, I decided I needed to get outside. It's what vacationing in dazzling Northern California is for, after all.

Carrying my book, I headed down to the pool. Perhaps expectedly, I couldn't concentrate on the words, not while my phone lay next to me on the lounge chair, conspicuously vacant from calls from Graham. He's hanging out with David. He's not going to call me. Finally, knowing I needed to just ignore the damn thing, I closed my book. Enjoying the gentle warmth of the noon sun on my skin, I walked into the water.

The temperature is perfect. Immersing myself fully in the pool, I push off from the wall to do laps. With each reaching stroke, I focus on the cool water rushing over my face. Sensory details keep my mind from wandering to Graham, or to my sister's painful brush-off. I just need to keep from dwelling on the hurt for a day longer, just one more day, so I can fully enjoy what's left of my vacation.

I keep swimming, pushing myself while the water douses the fires of exertion in my shoulders. With each lap I ignore the obvious metaphor in what I'm doing. I'm not outrunning my problems. I'm just swimming.

When I reach the end of a length, my lungs searing, I pop up to suck in air.

Instantly, I stop short. *Graham* is standing over me, not in pool-wear. He's in leather loafers on the pool deck, dressed in slacks and a white short-sleeve button-down, and looking very much like he wasn't on a run with David.

I blink water out of my eyes, reading his expression. His grimace. The tension in his features. He's upset.

"I've been looking everywhere for you," he says hurriedly. "Do you not check your phone?"

I'm immediately defensive, even indignant. "I was swimming, Graham. I can't check my phone while swimming," I say, not hiding the edge of sarcasm in my voice. "Besides, I thought you had *plans*." I hope he hears my hint of judgment. Whatever my faults, I didn't pick our anniversary to hang out with someone else.

"My parents are here," Graham replies.

I just stare, fighting to make sense of his words. The pool deck is silent except for the lapping of the crystalline water while Graham meets my gaze impatiently.

"They're expecting us at brunch," he grinds out, "in thirty minutes."

My mind unlocks. "Your parents are *here*?" I repeat, just to clarify that I'm understanding this unfortunate turn of events completely. "At this hotel?" The crispness of the day on my exposed shoulders feels suddenly chilly, the chlorine's stench pungent, the pool water itself clammy on my submerged legs.

Graham nods grimly. "Yes. They're staying in Carmel and decided they would *drop by*. I lied—I told them you were hiking on your own." His gaze shifts out over the ironically placid water of the pool.

Panic starts to pick up my heart rate. "Crap."

"Exactly," he says.

We spring into motion simultaneously. I haul myself out of the pool, spraying the concrete with water, while Graham is already reaching to hand me my towel. Wordlessly I rub my shoulders, my hair, into some semblance of dryness, not failing to notice Graham in the corner of my vision checking his smartwatch. I wrap myself in the towel and collect my things from the chair, my phone and my book in one hand and my dress in the other.

Graham holds the gate open for me in what I recognize is efficiency, not chivalry. This, I know, is husband Graham, not Investment Banker Graham. He doesn't need to point out the "emergency" in the present circumstances. Our pretense is gone, trampled under the arrival of in-laws.

It's not just the surprise of their visit I'm resenting. Graham's parents have a perfect marriage. Impossibly, irritatingly perfect. They're fierce proponents, not to mention living examples, of the idea of true love. Which, while lovely, leads them to put pressure on Graham—on us—to live up to their lofty romantic ideals. Whether this vacation was gifted out of their love of love or their pressure for perfection remains to be seen.

Either way, it puts undoubted pressure on this brunch. I figured Helen intuited there were problems in our marriage when she made us this reservation. Still, if we show the slightest sense of them now, it'll be the visible proof she needs to discount our marriage. To convince herself we're not the real thing.

It's something I refuse to entertain. Despite the problems we've had, I believe in us. In the vows we made, the love we've shared since, the laughter, the congratulations, the little kindnesses. The nights like our wedding night, the nights like last night. I'm holding on. I don't want someone, especially not someone who's known my husband his entire life, urging us to let go.

"I'll meet you at the restaurant," I say breathlessly. "Text me which one. I just need to shower and change first."

Graham shakes his head sharply. "We can't *meet there*. If we come separately, we'll have to admit to the separate rooms."

He's right, of course. I chew my lip in frustration. The last thing I want is to come clean to my Stepford-manufactured mother-in-law about the elaborate role-play I've been engaging in with her son. "Fine." I sigh. "Then . . . I guess you should come with me."

Our footsteps in rhythm provide the only reply. I start for the main hotel, Graham on my heels, both of us walking with haste. In the smothering silence, I think we're realizing this is the first time I've ever invited Graham up to *my* room. It's not the invitation either of us hoped for today.

We reach the sleek lobby. The temperature inside is refrigerator-like, worsened for me by my still-dripping swimsuit. I'm shivering when we get into the elevator. Graham moves to put his arm around me, but I pull away.

"Want to explain why half your shirt is wet?" I ask him.

He groans and drops his arm back to his side.

The bell dings, and I shuffle into the hallway, where I unlock my room. I'm already undressing as soon as the door shuts behind

Graham. His eyes catch on my nakedness for a second, which, despite our hurry, causes pink to flash into my cheeks.

I ignore the reaction, and Graham sits down on the bed, doing nothing. It's routine, mundane, the way a husband and wife change around each other after five years of marriage. I'm a little saddened at the casualness, at how the spark from hours ago is flickering out with the first hint of the real world returning.

Leaving Graham just sitting, where he'll probably peruse his phone—like he would while waiting for client meetings or picking up his morning coffee, not *in his wife's hotel room*—I rush into the shower. I wring chlorine out of my hair with frantic vigor. Without time to blow-dry, I settle for putting my hair up in a bun that will wreak havoc on my curl pattern when dry.

When I emerge from the bathroom in the hotel robe, Graham stands. "How can I help?" he asks.

"My yellow dress," I direct him. "The one I wore to Lexi's baby shower."

He drops to his knees in front of my suitcase, where he quickly pulls out the exact one I mean while I put on underwear. Graham holds out the dress for me, wordless efficiency in our every movement. When I step in, he zips me up.

I force myself not to remember other dresses zipped—or unzipped—by Graham. The black number I wore to his law-school formal, my wedding dress. I banish from my thoughts the way Graham then moved the zipper slowly, languishing his time so he could keep one hand on the dimples in my back. Ostensibly holding the zipper in place, but truly holding me.

He doesn't now. He finishes the job in one swift pull, then steps back so I can put on my shoes. Just one more way in which we're well-oiled machines in each other's presence.

The thought knots painful pressure in my stomach. I'm desperate to hold on longer, frightened of losing the progress we've made. The idea of the electricity we've found vanishing once more into flat, empty monotony makes me quietly frantic.

In Graham's expressionless features when I pivot to face him, I find no hints of whether he's similarly disconcerted. I'm not too proud or selfless to recognize I *want* him to be. I want him to hold on the way I'm desperate to. Charitably, I remind myself that maybe he's just stressed or pissed his parents have shown up uninvited.

"Let's go," I say quickly.

Like I've given him the cue he needed, he walks swiftly to the door. While he holds it open, I pause, starting to imagine sitting down opposite Conrad Cutler, with his man-of-the-world grandeur, and Helen, with her fine-china smiles.

"When we get there . . ." I start with strain. "I don't want them to know—"

"We're on the same page," Graham cuts me off with quick calm. I can't decode if he's being brusque or just prompt in his reassurance.

Either way, I swallow, relieved. Our marital issues will remain for us only.

Which means when we enter the restaurant, we'll be playing new parts, although not the ones we've been perfecting.

We'll be the happily married versions of ourselves.

44

Graham

THE RESERVATION MY parents made is at the same restaurant where Eliza and I shared crema catalana and danced to Spanish guitar. Thankfully, they're seated inside, where I don't have to pollute my perfect memories of Eliza's and my evening here with this tense parental brunch.

The restaurant is full, bustling for the midday meal. While the hostess leads us toward my parents' table near the windows, Eliza walks next to me. "Ready?" I ask her out of the corner of my mouth. I guess the question is in part for myself.

In response, Eliza entwines her fingers with mine and looks up at me, smiling gently. Her features practically shine, and not just with freshly showered scrub. From the love radiating in her eyes, this could be the morning we first saw our wedding venue or hung up one of our engagement photos in our living room.

I love every second of it, even while it hurts. I want to be walking hand in hand into our anniversary brunch because we *want* to, not because we don't want to embarrass ourselves in front of my parents. It makes the cracks in my real marriage feel wider, deeper. It makes them sting, like vinegar poured in delicately.

When my mom spots us, she stands up from the table to hug Eliza. "I'm sorry to surprise you like this," she says magnanimously into my wife's shoulder, then pulls back. "Graham said you were on a hike?" Her eyes search Eliza's expression—hunting, I know, for inconsistent reactions or flickers of disingenuity.

Eliza smoothly rolls with the lie. "Just a short one. It's perfectly alright."

While we sit, I notice the motherly satisfaction in my mom's eyes, like nothing is registering on her well-honed problem detector. Immediately, I reach for my ice water, feeling hot. My collar is scratchy, my belt buckle cold. I don't know how I'm going to get through water, then coffee—my dad never forgoes his French press—then brunch with unflinching, calm charisma.

I'm grateful when Eliza takes initiative in the conversation. Her smile, polite and friendly, is one fit for the first time meeting one's significant other's parents, let alone the hundredth. "So you two are staying in Carmel? What's the occasion?"

"No occasion," my dad replies cheerfully. "We decided we'd drive up for the weekend, which is why we had to drop in on you today. You're checking out tomorrow, right?"

"Right. As you know, since you made the reservation for us," I say. Instantly, I wish I hadn't. If I'm just going to lapse into sarcasm, I should stick to downing my water.

Eliza takes my hand on the table. "Which we're so grateful for," she adds. "We've had the best vacation."

Once more, I'm impressed by how flawlessly Eliza pulls on the clean costume of her role. She's hit exactly the right conversational emphasis, steering us on to uplifting subjects.

Sure enough, my mom lights up. "Well, what have you been up to? I want to hear everything." She shifts in her seat, like she's literally physically preparing herself for details of our marital bliss.

Eliza and I hesitate. We share a glance containing our wordless negotiation over who will lead our response. While we must look like fawning lovers, the moment for me hits closer to notepad exchanges with co-counsel on the courtroom table. We have to get our story straight.

Before either of us can speak, though, the waiter comes by to take everyone's orders. I opt for oatmeal, the most flavorless, unchallenging dish on the menu. When the waiter leaves, it's Eliza who speaks up, plunging forward.

"Where should we start? The room's been fantastic," she enthuses. Obviously, she's speaking about *my* room. Not hers. "We've really enjoyed the Jacuzzi in particular," she goes on, shooting me a look I don't fail to catch. It's genuine, wrapped in the warmth of real memories, cutting sweetly through our charade.

This unexpected gift steadies me enough to pick up the thread of our story. "Let's see," I say with vigor I hardly recognize. "We've done just about everything. There was the beach hike, jam tasting, couples' yoga, dinner with live music. Oh, and stargazing." I lock my gaze with Eliza's. "I think that was my favorite."

Her smile is real now, unmistakably. In her eyes I find reflections of the night we're each remembering, the soaring streak of the galaxy's curve. It occurs to me with quiet wonder—maybe this won't be difficult. My parents don't have to know we were pretending to be perfect strangers while enjoying the things I mentioned.

We laugh together, playing off each other. Describing our new friend David and his efforts to court a potential soul mate. Sharing how we spontaneously signed up for intermediate boxing, only to wind up with shoulders so sore we could barely move. It's easy. It's the us I want to be.

Until we're halfway done with our meals. Innocently, while reaching for his oil-black coffee, my dad eyes us. "Well, what are your plans tonight?" he asks. "After you've gotten rid of your intrusive parents, of course. How are you celebrating five years of perfect happiness?"

Right on cue, my stomach emits a loud, unexpected groan. Instantly I'm reminded why I resented my parents showing up, why their presence stressed me out. My dad's question wasn't probing or judgmental like my mom sometimes is, but the implicit expectation is no different. Just because Eliza's and my marriage hasn't been five years of *perfect happiness* doesn't mean it's not worth celebrating.

But I don't know how to bring us back to our real selves. Not with how deep into this game we've gotten. While I've been practicing asking questions, evidently, I haven't asked the right one. Or more accurately, I haven't had the courage to ask the right one. Who does Eliza want to spend her anniversary with? The real me, or the better me?

Chewing on these thoughts, I find myself unable to reply.

Eliza steps in gracefully. "I think Graham's planning a surprise."

I pull myself out of my rumination to glance up. Four eyes focus on me in expectation. "Yes," I say, forcing the words. "It's all worked out."

My parents exchange exuberant smiles, which feel like weights dropped onto my shoulders. It's been this way since my high school relationships, even. When I fell in love with Eliza, I hesitated to introduce her to my family for exactly this reason. My parents just want me to be *happy* and *in love* so intensely, I feel like I can't escape the smothering pressure. Honestly, it's probably part of why I've handled Eliza's and my growing distance so inexpertly. Whenever I'm not the picture of ideal companionship, I . . . don't know how to handle it. Why would I? In the house where I grew up, there's no room for discord.

The conversation moves on, my parents mollified by my vague anniversary plans. I don't follow. Somehow, my dad's innocuous question has shaken the very foundation of everything Eliza and I have spent the past week doing. What if it was all wrong? Just the perilously skewed design of our worst escapist impulses? Maybe nothing can fix us because the problem isn't with *us*. It's with me.

I'm not good enough for her. I can't pretend forever to be someone who is.

David was wrong, I decide in the moment. It *does* matter which me is the real me. Being my real self *is* different from shaping myself constantly, in incessant increments, into the me she wants. Even imagining it is exhausting. Waking up, pulling on the smile of someone cool, confident, concerned about nothing except the gorgeous woman with whom he's performing. Checking myself in mental mirrors hundreds of times every day. Even if I managed, what kind of marriage would I even be living? Certainly not the perfect one my parents imagine or expect. I'd be nothing but the cardboard cutout of a husband.

Eliza must notice something is off with me, though I doubt she intuits how deeply I've spiraled. I feel her hand squeeze my thigh comfortingly under the table. Her gaze is questioning, but I only shake my head subtly. I need to get ahold of myself and get through this brunch.

So I do.

I pull on my armor, my suit of charisma and sharp smiles. I charge back into the conversation, deploying anecdotes, jokes, questions. While it's not easy, the effort distracts me from darker worries for the time being. I'm losing the war but, damnit, I'm winning the battle. When the waiter comes by to collect our dishes, I'm relieved to find I did it. I made it through.

My mother places her napkin carefully on the table and folds her hands. "I have to say, I'm so relieved to hear you both so happy," she says.

I permit myself to look in Eliza's direction. There's nothing pretend in the smile I send her.

"Eliza, has your room been pleasant, too?" my mom goes on.

I see the moment it happens—the question freezes Eliza's expression into ice-sculpture rigidity. I feel the same thing happen to me, my blood running cold. Refusing to meet my mother's eyes, I find myself focusing instead on the leg of one of the neighboring table's chairs. "How—" I start.

"I called to try to send flowers to Eliza in the honeymoon suite when you first got in. The hotel told me Eliza wasn't staying in the honeymoon suite and asked if I'd like to send them to her in her room instead," she says.

Her voice holds nothing except concern, no *gotcha* glee. It doesn't mean she's not enjoying being concerned, though. I know her sympathy is genuine, but I know part of her *likes* being the worrying, monitoring mom.

"If I can confess something, it's why we decided to take this spontaneous little getaway," she continues.

Emotions roil in me, making me glad I opted for oatmeal. I know it's not just frustration pounding hotly in my cheeks, though

I'm pretty close to furious that she intruded on the privacy of her twenty-nine-year-old son and daughter-in-law this way. Deeper, there's shame. Embarrassment at the truth my mom's uncovered.

The effort I've upheld this entire meal just . . . crumbles. I hear the words I'm speaking like they're coming from elsewhere. "You caught us, Mom," my voice says, wavering with cornered spite. "Eliza and I have been staying separately. Things aren't as great in our marriage as we made you think. Sorry to disappoint."

Eliza's head whips in my direction. "Graham . . ."

"Might as well be honest, right?" I ask sharply, ignoring the shock in her eyes. I'm in the grip of something now, barricading myself inside my burning house.

"I don't understand," my dad says delicately, fiddling with one prong of his folded sunglasses. "Are you . . . separated?" He pronounces the word with mild horror. Of course he does. In my family, it's sacrilege.

"No, nothing like that." Eliza springs in, her voice unnaturally high. I register this, knowing if *she* can't control her pitch, she must be fraying. She goes on, racing to finish her sentences. "It's just . . . something we're trying. Like a game. It's really helping us." She's stumbling over her words, desperate to get out of this. But there's no way out. I would sympathize if I weren't caught within my own whirlwind.

My mom looks crestfallen. It manages to piss me off even more—she must know how embarrassing this is for me, for my wife, yet she just cannot restrain herself from this display of disappointment. No subtlety, no understanding. "You're staying separately, but you're not separated?" she manages. "You know, Uncle John knows a wonderful couples' counselor. I'll make a call and get you two in right away."

"Mom. Don't."

I slam the words onto the table with force no one can ignore. Everyone goes quiet for several seconds.

"I'm only trying to help," my mom says finally.

It's impossible to ignore how she really does sound genuine. It doesn't matter. All I hear are the ways in which we've fallen short. In which *I've* fallen short. Not just to Eliza, who only wants the smoke-and-mirrors, Central Casting version of myself I've invented—to everyone.

"Well, you're not. This"—I gesture to the table—"isn't helping." Like it came, the fight leaves me quickly. I'm exhausted. Exhausted by these games, by these pressures, by the gnawing knowledge of not being enough. I hear my voice go soft. "Maybe none of this is helping. I can't . . . I can't pretend for you anymore, Eliza."

I look over, finding her gaze fixed on me, filled with worry and hurt. I hate it.

"I'm sorry," I say to her. "I wanted to be the person you wanted. I really did." I have the unusual impression I'm reciting words I've practiced instead of saying them for the first time. Like déjà vu. Maybe I'm just realizing they're long overdue.

I stand up, feeling my parents' distraught gazes on me. I don't care. All I can see is Eliza's heartbreak. It's unbearable.

I walk out, hating myself.

45

Eliza

I SIT, HELPLESSLY watching my husband leave the restaurant. Heartbreak and mortification are pulling me in opposite directions, and I'm not certain either is winning. Maybe neither of them will. Instead, they'll end up ripping me in half, going their separate ways.

The harsh echo of Graham's words resounds in my head. *I wanted to be the person you wanted. I really did.* The unyielding repetition surrounds me. *I wanted to be the person you wanted. I really did.*

It's not just misery leaving me motionless in my chair, with my pulse choking my chest. It's confusion. Did he mean *Investment Banker Graham?* Could he have possibly thought I wanted him to make himself into another person, entirely distinct from the man I married? While I retreat into my head, the silverware sounds and the movement of waiters fading, I replay Graham's and my week. I've worked to point out to him the ways *he,* my Graham, not the fabricated hotel Graham, was everything I wanted. How the character did nothing except emphasize the charisma, the humor, the creativity, the *sexiness* I know he has.

So why couldn't he see that's what I was doing?

Either I miscommunicated horribly, which is my fault, or Graham couldn't understand what I was showing him because he's so deeply convinced he's not enough.

When I've wound over and over these thoughts a couple times, I return to myself in the restaurant, gradually conscious of my in-laws gaping. They're watching Graham, Helen looking the loveliest shade of porcelain and Conrad's eyes huge.

Then, though, their gazes swivel to me. I swallow painfully. Their flabbergasted scrutiny is nearly impossible to withstand. *Oh, I see you've remembered me, the harpy who broke your son's heart.*

New warring urges rear up in me now. Part of me wants to rush out of the restaurant, to escape their stares, to find Graham and demand he explain himself. But part of me doesn't want to have that conversation with him. Because I'm terrified. I can imagine vividly the way the exchange would go—Graham telling me there's nothing I can do. *It's over.*

I notice my hand shaking on the table. Quickly I shove it into my lap. I drop my gaze from the shocked expression of Graham's parents while a third option forms in my mind. I'll calmly leave, I won't confront Graham, and I'll watch everything crumble from the comfort of my small, solitary hotel room. Perfect. Poetic, even.

"Are you alright?"

I look up. The unguarded sympathy in Helen's question is, frankly, surprising. Meeting her eyes, fresh shame scalds over me.

I start forcing words out. "Do you want me to go? I mean, do you want us to check out? Maybe you can get some of the money back for the night."

My mother-in-law has the good grace to look horrified. Or maybe she really is horrified. I don't know. I don't know. *I don't know.* "Goodness, no," she says gently. "Why would you think that?"

Despite her kindness, I honestly don't understand her question. How could I possibly think otherwise? I gesture miserably in the direction of the now-gone Graham. "You gave us this stay to cele-brate our anniversary. Not . . ." *Come on, voice. I hear you wavering. Don't crack now.* "Not this," I finish effortlessly.

Graham's parents exchange glances. They're probably relieved I brought this up. *Well, now that you mention it, you hasty interloper into our perfect family . . .*

"A gift is a gift, hon," Conrad says with quiet compassion I've never heard in his ordinarily stentorian tones.

"Don't worry about us," Helen adds, clasping her husband's hand on the table the way I did Graham's.

In the middle of this perfect, polished restaurant, I surprise my-self. I burst into tears. Not trickling, stinging tears either. The sob kicks into me hard, forcing me to suck in one loud, rattling breath. Instantly self-conscious, I lift shaking hands to my face, hoping to hide my face-warping anguish and my ragged breathing. It doesn't work. I feel myself losing control, feel the seconds stretch while I cry and cry.

I just wasn't expecting such compassion. I—and Graham, I know—feel ever-present pressure from his parents to have the flaw-less relationship they do. Even from the distance of Los Angeles to La Jolla, the weight of expectation hovers over us. I knew what they thought when we got engaged. The same thing my parents did, though my in-laws expressed their misgivings with subtle concern instead of my mom's unmistakable judgment. I wasn't naïve. I heard Helen's skepticism in her inquisitiveness about how we met and whether dating online was a solid enough foundation, her proud pronouncements of how long she and her husband had known each other before marrying. Scalpel cuts where my mother used steak knives.

Right now, Graham's mother is silent. The fact she's not interrogating me, not trying to "fix" us, is an impossible relief. It keeps my tears flowing. I draw in a particularly noisy, wet breath, earning uncomfortable glances from the rest of the restaurant.

"Oh," I hardly hear Helen say over my carrying on. Past the tears in my vision, I see her pat Conrad on the hand. "Why don't you go get our car from the valet? Give us a moment," she mutters to him.

He stands up and squeezes my shoulder comfortingly on his way out.

I cry harder. Honestly, with my own family messed up right now, I know part of the reason I'm reacting this way is because I'm overwhelmingly grateful for parental affection. The fact it's no secret to me where this outpouring of emotion is coming from, though, does nothing to distance me from the feelings.

Helen scoots her chair closer to me and hands me a clean napkin, which I gratefully receive.

"I'm so sorry," I say, wiping my dripping nose. "I—" My breath hitches with perfect timing. "I'm making a scene."

"It's okay," she reassures me. Her voice is pillow-soft. Not the kind of pillows on fancy couches you're not supposed to touch, either, laced with starched sequins. Really wonderfully comfortable ones. "Graham will be back. He's wild about you, you know that?" she goes on.

I inhale deeply, steadying the lump in my throat. I'd been trying to avoid my unhappiness for so long, and now it's like a dam has burst. Every insecurity, every inadequacy, every failed effort is cascading over me while I'm exhausted, unable to fight my way to the surface. Tears keep streaming down my face, though I'm quieter now. "I'm just so scared I've messed things up with him," I confess, hearing the defeat in my gravelly voice. "He's . . . everything to me."

Helen nods. "I understand."

I look up, blinking waterlogged lashes. "You do?" I ask. I don't hide my doubt, even if it's impetuous. Here Helen is comforting me for the first time ever, and I'm questioning her. "But you and Conrad have the perfect marriage," I explain.

Her lips twitch, her eyes drifting to where her husband just exited the restaurant. "I'm going to let you in on a secret," she tells me. I feel myself lean in. "Our marriage *is* perfect," Helen continues. "It really is. But we pretend, too."

I meet her eyes. She only caught Graham's dismissive parting remark. She doesn't know what we've been pretending this week, the extent of our elaborate game, with its joys and its unexpected heartbreaks. She doesn't know how much her words resonate with me—how much they're exactly what I needed to hear.

"Everyone pretends," Helen goes on gently. "They pretend they're brave. They pretend they can predict the future. They pretend they can carry fears or difficulties, but they don't know if they can. They pretend they have hope they don't know if they've mustered quite yet. When we need to, it's what we do for each other." She reaches for my hand with hers, which I grasp. "Perfect sometimes . . . requires a little pretend."

I stay silent, clinging to what she's saying.

"Perfection is only something you can see from the outside," she continues. "I know you and Graham are working something out right now, but that doesn't mean your marriage is any less perfect than mine. I just hope you won't give up on it."

"I won't," I whisper unhesitatingly. "I don't want to. Ever." In fact, it's this truth I've protected even in my lowest, saddest moments with Graham. On the nights I felt like I really didn't know him, or the mornings when I was guiltily relieved we wouldn't have to make small talk over breakfast. That truth was there.

Helen smiles fully. "Then Conrad and I need to get out of your hair. Go find your husband."

She stands suddenly. Her decisiveness in ending the conversation gives me the momentum I need to do the same. I'm grateful for it. I get up, feeling better, and walk with my mother-in-law out of the restaurant.

The Cutlers' BMW is waiting when we reach the valet. Surprising myself for the second time today, I hug Helen. She doesn't stiffen or seem thrown in the slightest. Her arms come around me, and I'm inexpressibly thankful to have this entire other family through my bond with Graham.

It makes me miss my own parents. I feel this sliver of sadness keenly inside my gratitude. While they're not perfect, they're *my parents*. Avoiding them over the problems I'm having with Michelle is starting to get exhausting.

I release Helen, renewed. I have so much I can't avoid anymore. Starting now.

46

Graham

I COME TO a hard halt, sucking in air with my hands on my knees.

I hear David stop gracefully next to me. He doesn't even sound winded, somehow. We're farther from the hotel than I've been all week, having taken the long, looping trail for our makeup run. The dirt path is uneven, my legs searing with every incline. The sun filters through the trees surrounding the trail in ever-changing patterns of glittering light. It's quiet—I seem to have scared off the birds with my wheezing.

I give up and drop down onto the grass, head between my knees. What if I just lay down right here instead of returning to the hotel? I start to like the sound of the idea.

"Do you want to talk about it yet?" David asks from overhead.

Squinting up, I find him ringed in sunlight. My temples pound with the blood fighting to reach the rest of my body. When my thoughts shift to Eliza—to my parents, to all the doubts and questions I have—I feel dizzy. I'd hoped running would distance me from the emotions I couldn't fend off in the restaurant, feelings of not being enough. It didn't. They were waiting for me, like they have been every day, no matter how difficult my work or how delightful my distractions.

"Tell me about your plans with Lindsey instead," I deflect.

David sits down across from me in "crisscross applesauce" like I'm sure he demonstrates for his students. He eyes me but allows me to redirect the conversation. "We're getting dinner tonight somewhere off hotel grounds," he says. "She picked the place, and she's going to drive us over there. I've been thinking about what you said, though."

I wipe my forehead with my shirt, waiting.

Something sad has entered David's expression. "I know I need to be honest with her before we really start something."

"Honest about how you're not actually an expert on marine-life conservation?"

He idly rips a blade of dead grass into smaller and smaller pieces. "Well, honest that I only started reading up on those subjects after meeting her." His gaze rests on the papier-mâché grass pulp he's creating. "I can't pretend with her, not if I want something real," he goes on. "Which I do."

When he looks up, I find I can't quite meet his eyes. His words touch too sore a place in me. I want to flinch away. To put off these questions just a little longer. But I can't. While I know this week's pretending with Eliza has held us together and even brought us closer, I can't help wondering, *closer to what, exactly*? To a promise I can't keep? Not while I'm *still* not enough for her.

I force myself to focus on David. It's him we're talking about, his relationship. If I can't be enough for Eliza, I can at least be a good friend to David.

"You're worried about how Lindsey will react," I say, reading the concern furrowing his brow.

"She's going to think I'm a creep or . . . or, best-case scenario, I'll be a letdown. A disappointment," he replies morosely.

"Hey, would your soul mate see you in any of those ways?" I ask, letting light humor into my voice.

It cracks a slight smile on David's face. "I see what you did there," he says. "So either she's my soul mate and she gets it, or she doesn't and . . ." His smile slips.

I hurry to catch his spirits before they sink completely. "No need to go there yet. I think it's great you're going to be honest. Tonight could be the start of something really incredible for you."

David looks earnestly encouraged. "Thanks, man," he says. "Okay, your turn. What's going on with you and Eliza? You had a fight?"

On cue, the sun seems to slide behind the day's sparse clouds. The grassy patch where we're resting darkens in cooler light.

I shift my gaze, staring up the trail, the who-knows-how-many-more miles we have left to run. "I don't know. Yeah. I mean, I guess. Not exactly," I start, hearing how confused I sound, which is fitting given how confused I feel. Focusing, I find coherence. "I love Eliza, I really do. Still, I don't know if I can be the man she wants."

David considers, watching me. While I continue to stare out into the forest, he starts to speak slowly. "When you two are . . . role-playing—"

"It's not like that," I interject, hearing the connotations he has in mind. "Okay," I correct myself. "It's mostly not like that."

Waving his hand passively, David goes on. "Whatever it is," he says. "When *she's* pretending, do you really see her as a different person? Even with the voice, the stories you come up with, the everything? Or do you just see your wife underneath it all?"

Finally, I pull my eyes from the path leading into the forest. I consider David's question—really, honestly consider—even while realizing I don't need to. Of course I only see Eliza. In every detail she creates of Vacation Planner Eliza, I only see my wife's gorgeous smile, her ingenuity, her vibrance. I'm not interested in someone else, don't want to date some random woman I meet on vacation. I see only Eliza. I want only Eliza.

David smiles, the asshole. He knows exactly how I've answered his question in my mind. The conclusions it's led me right into.

"So maybe," he says—and I have to applaud him, I don't know if I've ever led a jury with his deftness—"Eliza just wants *you*."

The sun emerges from the cover of the clouds.

Closing my eyes, I say nothing. I want to believe what he's saying, want to feel his faith. I've caught my breath from our run, but the fire ripping through my chest now is hope.

Even if David is right, I start to reason while the sun warms my shoulders, I still feel questions holding me back. While Investment Banker Graham's charm, quick intelligence, and, even on occasion, charged confidence come from me—will I be enough for Eliza if I can't be those things every day? Will I be enough even if I can? Not just to have fun with for a weeklong getaway. Will I be enough when days stretch into the monotony of life?

Or will I always be striving for her to let me in—feeling her holding me from the same distance she did this morning?

With sweat sliding down my face, I decide I don't know.

47

Eliza

I'M IN MY room, packing in a huff. When I came up here, I felt full of new resolve, determined to face my problems with Graham.

Graham, whose suite is on the opposite end of the resort. Graham, who won't pick up his phone. More than ever, I regret my decision not to share a room with him. I'm his wife, not his girlfriend. I shouldn't have trouble trying to reach him. Helpless here in my mountain-view room, I have nothing to do except get progressively more brisk as I grab toiletries and unzip zippers, like a little hurricane of nervous resentment.

The trip is over. We need to go home, to return to our real lives, where Graham can't avoid me. Where we can put to use everything we've learned about each other. I'll recognize his creativity, his confidence. He'll ask me questions, real questions, instead of leaving me lonely. He'll see the ways in which this week has helped us, the ways it hasn't been just pretend.

I'm folding my lingerie into my suitcase, slightly sad about the happier memories I have of it and hoping it won't stay in the dresser like it did before this trip, when I hear a knock on the door.

It's embarrassing how fast I move from my suitcase into my room's short hallway. Innately, I know it's Graham. My heart pounds with static-shock hope. It physically hurts how much I want things to be okay.

But when I open the door, I see things are very much not okay. In seconds, I catalogue every stinging way this is not the Graham I wanted to see. He's dressed in exercise clothes stained with sweat, but his features aren't beleaguered from exertion. He's crestfallen. His green eyes have the dull emptiness of sea glass, a flat-tire frown hanging on his face.

"Would you like to come in?" I force out. I hate the sound of the invitation—that an invitation has to be made at all.

He steps inside, then stops, lingering in the hallway of my room like he doesn't want to move farther without saying what's on his mind. "I'm sorry for leaving you with my parents. I shouldn't have stormed out like that," he says dutifully, facing me at an unnatural angle.

"Graham, it's fine. They were surprisingly chill about it." I gesture into my room. "Do you . . . want to sit?"

He shakes his head. The immediacy of his response wraps me in nervous wire, and I fight the fear working its way into my stomach.

"I can't pretend anymore," Graham declares with neutral intensity. "I'm not saying this week hasn't helped. It has. I used to think I knew you just because I once *did* know you, but I understand now that knowing a person is never finished. Even if the answers stay the same, the questions you ask on a first date are still worth asking seven years later. I think it's helped me know *me* better. But—"

His gaze locks with mine, decisive now. I find I'm holding my breath.

"We can't do this forever," he continues. "*I* can't do this forever. I can't keep pretending every day I'm this other Graham, the *fun* Graham. The Graham you want."

I'm doused in horror. Quickly, I close the distance separating us in my cramped hallway, reaching for his hand. Something flickers in his stony expression, his fingers grudgingly entwining with mine. "You are the Graham I want," I say emphatically.

Graham's eyes linger on mine. The sun coming in my room's windows illuminates him fully, leaving no trace of his expression— no detail of the features I've loved since I was twenty-three—in shadow. I know this is hard for him. He doesn't give up his side of an argument easily. It's part of what makes him a good lawyer.

Right now, however, I can see him working not to interrogate every angle of what I've said. He's letting himself listen.

"I'm trying to believe that," he replies finally. "But when you won't let me in all the way, it's hard not to feel like you only want the vacation version of me."

I hold his hand tighter, willing him to feel my certainty. "There *is* no vacation version of you," I tell him. "Don't you think I saw who really swept me onto the dance floor on our anniversary trip? Who somehow learned to box in one night? Even with every spontaneous surprise, don't you think I felt who I was spending every day with?"

When he looks at me, there's tentative hope in his expression. The sun flints on his green irises, making them shimmer with un-canny poetic timing. I watch him closely, searching for whatever he's starting to hold on to.

Then something new clouds over in his eyes. I have to fight down my discouragement.

"Maybe, but I can't be *that* me every minute of every day, either," he says firmly.

"I don't need you to! Maybe—maybe the game we played this week overdid it, with the staying in character. But I think we needed to overdo it in order to get out of doing nothing at all," I say. "Being spontaneous, being flirtatious, being surprising from time to time is not the same as being a different *person*. You're the man I see. You're the one I want." I pause, honestly not knowing if what I'm going to say next is a step into a conversational chasm. "You're the one who thinks you aren't worth as much as the Graham you've been pretending to be."

I'm expecting him to react defensively, to push or to evade. Instead, he pauses, the weariness of self-recognition crossing his features.

"I'm working on that," he says quietly. "But I need to feel like you want to let me in regardless of which me I'm playing."

My shoulders slump in exasperation. I remember the hike to the beach, the morning we did yoga. Desperately, I sift the sands of those memories for ways I've fallen short. "I have let you in," I insist. "What has this whole week been but letting you in?"

"You haven't, though. You've only said you wanted to *be on vacation*. You didn't want to share what's going on with your sister because we're *on vacation*. But, Eliza, you treat these conversations the same way when we're home." Graham's gaze pries on closed doors in my heart. "Will you ever want to talk about them? Will you ever want to talk about *anything*? I know you felt our relationship was suffering before we got here. I know I could've done more, been better, to prevent that from happening. But you said nothing. Instead of trying to work through what was going on between us truthfully, you invented this whole elaborate game for us."

"It worked, didn't it?" I reply. My heart is pounding—not with the nerves of a fighter in the ring, but those of someone far out to sea.

Graham softens momentarily. "It worked wonderfully," he says. "But, when we're home, when we're not playing these parts, will you ever want to share when you're upset? Or concerned? Or dissatisfied? I can ask all the questions I want, but I just can't keep guessing what the right questions are."

I'm struggling under the gravity of what he's saying. My cheeks feel horribly hot, like I have a fever. Graham isn't accusing, he isn't angry. I might find it easier if he was. If I could pin a litigator's fierce vindictiveness on him. Instead, he's just explaining. He's giving me no room to retort, no room to resent.

"You hide in silence. In your performances," he continues. "It's the shadow on the other side of this week. I know you want to pretend we were just having some unconventional, therapeutic fun. But it's not true, is it? You weren't just enjoying being and meeting someone new. You were loving being *not yourself.* This wasn't just about asking questions, or rediscovering surprises, or whatever. It was about hiding." He shakes his head sadly. "Until you're ready to open a door to me, I don't know how I can be here for you."

I'm speechless, caught in the cold grip of this impossible reality. Not just wordless-speechless, either. He's sucked the breath clean out of my lungs. I want to defend myself, want to point out the reasons why he's wrong. Under his gaze, though, I can't find them.

Sparing me, his eyes shift to my open suitcase on the bed. "I'll let you finish packing," he says, sounding like something has frozen over the fight in him. "We should drive out tonight. No point in staying."

Not hesitating, he walks to the door.

Before he opens it, he speaks to me over his shoulder. "Meet me in the bar when you're ready. We'll figure . . . the rest out from there."

Silently, I watch him walk out into the hallway. Unlike in the restaurant, I don't have the urge to rush after him. I don't have the energy. I don't have the hope.

I don't have anything at all to say.

48

Graham

IT'S FUNNY HOW different hotels feel with no excitement in them. They're just spaces, just logistics, just people showing up for work in rooms engineered for relaxation. Just beautiful frames on empty canvases.

Over the past week, I guess I'd gotten used to seeing something more in the mahogany corridors of this one. Now, standing in front of the reception desk with my bags packed, I feel exactly like I did when we first got here, when Eliza suggested we stay separately. I hand over my bags to the same bellhop who watched me with tentative curiosity when he escorted me down to my lonely honeymoon suite on our first night.

I don't know what's going to happen when we get into that car, when we start the six-hour drive back home to the problems now brought out into the daylight, still unresolved. Problems I couldn't even name on my way out of Eliza's hotel room. *We'll figure the rest out,* I said. The rest. I had to disguise the enormity of the rift between us behind the simple idiom. In this, I guess I'm hiding, too.

The receptionist smiles when she comes out from the back office and sees me. *Rosie,* I remember miserably. The cyclicality of everything is starting to grind on my nerves.

"Hi, Mr. Cutler," she greets me. "Happy anniversary."

Impossibly, I feel even worse. Part of me had forgotten. My parents must have mentioned it when they tried to send Eliza flowers.

"Would you like me to have champagne and roses sent over to your room tonight?" she offers. "What time are you dining? We can have them brought in while you and Mrs. Cutler are out."

Forcing my smile feels like carving into greased stone while holding my chisel with broken fingers.

"Actually," I say, "I'd like to check out."

Rosie maintains her pleasantly neutral demeanor despite the huge reversal I've delivered her. "All right," she complies quickly, her nails clicking quietly on her keyboard. "I hope there weren't any problems with your room or your stay."

"No, nothing like that," I reply. It's the truth, which is heartbreaking in its own way. Everything here was perfect. Practically paradise. It was our best shot.

But if Eliza and I couldn't succeed here, couldn't find each other here, there's no way we'll manage to in the midst of work, routines, ordinary life. The thought returns two looping, looming words to the fore of my mind—*the rest.*

Rosie prints out a receipt. "Just sign here," she instructs me gently, passing the hotel pen to me over the desk. "When you're ready to leave, you can recycle your keys with me."

I nod, staring down at the list of charges. Neat, itemized reminders of everything Eliza and I did this week. There's dinner and dancing. Higher up, the boxing class neither of us was prepared for. Everything. It's painfully perfect, seeing them reduced like this. Stripped of emotion in precise ink.

I hesitate for a second, then sign my name in fast, sure strokes.

Returning the paper to the receptionist, I feel sadder than I thought I would. I imagined we'd be leaving this hotel renewed, our marriage fortified. Instead, part of me feels like I'm throwing in the towel. But I've truly done everything I can think to do. We don't need to have the impending long conversation in the same room where I undressed my wife down to her lingerie. Better it be in our cluttered dining room.

I'm turning to leave when the front doors open. David and Lindsey walk in. Remembering the plans David detailed to me for their date, I check my watch. It's only 7:30, which doesn't bode well for a first date. Neither do the looks on their faces—David is plainly crestfallen, the emotion out of place on his usually exuberant features, while Lindsey is grimacing like she just stepped in a puddle while wearing socks.

They're not speaking. Feet of distance separate them without the slightest chance of hand-holding.

"Have a nice trip home," Lindsey manages when they get inside, not quite meeting David's eyes. David mutters something I can't hear in reply.

My heart sinks for my friend. While I haven't known David long, not only was I really rooting for him—I'd started to find in his hope the hope I needed myself. It's difficult not to see in this obviously dismal turn of events one more sign from the universe that things weren't going to turn out well. Not for me, nor for my large-hearted new confidant.

Only once Lindsey has disappeared into the back does David

notice me. His somber expression unchanging, he walks up to me with his hands in his pockets. I wait, expecting the full rundown. If I know David, he's going to need to give me a detailed report, to strategize, to figure out and fix what went wrong. He's going to need hope.

Instead, he only sighs.

"I need a drink," he says.

49

Eliza

I WALK MY luggage from my room to the car, moving methodically, with empty calm. The car is parked in the small lot where we first drove in, and I can't help feeling the finality of my every step, each one carrying me closer to saying goodbye to the chances I once found here.

The night is shifting from twilight blue into black over the trees surrounding the hotel. I load the suitcase into our trunk, remembering how frayed my wits were when I got out of this car six days ago. How hopeless I felt.

Miserable, I shut the door. I really don't know what to do. Marriages, I think, run on the conviction of having a certain invincibility. To make the promises they involve, you have to believe you could, if called upon, do *whatever* your spouse needs. It's a faith you need to keep.

But it's a perilous one, isn't it? If Graham *needed* me to compute multivariable calculus right now, I couldn't do it—no matter the promises I made to him on the lawn of the Huntington Gardens.

What if this is emotional multivariable calculus?

I'm confronting the possibility that Graham needs something from me I don't know how to give. Leaning against the car, I stare at the hotel. I don't want to go to the bar to meet him just yet, not when it puts me one pace closer to embarking on the journey home. Leaving here doesn't just mean leaving the celebration of our anniversary, leaving the progress we made. It means leaving the performance behind—its joys, its surprises, its memories.

So I say goodbye. Under the night sky, I pause in silent farewell to my character, the vacation planner who helped me to loosen up around my husband, who could see Graham in so many new lights.

The feeling isn't entirely new. Whenever I finish a job, I mourn just a little the small death of the character I played. This is worse, though. This other Eliza brought so much to my life. I'm going to miss her, and her fling with a man she was already falling for, and her business with her three sisters.

My heart clenches painfully, tears catching me by surprise for the second time in one day. I open the passenger door and get inside, then pop open the glove compartment, searching for napkins. The tearful feeling doesn't pass, my throat throbbing painfully. I'm upset about Graham, of course, about how I guess I failed him in some way I couldn't see coming today.

But I'm crying about Michelle, too. About how childishly transparent it was that I invented this perfect little professional life for my character with her merry group of vacation-planning sisters, like we're some upbeat Netflix comedy. What a joke. What a fucking sad joke.

Returning to the real Eliza means fully dealing with everything going on with my sister, not just escaping into this fantasy version of myself. The tears come harder now. In the echoing quiet of the car, I hear myself gulping sobs while everything crashes over me.

How *did* I let things get so messed up with my sister? Yes, Michelle shouldn't have jumped to the conclusion that I missed her engagement party because I was flippant or selfish, but I didn't explain myself, either. I didn't try. Not once. Maybe Graham was right when he said I don't make it easy to know me. Maybe I hide from problems, preferring to ignore them until the point where they become daunting, impossible, consuming.

How do I stop, though? Somehow, I need to open the door not just to Graham, but to Michelle, too. Because—I realize with panicky hurt so profound it makes me crumple over the dashboard—they're just different parts of the same problem. In my battered heart, I know feeling rejected and judged by Michelle is why I've been closed off with Graham these past months. I was scared. If my only sister, once my best friend in the whole world, could write me off, then the man I loved could, too.

But not if I wrote us off first.

It's why, this whole trip, I've resisted getting into anything real with Graham. I didn't want to be in the position to get rejected the way Michelle rejected me.

But that ends now, I hear in my head in a firm voice I don't entirely recognize. I need to open the door to them and face what could hurt me. Pushing myself not to lose my nerve, I unlock my phone, and with unsteady hands, I call Michelle. In the seconds while the call rings, I compose myself, casting off my tears with deep breaths.

My sister picks up, her voice prickly. "Hello?"

I don't hesitate. "I didn't mean to miss your engagement party. I promise—I tried to get out of the studio but it wasn't just my job that would have been affected by cutting out early. I couldn't do it to the producer, the sound technicians, the people who needed my work done. Then when I *could* get out, I spent forever on the phone with the airline searching for whatever wild connecting flights would get me there in time, but there just was nothing. Truly there wasn't," I say, pausing only to catch my breath. "I'm so*, so* sorry. I wanted to be there more than anything. I still have the toast I wrote in my phone. I know it looked flaky or selfish of me to miss it, I know that. But . . . Michelle, it really fucking hurt that you didn't even ask me what had happened. You just assumed I was making it about me."

I finish my speech, dazed, sort of in disbelief I said everything I envisioned saying. I'm grateful Michelle didn't interrupt me or hang up. I don't know what will come next, but I know this step was important.

When Michelle speaks, her voice is soft, if grudging. "You're right," she concedes. "I shouldn't have assumed."

She doesn't sound warm, but I hear real emotion in her voice, real feeling she wouldn't let in during our last call. I wait for her to continue, curled up in the cool leather of the passenger seat with my heart pounding.

"It's not that I think you're selfish," she goes on. "But . . . throughout our lives, I've sometimes felt like a giant spotlight follows you around. You're an actress, and you're older, and you're married, and you're . . . everything you are. And I'm not jealous of you, I'm not. I just felt like maybe my wedding could be the time where *I'm* the center of attention. God, I sound like a spoiled brat even saying that, don't I?"

She says her final words with a flicker of self-effacing humor, and it's enough for me to laugh with immeasurable relief. "Of course you don't sound spoiled. It's your wedding," I reassure her. "You *should* be the center of attention." I wipe my nose, exhaling, finding my reply. "I'm sorry that my missing your party stole even a fraction of your spotlight. And I'm sorry if, at any other times in our lives, I haven't been as sensitive as I could be about that. You deserve your own spotlight—not just on your wedding day."

Michelle is quiet for a moment. "Thank you, Eliza," she finally says. "I . . . really want you to be at my wedding."

I'm crying again now, but they're good tears. Not just happy tears, though there is happiness in them. They're *good* tears. The release of things needing freedom from my heart, new beginnings rolling down my cheeks.

"I'm going to take the whole week off work," I tell her with hic-cupping breaths. "Trust me. I'll be there. There's nothing more im-portant to me."

"Thanks." I hear a sniffle on Michelle's end. "You said you still have that toast?"

I smile. "I can send it to you right now, if you want."

"How about you save it for the wedding?"

My heart swells. I nod like she can see me, even though of course she can't. "You got it."

I know this is when we say goodbye, but not a real goodbye, not the goodbye we've been living for months. Just a temporary break in our lifelong conversation. Still, though, I don't want to hang up. Not yet.

"Eliza?" Her voice sounds scared. "Can I ask you something?"

I squeeze my eyes shut, afraid. *No.* I can face this. Whatever she wants to know, I can face it for her. I open my eyes and fix them on the sea ahead. "Anything."

"Do you think Ben and I will be good together? The way you and Graham are, I mean."

Even though I know her words should make me sad, I don't just smile. I beam. "You two will be perfect, even when it feels like you're not. Which—sometimes, you'll really, really feel like you're not."

It's a moment before she replies, and I just know my sister is smiling one of her small, dazzling smiles. "Thanks."

When we hang up, I feel lighter. No, not lighter—stronger. The lightness isn't the weight of emotions leaving me. It's the understanding that I'm courageous enough, honest enough, to carry them.

I wipe my tears and get out of the car. Calmly, I go to the trunk, where I remove my suitcase. We won't be checking out tonight.

With the evening drying my cheeks, everything feels clearer. I'm done hiding. I'm done concealing truths I don't want to face. Whenever things get dark or frightening, I'm going to hold on to how I feel right now, walking toward the hotel with my suitcase in hand.

But performance doesn't just mean hiding. It means growth, too. It means self-discovery.

Graham was right about certain things, but there are others he doesn't understand. He doesn't think our performances can stay with us. He doesn't understand that the parts we played *weren't* just a game. No performance ever really is. Ours helped us explore who we are and who we can be to each other. I know I'm going to carry parts of Vacation Planner Eliza with me even when we go home, and I hope we can hold on to parts of the relationship we started to rebuild together here. We can discover and rediscover new lives and new loves. We can do it without hiding.

I walk swiftly into the lobby, needing to make arrangements for the night.

50

Graham

DAVID LEANS WITH his elbows on the bar, looking lost. I'm sitting next to him with our drinks in front of us, half empty.

Half full, some would say. Not us.

Truthfully, while I'm not *happy* David's date got cut short and he's heartbroken in this bar with me, I'm not ungrateful for the distraction or for the chance to have this last drink with him before we return to our respective normal lives. I know what's waiting for me, but I have one hour left of vacation, and I'm going to take every glorious, mopey second of it.

"Do you want to talk about it?" I ask. I've let David nurse his drink in silence for fifteen minutes, but I don't know when Eliza will show up. Besides, I do want David to know I'm here for him. I've never been the kind of guy who's afraid of sharing his feelings. David obviously isn't, either.

David sips his drink morosely. "The date started out fantastic," he says, staring vacantly forward. I note his word choice. Even down in the dumps, he's effusive. "We shared a hummus platter, and she told me about her hiking plans," he goes on. "We talked about the seminar. I made her laugh a couple times, too."

I nod encouragingly, knowing there's more to the story.

"I was feeling *so* good that it seemed like the time to tell her." He winces from the pain of this confession. "So I did. I told her the truth—that my hobbies back home look less like climbing mountains in my free time and more like hunting for glue stick deals and memorizing the new Pokémon—but I said I really was enjoying learning about all the things she's interested in."

He's emphatic on his final words, presenting them with passion. He's talking to me the way I imagine he did to Lindsey. I've heard partners do this on the phone with clients, orating case points to them with the same intonation, the same conviction they did for the jury.

"It was the right thing to do," I tell him gently. "I'm sorry she didn't take it well."

Frowning, David swirls his drink. "She did, though. She took it great. She wasn't mad. She didn't think I was lying or being weird. She admired that I was taking an interest in what interested her."

I furrow my brow. Often when partners overemphasize case points to clients, it's because we lost. "Okay, then . . ." I say. "What went wrong?"

When David sighs, I don't just hear resignation in the sound. He's hurt. "She didn't want to know what interested *me*. I guess I can't blame her. She went on this date expecting me to be someone who perfectly aligns with her passions. Still, though, I realized while sitting there that I wanted to tell her about my students and the field trips I have planned. And she just . . . didn't want to know. She didn't like me for *me*."

Unexpectedly, his face crumples. The open display of emotion sort of moves me—not only out of sympathy, either. There's impressive honesty in the expression, even courage. I reach over to pat him on the back.

"It's okay if you need to cry, man," I say.

David sniffles a little, then straightens. "No. I . . . didn't really know her that well." He forces a smile that doesn't fully reach his eyes. "*Next* time I fall in love, I'm going to be true to myself."

I smile. "You're a catch," I say honestly. "It won't be long."

Now he glances up intently, with comedic bewilderment. "I am, right?"

My laughter echoes in the dark bar. "Dude," I reassure my friend. "You're like seven feet tall. Built for boxing. Great with kids. Of *course* you're a catch."

David looks like he's grinning despite himself when I finish my litany of compliments. "You just wrote my dating profile bio for me. Better than the workshop's." He finishes his drink. "Hey, San Diego and SLO aren't that close, but LA is in the middle-ish. You think we can hang out after this week?"

I feel some of the day's heartache leave me. "Yeah," I say. "Yeah, I'd really like that." In this week of pretend, my friendship with David is something undeniably real, something I can take home with me.

Neither of us speaks now. The silence isn't sad like when we first sat down, though. I can savor the end of my final hour here in quiet companionship. While it's not how I wanted to celebrate my anniversary, I'm grateful that I'm not alone.

51

Eliza

"ARE YOU SERIOUS?"

I'm at reception, interrogating Rosie, who is wholly undeserving of my frustration. It's just, I can't believe him. I was only in the car having a life-changing epiphany for ten minutes, and *this* is what my husband does?

Rosie nervously checks the computer again, her fingers racing over the keys. "I'm so sorry," she says sounding genuine, her concerned eyes scouring the screen. "He's already checked out of the room. His bags are waiting at the bellhop. His key won't even work anymore."

I sigh. In my head, I fight to regroup. My plan was perfect. On the short walk from the car up to the reception desk, I guess I . . . got my hopes up. I imagined. I was proud of the idea I feel collapsing under the weight of logistics.

"He didn't check out of your room, though, if you'd like to make your arrangements there," she says.

In the one foot between my queen bed and the wall? I appreciate Rosie's effort, I do. I just know with certainty my little, lonely room won't accommodate what I have in mind. Not like—

A wild impulse grips me. I place my card on the counter.

"Can I rebook his suite for tonight?"

ON MY WAY to the bar, I'm on the edge of frenzied. I rehearse my mental checklist, hoping I got everything set despite Graham's unknowing efforts to thwart me.

In inexplicable ways, every detail of this hotel feels incredibly significant to me. The earthy geometry of the lobby, the slate in the hallway to the bar, the echo of my heels on the floor. This place was only supposed to be our vacation spot. Right now, it feels like it could be much, much more.

Pausing in the doorway to the bar, I smooth down my dress. It's the white one I packed for our anniversary dinner. The costume choice, I recognize, is high stakes. If this goes wrong, I'll feel stupid, dressed up in my wishful thinking.

If it goes right . . . it'll be the sort of perfect I hardly dare to hope for.

With my heart pounding, I work to calm my jumpy nerves. Is this how Graham felt right before he proposed? No, this is definitely worse. Because I don't just have to pop one iconic four-word question. Having my epiphany was one thing, but doing it is something else entirely. I have to make real, vulnerable changes. I have to open up.

Mustering my strength, I walk in.

I find Graham and David seated at the bar, in practically the same stools as the first night I found them here. The night one innocent misunderstanding sparked the game we've spent the week playing. Hit with overwhelming déjà vu, I shake off the feeling. The bar might look the same, the way my husband is sitting, his friend with him—fine, pretty much everything seems the same— but *I'm* not the same. We're not the same. We're not in the same spot we were a week ago.

I remind myself of the differences. The ways I've changed, the ways we've learned how to be better with each other. The reasons why we'll work.

These thoughts carry me up to the bar with my head held high, projecting confidence I'm still working on feeling. It'll come, though. I know it will.

David notices me first, glancing up from his empty glass. "Hey, Eliza," he says. "Want to join us?"

Graham follows his friend's gaze to me. I watch his double-take when he registers what I'm wearing, my white dress lit up under the dim overhead lights. Questions I can read easily spring into his eyes. They begin with, *You changed into your dinner dress for our six-hour drive home?* But where they end is somewhere else, some realm of closely guarded hope.

When he opens his mouth—probably to point out the car attire thing—I cut him off, holding my hand out to David.

"David, I want to introduce myself for real," I say. "Hi. I'm Eliza Cutler, Graham's wife. Thanks for being such a great friend to my husband this week."

David blinks. I have to smile. He wears his bemusement at my unconventional second introduction right on his sleeve, just like everything else. Rewriting this moment feels sort of strange—playing out my conversation with David without the crossed cues, the mixed signals, the sudden pivots. It reminds me of the weird clashing juxtapositions of getting coffee with classmates right before running some traumatic Shakespearean death scene with them in college.

But this is right. It's time to be me. It's time to do this for real.

David takes my hand, his eyes darting uncertainly to Graham. "It's nice to meet you, too, Eliza. You've got a good guy here."

I look to Graham, my smile softening. Nothing, I think to myself, is more real than that. "I know," I say. I turn back to David, who's watching my husband, no doubt trying to figure out what's going on here. "Do you mind if I interrupt you two?" I prompt gently.

David searches Graham's expression before replying. It's endearing to see their silent exchange. When Graham introduced me to Nikki, it didn't take long for Nikki to become more my friend than his. I'm glad Graham has David now—glad Graham has more proof of how easy he is to love. If tonight goes the way I hope it will, I'll make sure David's invited down to San Diego for long weekends. Maybe they can go camping in Joshua Tree, making up for the trip I made Graham cut short.

Graham dips his chin in the subtlest of nods, and David stands up. "Of course not," he says, his eyes returning to me. "I should go back to my room and pack anyway." He claps Graham on the shoulder on his way out.

"I'll text you later, man," Graham says to his friend.

David grins. Behind Graham's back, David shoots me two encouraging thumbs up before walking out.

I don't take David's now-empty seat.

"Are you really going to wear that for our drive back?" Graham asks. "It's six hours, you know."

I bite the inside of my cheek to keep from smiling at the question I just knew Graham has been thinking since seeing me tonight.

It's nice, to have this small moment of knowing what he was going to say. Of knowing him. It feels like the universe's tiniest tongue-in-cheek promise that things will be better now, or they'll start to be.

"No," I say. "Would you come with me, Graham? Please."

I know he's hesitant, frustrated, even hurt. But his expression betrays him. He must hear the lifetime I meant to promise in my short, simple request, because his eyebrows rise, and when hope steals into his eyes, it sparkles like stars scattered in the night sky. He looks like it's surprised even him.

"Why?" His question is scarcely audible over the noise of the bar. "We were going to head home."

I reach for his hand. When mine finds his, his expression flickers, like it's nearly too much for his heart to bear. I feel the same way.

"I was thinking," I say, "we could celebrate our anniversary."

52

Graham

I FOLLOW MY wife down the now-familiar path toward the suites, not knowing where we're headed. I feel like I'm very high up but haven't looked down yet. The risk is there—the precariousness of my position—but the thrill is there, too, the dizzying clarity of my heart starting to soar. I've never felt more frightened of falling, but I've never felt closer to heaven, either.

When we take several turns I know I recognize, confusion settles over me. "Eliza, I checked out of my room."

She doesn't slow down. "I know," she says.

Undeniably curious, I keep following her. In the quiet of the evening, the trees feel like they're welcoming me back home, their limbs motionless while we continue down the gravel pathway. It's jarring, returning to this private world I thought I'd left for good. My mind can't decide whether I'm stealing in uninvited or whether I'm right where I'm supposed to be. Maybe it's both.

When Eliza stops outside my old room, I raise my eyebrows in inquiry.

She only grins. Then she produces a keycard, which she uses to click open the door.

I watch in bewilderment. "How . . ."

"The suite happened to be vacant for the night," she replies with coy innocence. "So I checked in."

She enters, the lights turning on gradually with the unlocked door. I cross the threshold and feel fully like I'm walking into a dream. When I take in the room, my questions disappear.

It's been prepared exactly the way we wanted to avoid when we first checked in. Every detail is impossibly, perfectly in place. Candles line the hallway leading to the bed, where rose petals spell out "Mr. and Mrs." On one nightstand is a sweating champagne bottle and a pair of crystal-clear glasses. It's romance epitomized, and it makes my heart pound with joy struggling under so much uncertainty.

I turn to Eliza, who looks nervous, watching my reaction closely. She's a good enough actress to hide her nerves if she wanted to. That she didn't is unfairly endearing.

"I don't want to drive home tonight," she explains. "I don't want to give up. Instead . . ."

She pauses. Her eyes, full of daring conviction, find mine.

"I want to renew our vows," she says.

I blink. While I'm finding nothing to say—not yet—excitement and hesitation share my speechlessness uneasily. Eliza steps forward, her hand taking mine. Instinctively I interlock my fingers with hers, the dance we've done hundreds, even thousands of times.

"It's been five years since we did this, and I think it's clear we've changed," she goes on. "We're not the same couple we were when we stood before all our friends and family and promised to love each other through everything. I think we need to update those promises. We need to make them match the people we are now."

I want so badly to say yes. To go with empty confidence into the plan she's proposing—to never look down from this heartrending height.

But what she's saying doesn't undo my doubts. I can't ignore them, even if I wish I could.

"Eliza, I—I told you what I needed from you," I get out.

"I know. I know—" Her words pick up speed. "You were right. The game we were playing did bring us closer, but it let me hide from being myself, too. Which I do too often. It's . . . something I have trouble with." She sighs, half frustration, half discomfort from this confession. Sympathy flickers in me. "I'm afraid of being rejected by the ones I love," she goes on. "You, Michelle—it *was* the same thing. I thought I was protecting myself from you, and I couldn't see how it was hurting us. But I'm fighting it now. I called Michelle, and I told her everything."

My surprise rushes blood to my face. The room comes into sharper focus. Eliza comes into sharper focus. I see she's still wearing her rings around her neck. "What happened?" I ask.

She smiles bashfully. "I'm hoping you'll be my date to her wedding."

The news fills me with instant, instinctive happiness—not only from Eliza reconciling with her sister, but because she's telling me. It *is* what I said I needed from her, or some small beginning of it.

But it only makes me feel more pulled in opposite directions. I don't know how to respond to Eliza, not when my mind and heart still feel out of sync. Surrounded by rose petals, with champagne on the nightstand, I want so desperately to give in to the romance she's put on, the promises she's inscribed everywhere in this room. I want to trust she's heading to where I'm waiting.

Eliza's intensity softens. "I won't keep shutting you out, Graham. I promise. We have to talk about the hard stuff," she says. "Starting right now."

Just like it came into her features, the imploring in her eyes is suddenly gone. She straightens up, looking me squarely in the face. In her moment's pause—with her chin up, her perfect lips set, her spun-gold hair curling over one shoulder of her ivory dress—I have the chance to think to myself, *What a profoundly gorgeous woman I married.*

"I vow"—she starts—"to open the door to you. To tell you when I'm upset, when I need something. To let this be a partnership not just in fun, but in everything."

She pauses like she's choosing her words. I wait.

"Which includes us," she continues. "Part of sharing even the hard stuff is letting you know what I need—trusting that you want to know and won't reject me for it. So," she says, "here it goes."

I start smiling with her. The quiet wonder of her words begins to settle over me, too. What she's saying isn't the only surprise. What's also surprising is that she's saying it herself. She's not hiding in character. She's Eliza, Eliza Cutler.

"I wish you, Graham, would dance with me more," she declares.

Her no-nonsense tone lifts my eyebrows. Eliza's posture only sharpens, wild confidence entering her gaze.

"I wish you would ask me about my day. About anything. I need to keep exploring, stepping outside of my normal routine, and I want you there with me when I do. I need you to be up for the challenge," she continues.

Her words wrap around my heart. "I vow to never stop dating you," I reply. While Eliza had the opportunity to figure out what she wanted to say while she was putting this together, I'm coming into this vow renewal pretty much cold. Even so, I find my words come easily. "I vow to never stop getting to know you. To believe in myself because—believing in myself is believing in us."

Eliza's smile is iridescent. It fills her face—it fills the room. My own private moonlight.

"I love you," she says.

"God, I love you so much," I rush to reply.

Pulling her to me, I kiss her fiercely. She kisses me back. There's nothing else, no layers, no charged questions, no one here except me and the woman I love, my best friend in the world. It's impossibly, incredibly real.

When I step back, I thumb the rings hanging from her neck-lace. I know their contours as well as the hand on which I've seen them worn for five years, studied the stone's winking facets while Eliza cooked or drove or flipped the pages of whatever she's reading for work.

In unspoken reply, she turns around. I brush her hair aside, exposing her neck, and with featherlight fingers, I undo the clasp of her necklace. She catches the rings as they slip from the chain. Then, her eyes questioning, she holds them out to me. When I take them, the platinum and diamond feel at once delicate and unbreakable in the palm of my hand. Facing me once more, Eliza puts out her left hand.

For the second time in five years, I slide the rings onto her finger.

Once I have, Eliza reaches for my right hand and deftly removes my wedding band from where I've worn it for a week. We watch together, our heads bowed over this quiet dance of hands, as Eliza returns it to where it belongs.

"I vow never to take this off again," I say quietly.

She doesn't reply. She doesn't need to. I hold her hand tightly, making more vows silently to myself. I will never give up. Our marriage will change over the years, but I will always remember this—there's a way back. We just have to be brave enough to find it.

53

Eliza

WE STAND ON the balcony, wrapped in a sheet, staring at the vista that stretches forever in front of us. In the distance, the details of the trees disappear, the foliage reduced to one continuous expanse, darkly carpeting the cliffs. Nevertheless, they're there. Growing, reaching. Ever changing.

The night is perfectly calm. There's no whisper of wind. The soft roar of the ocean surrounds us, its own faint, ever-present reminder of the enormity of the world outside this private universe we've created for ourselves this week. It's breathtaking. It's endless.

It's waiting for us.

The idea doesn't make me nervous. It would've when we got here, would've even yesterday. In this moment, though, I feel comfortable enjoying the sweetness of tonight while looking out into the inescapability of tomorrow.

Graham is behind me, his body flush with mine in the bedsheet covering us, his lips pressed to my bare shoulder. I gaze up into the sky, my breathing even. On my left hand, the feeling of my wedding rings is inexpressible comfort. Searching the skyline, I follow the swirl of stars to one bright spot in the distance, smudged like iridescent ink on the black page of the night. On our balcony, we don't have quite the view we did last night, when we stood on the hilltop now partially obscuring the curve of the Milky Way, the band of stars overhead.

I don't need the full view, though. I remember everything. I'll never forget it.

Behind me, Graham's deeper breathing moves out of sync with mine, like two rhythms in one song. I guess it's cliché or mushy, but with his smoothly shaven chin resting on my shoulder, his body close enough for me to smell his familiar scent, I'm happy. In his arms, I feel like I'm exactly where I'm supposed to be. Like I'm exactly *who* I'm supposed to be.

I understand myself better—I understand us better. I think something starts to happen in the different ways you see your partner over the years. There's the concept of them—their human résumé, their vocation, the collection of things you're proud of in them, the good qualities you know they embody—but then, separately, there's the day-to-day person. The person who reminds you to do the laundry, or who microwaves dinner, or who wakes you when he gets up in the morning. It's not like they clash, one the disillusionment of the idealized other. It's more like the quotidian sometimes eclipses the more fundamental picture.

I understand now that Graham didn't know how much I see the wonderful light in his full picture. But I do. With this week behind us, I think he finally knows I do. The idea is its own profound peace, perfectly in tune with the calm night.

Over the whisper of the ocean, I almost don't hear my husband's murmured question.

"What do you think they're doing right now?"

I twist to see his face. He's staring out into the stars like I was, their patterns reflected on his irises. He looks down to meet my gaze, the promise of a smile on the lips I'd just felt on my skin.

"Who?" I ask him.

Now he smiles, like he expected the question. "You know who."

Matching Graham, I curl my lips, returning my eyes to the vast, dark view. I *do* know who. In the distance, where the road winds into the hillside, I can practically see them. The other us, in separate cars to the airport, for separate flights to separate cities. I let myself conjure them in my head. "Hm," I start. "I think they'd spend one last night together. They'd stay up all night talking, and not talking. In the morning, saying goodbye would be very hard."

"How sad for them." I feel Graham's smile brush my neck.

"Very."

Graham goes quiet, kissing my shoulder gently. "Graham would get on his plane home to Santa Fe," he says. "He'd tell himself it was just a fling, but he wouldn't stop thinking about her, no matter how much he tried to."

I follow his imagination, privately glad this flight of fancy isn't over. "Even with wild late-night hookups after leaving the office?" I ask goadingly.

"Especially then."

I turn to face him fully. He gazes down, our eyes, our lips, thrillingly close. It's been fun—better than fun—inventing these characters by embodying them. But carrying them on like this, like they're old friends or, closer to the truth, treasured memories, is wonderful in its own way. "I think Eliza would return home to her sisters and then immediately find a reason to research hotels in Santa Fe."

His grin sharpens playfully. Inspiration sparkles with the stars in his eyes, his hand ever so softly finding my hip under the sheet. "Then they'd surely run into each other," he says. In the undercurrent in his words, I don't just hear the fun he's having. This story we're telling is meaningful to him. "Maybe Graham is having dinner with an investor at a swanky hotel and he looks up to see a familiar face at the bar."

I pick up the story. "She saw him, too, of course. But she wants to play coy. She just waits, making sure no one sits next to her."

"We both know what happens next," he replies.

With Santa Fe and stylish hotels filling my imagination, I start to realize something. Our characters no longer feel like us. Yes, they're figments given life by little pieces of our souls, but their story isn't one we're living. It's one we're watching from our own lives, our own selves.

"Is it silly to say I'm going to miss them?" I ask softly. I'd let my gaze drift out into the night, but now I pull my eyes back to Graham's. "Don't get me wrong, it's not Investment Banker Graham I miss. I prefer you in every single way. But . . . I'm grateful to them. I'm grateful for the gift they gave us."

When I finish, I hear emotion in my voice I didn't expect. I search Graham's expression for signs of whether he feels the same. Whether he understands. Whether sadness streaks the edges of this story for him like it does for me.

"No, it's not silly," he says.

I rest my head on his chest. Every contour is wonderfully familiar.

"I don't think we need to say goodbye to them, not completely," he goes on.

Biting my lip, I look up with a raised eyebrow. "Is that so?"

Graham leans down, nipping my lower lip. "On occasion, it might be nice to check in on them," he murmurs, his face near mine, his mouth within kissing distance.

"Graham Cutler, just when I think I know exactly who you are, you never stop surprising me," I say.

He pulls me to him in reply, our lips coming together. With the sky at my back, he holds me while the galaxy gently spins.

Epilogue

Eliza

THE DRESS I'M wearing to Michelle's wedding is hanging up in the car. I'm in the house, packing the rest.

Graham and I decided to take time off of work for the two-day road trip we're making out to Boulder, Colorado, where my sister is tying the knot, then to Santa Fe for the weekend, complete with itinerary and restaurants Graham planned. Truthfully, I'm really excited. Not just for Michelle, obviously, or the gorgeous venue she's chosen in the mountains, or New Mexico's desert charms. No, I'm excited for the drive. I'm excited for time with Graham.

With my suitcase open on our bed, I've layered in most of what I'll need. Heels in the top zip pocket, flats for brunch on the sides, the non-work book I'm planning to read stuffed between sweaters. I smile, knowing Graham's eyes will light up when he notices it—it's book three in a series he's effectively caught up on via my enthusiastic descriptions over dinner.

Now I'm making sure I have enough underwear for the trip. My eyes snag on the red lingerie in my drawer. Without hesitating, I reach for it right as Graham appears in the doorway. I lay the lingerie in my suitcase, in full view.

The lace snares his gaze just like it did mine. When he raises an eyebrow, I know exactly what he's thinking. "Those remind me of someone," he says, folding his arms across his chest.

I don't hide my grin. "Mr. Cutler," I say in mock inquisition, "are you thinking about another woman?"

He crosses the room in quick strides. I let his hands find my waist, let myself lean into his chest. "Just a vacation fling," he says. "She has nothing on you."

Warmth fills me, his words melting my playful posturing. We brought more than this lingerie home from our anniversary trip. We've kept going to boxing classes—the beginner level, though. Every now and then, Graham surprises me with dance lessons or cooking classes or nights out. Over a long weekend, David visited, and while we hiked in Torrey Pines, he enthusiastically shared with us everything about the new woman he met online using the dating profile he set up in the workshop. He promised to invite us to the inevitable wedding.

On occasion, it isn't Graham who works in downtown San Diego who comes home from the office, nor the Eliza who spent the day in the recording studio who meets him. From time to time, we slip on the roles of our characters for some fun. We reignite their chemistry, we continue their stories. For the night, we become the couple who found each other again, who fell for each other again, who remind us of ourselves in the sweetest ways.

The roles remain easy opportunities to keep getting to know the new and ever-changing sides of each other, and to remind ourselves of just how many versions of each other we love. They're hours-long vacations into parallel lives. What's more, they've strengthened our marriage in every way, so much so, I can hardly imagine the me of four months ago who dreaded six silent hours in the car with my husband.

They're helping us find our future, too.

When we got home, conversations happened over dinner in which we confirmed it wasn't just Graham in character who was ready to have kids. In short, I fell in love with the idea, which now sparkles on the horizon. I'm not pregnant yet. But Graham's researching his firm's paternity leave policies in earnest, and sometimes when I look into rooms in our home, I start to imagine different furniture in them.

"Not to rush you," Graham says, stepping out of our embrace, "but we have to get on the road if we want to beat traffic."

I smile to myself. Some things haven't changed between us. But I know how to talk to my husband now. Shutting my suitcase, I turn to Graham. "Exactly how much time have you spent on Google Maps this morning?" I put the question to him with playful suspicion.

He laughs good-naturedly. "It's good to be prepared. Wouldn't want something to make you late to this wedding."

I soften, recognizing the kindness in Graham's thinking. It's not unwarranted—I might have had a little travel anxiety about making it to Michelle's wedding, given what happened with the engagement party. I don't know if I could take disappointing my sister for the second time. Instead of concealing my fears, though, I told Graham what I was feeling. I let him in. He was the one who suggested we drive out early, ensuring nothing keeps us from my sister's wedding.

I brush a quick kiss to his lips on my way out of the room.

He follows me through our house, which hasn't looked cluttered to me since we got home from Big Sur. Graham's paperwork on one end of the dining table, the scripts I've stacked on top of the books on our bookcases, the handheld fan we keep in the kitchen for when Graham's recent forays into cooking upset the smoke detector. They don't feel like the signs of increasingly non-overlapping lives. They feel like us.

"Are you going to be recording something while we drive?" he asks.

He holds the front door open for me while I walk out into our familiar driveway. The conditions closely resemble the day we drove out for the trip we didn't know would change our lives, the silver sky overhead, the fog condensing in droplets on our recycling cans. It's nothing like the gorgeous greenery, the rolling hills, the unique majesty of the Treeline Resort—and yet, I feel like we bottled up and brought some of the hotel's romance home with us.

"I might," I reply. "If it doesn't bother you."

Graham pops the trunk. "Is it sexy stuff?"

His boyish phrasing makes me laugh. "Not today," I say, swinging open the passenger door. A hint of regret colors my voice.

Graham hums. "Damn. That's unfortunate."

I grin. "Well, if *that's* what you're looking for, I'm certain we can come up with something on our very long drive."

The car shudders as Graham shuts the trunk. He reappears on the driver's side. "Yeah? Because I've been brainstorming, and I think I might outdo you this time."

We get into the car at the same time. I feel a pleased flush rise on my neck, while Graham looks like he can't resist. He leans over the center console to take my lips with his. His mouth is hot, wanting in his every caress, weakening my limbs with sweet static electricity. Suddenly, I find myself running the same calculations he was all morning—exactly *how* long until we're in our hotel room for the night?

"I'm sure you will," I whisper in the post-kiss lull. "You're very creative, you know."

Flashing me a cheeky grin, Graham starts the car, his motions hurried, like he knows what every wasted second will cost him. I don't fight the flush in my neck from raging onto my cheeks. Graham will notice. I don't care. He knows what I'm thinking, because he's thinking it himself. There's no use pretending.

He pulls out of our driveway, and my face aches from smiling. With the open road ahead, I settle into my seat, looking forward to every us we'll be tonight and for the rest of our lives.

Acknowledgments

What's left to say on second books? They're challenging, nerve-wracking exercises in sustained hope. Self-doubt waits in every stumble. Encouragement is essential. While *Do I Know You?* is not our second book, it is our second foray into this genre—one we couldn't have made without the invaluable help of so many.

Katie Shea Boutillier, you're the greatest. We literally couldn't have done any of this without you. Thank you for being our champion on every single book, not to mention the sort of wonderful friend one is lucky to find in publishing.

Kristine Swartz, you're our dream editor. Thank you for making us part of the fabulous Berkley family. We're deeply grateful for the incisive, completely spot-on editorial guidance you gave us to make this the very best version of the story we envisioned. We feel so, so lucky to work with you!

We do not exaggerate when we say we were stunned by the gorgeous design of every component of this book. Vi-An Nguyen—

we've got to be honest, we didn't know how you would rise to follow up the cover of *The Roughest Draft*, but this marvelous design is in its own league. The way you've captured the concept is nothing short of ingenious. Alison Cnockaert, thank you for making every page lovelier than we could have ever imagined, the perfect invitation into this story. Thank you to Megha Jain, Christine Legon, Jessica McDonnell, Alice Dalrymple, Claire Sullivan, and Mary Baker for turning our manuscript into this book.

Every word we write is for readers. Tina Joell, Kristin Cipolla, Fareeda Bullert, Jessica Plummer, Hillary Tacuri, we feel very fortunate for your incredible work getting this story into their hearts and hands. We love working with you.

The wonderful romance community continues to feel like home. We're very grateful for the kind words and support of fellow authors—Lyssa Kay Adams, Kate Clayborn, Jen DeLuca, Trish Doller, Rachel Hawkins, Ali Hazelwood, Emily Henry, Sarah Hogle, Libby Hubscher, Kosoko Jackson, Amy Lea, Maureen Lee Lenker, Sarah Grunder Ruiz, Sophie Sullivan, Elissa Sussman, Alicia Thompson, and Denise Williams. Jodi Picoult, thank you for encouragement we never imagined from one of our genuine idols.

Bridget Morrissey, words fail us. In every time line, we're in your corner. Thank Sim we found each other. Maura Milan, steadfast writing companion, action movie connoisseur, we love you. To Gabrielle Gold, Gretchen Schreiber, Rebekah Faubion, Kayla Olson, Kristin Dwyer, Diya Mishra, Farrah Penn, Amy Spalding, Kalie Holford—your friendship brings us invaluable joy.

Finally, thank you to our family, without whom none of this is possible.

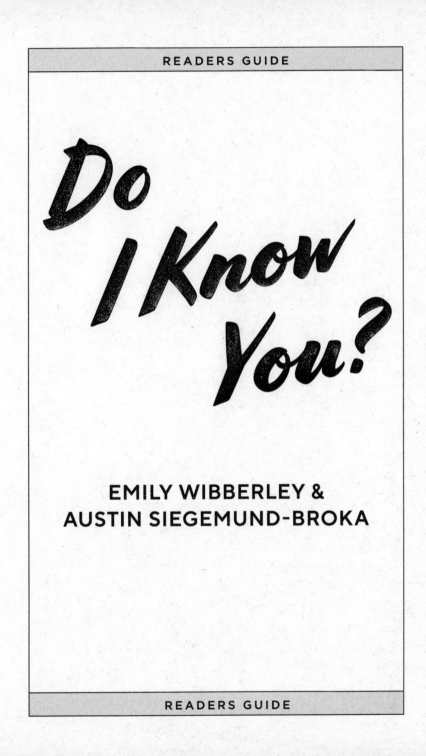

Do I Know You?

EMILY WIBBERLEY &
AUSTIN SIEGEMUND-BROKA

Discussion Questions

1. What is the main problem in Eliza and Graham's marriage at the outset of the book? In what ways does their role-play help bring them together?

2. *Do I Know You?* features a "marriage in trouble" trope. Have you read any other books exploring this trope?

3. The persona Graham chooses has a career similar to his real one, while Eliza's is completely different. Why do you think they chose the roles they did?

4. How does Graham's friendship with David help restore his self-confidence?

5. David exaggerates his interest in Lindsey's passions. Is this

disingenuous or is it a good effort to connect with someone he has a crush on?

6. Do you think Eliza or her sister was in the wrong in their fight?

7. Why do Eliza and Graham feel freer to share their hopes and insecurities while playing characters?

8. What do you think of Eliza's statement "You can still date your spouse"?

Keep reading for an excerpt from

The Roughest Draft

Available now!

Katrina

THE BOOKSTORE IS nothing like I remember. They've remodeled, white paint covering the exposed bricks, light gray wooden shelves where there once were old metal ones. Cute candles and Jane Austen tote bags occupy the front table instead of used books.

I shouldn't be surprised it looks different. I've pretty much given up buying books in public in the past three years, including from Forewords, where I've only been once despite the bookstore being fifteen minutes from our house in Los Angeles's Hancock Park. I don't like being recognized. But I love books. Doing my book buying online has been torture.

Walking in, I eye the bookseller. She's in her early twenties, not much younger than me. Her brown hair's up in a messy bun, her green nose-piercing catching the overhead lights. She doesn't look familiar. When she smiles from the checkout counter, I think I'm in the clear.

I smile back, walking past the bestseller shelf. *Only Once* sits imposingly right in the middle, its textured blue cover with clean white typography instantly identifiable. I ignore the book while I move deeper into the store.

This visit is something my therapist's been pushing me to do for months. Exposure therapy, conditioning myself to once more find comfortable the places I used to love. Pausing in the fiction section, I collect myself, remembering I'm doing fine. I'm calm. I'm just me, looking for something to read, with no expectations pressing on my shoulders or stresses jackhammering in my chest.

Covers run past me in rows, each waiting to be picked out. Everything is crisp with the scent of pages. I knew the Los Angeles independent bookstore scene well when Chris proposed we move here from New York for the job he was offered in the book department of one of Hollywood's biggest talent agencies. Each shop is varied and eccentric, indignant icons of literacy in a city that people say never reads.

Which is why I've hated avoiding them. The past three years have been a catalog of changes, facing realities of the life I no longer knew if I wanted and the one I decided I didn't. I've had to remember the quiet joys of my ordinary existence, and in doing so, I've had to forget. Forget how my dreams hit me with devastating impact, forget how horrible I felt coming close to what I'd once wanted. Forget Florida.

Everything's different now. But I pretend it's not.

The bookstore is part of the pretending. When I lived in New York on my own, before Chris, I would walk to Greenpoint's independent bookstores in the summer, sweating into the shoulder strap of my bag, and imagine the stories in the spines, wondering if they'd lend me inspiration, fuel for the creative fire I could never douse. Reading wasn't just enjoyment. It was studying.

I don't study now. But I never lost the enjoyment. I guess it's too integral a piece of me. Reading and loving books are the fingerprints of who I am—no matter how much I change, they'll stay the same, betraying me to myself for the rest of my life. And bringing me into this bookstore, wanting to find something new to read until Chris gets home in the evening.

"Can I help you find anything?"

I hear the bookseller's voice behind me. Instinctive nerves tighten my posture. I turn, hesitant. While she watches me welcomingly, I wait for the moment I've been dreading since I decided earlier today I needed something new to read *tonight*. Why should I wait for delivery?

The moment doesn't come. The bookseller's expression doesn't change.

"Oh," I say uncertainly, "I'm not sure. Just browsing."

The girl grins. "Do you like literary fiction?" she asks eagerly. "Or is there a subgenre you prefer?"

I relax. The relief hits me in a rush. This is great. No, wonderful. She has no idea who I am. It's not like people overreact in general to seeing celebrities in Los Angeles, where you might run into Chrissy Teigen outside Whole Foods or Seth Rogen in line for ice cream. Not that I'm a celebrity. It's really *just* bookstores where the possibilities of prying questions or overeager fans worry me. If this bookseller doesn't know who I am, I've just found my new favorite place. I start imagining my evening in eager detail—curling up with my new purchase on the couch, toes on our white fur rug, gently controlling James Joyce so his paws don't knock green tea everywhere and stroking him until he purrs.

"Yeah, literary fiction generally. Contemporary fiction more specifically," I say, excitement in my voice now. I'm going to enjoy telling Chris tonight that I went to Forewords and no one knew who I was. It'll probably piss him off, but I don't care. I'll be reading while he's working out his frustration on his Peloton bike.

"I have just the thing," the girl says. She's clearly delighted to have a customer who wants her recommendation.

When she rushes off, my nerves wind up once more. The horrible thought hits me—what if she returns, excited to pitch me the book she's chosen, and she's holding *Only Once*? I don't know what I'd say. The couple seconds I have right now aren't enough for me to come up with even the first draft of how I could extricate myself from the conversation.

Instead, it's worse.

"Try this." The clerk thrusts the hardcover she's chosen toward me. "It came out last week. I read it in, like, two days."

Under the one-word title, *Refraction*, imposed over moody black-and-white photography, I read the name. Nathan Van Huysen. I look to where she got the book from, and I don't know how I didn't notice when I walked in. The cardboard display near the front of the store holds rows of copies, waiting patiently for customers, which tells me two things: high publisher expenditure, and it's not selling.

His name hits me the way it does every time I see it. In *New York Times* reviews, in the profiles I try to keep out of my browser history—never with much success. The first is wishing those fifteen letters meant nothing to me, weren't intertwined with my life in ways I'll never untangle.

Underneath the wishing, I find harder, flintier feelings. Resentment, even hatred. No regret, except regretting ever going to the upstate New York writers' workshop where I met Nathan Van Huysen.

I was fresh out of college. When I graduated from the University of Virginia and into the job I'd found fetching coffee and making copies in a publishing house, I felt like my life hadn't really started. I'd enjoyed college, enjoyed the rush I got learning whatever I found genuinely interesting, no matter the subject—fungal plant structures, behavioral economics, the funeral practices of the Greco-Roman world. I just knew I wouldn't be who I wanted to be until I wrote and published. Then I went upstate and found Nathan, and he found me.

I remember walking out of the welcome dinner, hugging my coat to my collar in the cold, and finding him waiting for me. We'd met earlier in the day, and his eyes lit up when he caught me leaving the restaurant. We introduced ourselves in more depth. He mentioned he was engaged—I hadn't asked. I was single—I didn't volunteer the information. It wasn't like that between us. While we walked out to Susquehanna River Bridge in the night wind, we ended up exchanging favorite verses of poetry, reading them from online on our phones. We were friends.

For the whole lot of good it did us.

When I take the copy of *Refraction*, the clerk's voice drops conspiratorially. "It's not as good as *Only Once*. But I love Nathan Van Huysen's prose."

I don't reply, not wanting to say out loud his prose was the first thing I noticed about him. Even at twenty-two, he wrote with influences fused perfectly into his own style, like every English course he'd ever taken—and Nathan had taken quite a few—was flowing out of his fingertips. It made me feel the things writers love to feel. Inspired, and jealous.

In my silence, the clerk's expression changes. "Wait," she continues, "you have read *Only Once*, haven't you?"

"Um," I say, struggling with how to reply. *Why is conversation way easier on the page?*

"If you haven't"—she starts toward the bestseller shelf to fetch the paperback. I know what'll happen when she catches sight of the back cover. Under the embarrassingly long list of starred reviews, she'll see the author photos. Nathan's blue eyes beneath the immaculate black waves of his hair, the dimple he only trots out for promotional photos and press tours. Then, next to him, she'll find his coauthor, Katrina Freeling. Young woman, sharp shoulders, round features, full eyebrows she honestly loves. Professionally done makeup, dark brown hair pressed and polished, nothing like it looks when she steps out of the shower or she's reading on the patio on sweaty summer days.

The differences won't matter. The bookseller will recognize the woman right in front of her.

My capacity for speech finally returns. "No, I've read it," I manage.

"Of course," the girl gushes. "Everyone's read it. Well, *Refraction* is one of Nathan Van Huysen's solo books. Like I said, it's good, but I wish he and Katrina Freeling would go back to writing together. I've heard they haven't spoken in years, though. Freeling doesn't even write anymore."

I don't understand how this girl is interested enough in the writing duo to know the rumors without identifying one of them in her bookstore. It might be because I haven't done many signings or festivals in the past three years. Following the very minimal promotional schedule for Nathan's and my debut novel, *Connecting Flights*, and then the exhausting release tour for our second, *Only Once*—during which I made my only previous visit here, to Forewords—I more or less withdrew from writerly and promotional events. It was difficult because Chris's and my social life in New York centered on the writing community, and it's part of why I like living in LA, where our neighbors are screenwriters and studio executives. In LA, when people learn you're a novelist, they treat you like a tenured Ivy League professor or a potted plant. Either is preferable to the combination of jealousy and judgment I endured spending time with former friends and competitors in New York.

If you'd told me four years ago I would leave New York for the California coast, I would've frowned, or likelier, laughed. New York was the epicenter for dreams like mine, and Nathan's. But I didn't know then the publication of *Only Once* would fracture me and leave me reassembling the pieces of myself into someone new. Someone for whom living in Los Angeles made sense.

While grateful the Forewords bookseller hasn't identified me—I would've had one of those politely excited conversations, signed some copies of *Only Once*, then left without buying a book—I don't know how to navigate hearing my own professional life story secondhand. "Oh well," I fumble. "That's too bad." No more browsing for me. I decide I just want out of this conversation.

"I know." The girl's grin catches a little mischievousness. "I wonder what happened between them. I mean, why would such a successful partnership just split up right when they were really popular?"

The collar of my coat feels itchy, my pulse beginning to pound. This is my least favorite topic, like, ever. *Why did you split up?* I've heard the rumors. I've heard them from graceless interviewers, from comments I've happened to notice under online reviews. I've heard them from Chris.

If they're to be believed, we grew jealous of each other, or Nathan thought he was better than me, or I was difficult to work with.

Or we had an affair. There'd been speculation before our split. Two young writers, working together on retreats to Florida, Italy, the Hamptons. Photos of us with our arms around each other from the *Connecting Flights* launch event—the only launch we ever did together. The fact *Only Once* centered on marital infidelity didn't help. Nor did the very non-fictional demise of Nathan's own very non-fictional marriage.

This is why I don't like being recognized. I like the excited introductions. I love interacting with readers. What I don't like is the endless repetition of this one question. Why did Katrina Freeling and Nathan Van Huysen quit writing together?

"Who knows?" I say hastily. "Thanks for your recommendation. I'll . . . take it." I reach for the copy of *Refraction*, which the girl hands over, glowing.

FIVE MINUTES LATER, I walk out of the bookstore holding the one book I didn't want.

Photo by Sue Grubman

EMILY WIBBERLEY and **AUSTIN SIEGEMUND-BROKA** met and fell in love in high school. Austin went on to graduate from Harvard, while Emily graduated from Princeton. Together, they are the authors of several novels about romance for teens and adults. Now married, they live in Los Angeles, where they continue to take daily inspiration from their own love story.

CONNECT ONLINE

EmilyandAustinWrite.com

Ready to find
your next great read?

Let us help.

Visit prh.com/nextread

Penguin
Random
House